KILLSTREAK: BOOK ONE
RESPAWN
AN EPIC FANTASY LITRPG

STUART THAMAN

NEF HOUSE PUBLISHING

Killstreak: Book One
Respawn

Copyright © 2017 Stuart Thaman
Nef House Publishing
www.stuartthamanbooks.com

All rights reserved. Without limiting the rights under copyright reserved alone, no part of this publication may be reproduced, stored in or introduced into a retrieval system, or transmitted in any form or by any means (electronic, mechanical, photocopying, recording, or otherwise) without the prior written permission of both the copyright owner and the above publisher of the book.

This is a work of fiction. Names, characters, places, brands, media, and incidents are either the product of the author's imagination or are used fictitiously. The author acknowledges the trademarked status and trademark owners of various products, bands, and/or restaurants referenced in this work of fiction, which have been used without permission. The publication/use of these trademarks is not authorized, associated with, or sponsored by the trademark owners.

ISBN-13: 978-0692122105
ISBN-10: 0692122109

Cover by J Caleb Clark (www.jcalebdesign.com)
Interior layout by Bodie D Dykstra (www.bdediting.com)

ALSO BY STUART THAMAN

THE GOBLIN WARS SERIES
The Minotaur King
Siege of Talonrend
Death of a King
Rebirth of a God

THE UMBRAL BLADE SERIES
Shadowlith
More coming in 2018!

THE CHRONICLES OF ESTRIA SERIES
Blood and Ash
More coming in 2018!

THE KILLSTREAK SERIES
Respawn
Heavy Armor (coming in 2018)

HORROR BY STUART THAMAN
For We Are Many

I vow to fill my grave with a life not wasted.

I am a storm that's grown in the winds of woe.

I built these wings with bones that broke on the grounds of weakness.

I am a phoenix reborn!

Death from Above, "Oh, Sleeper"

CHAPTER 1

"What do you think?" Lord Kadorax Darkarrow whispered to his sole companion, a thin half-serpent with a scaly head and flat ears.

The bipedal snake-man's gaze darted around nervously as his tongue licked the air. There were torches on the walls, but most of them had already sputtered out. Ahead, down a stone ledge slick with old moss, a ring of robed humanoid figures stood around an altar. "Five against two," Syzak hissed. "And none of them are above your level, my lord, not even close."

Kadorax nodded. "Good. Which one is the strongest?"

Syzak scrutinized the ring of priests once more, using his *Detect Strength* ability to read their stat sheets. "There," he pointed with one of his three green fingers, "the one on the left is two levels higher than the others. That one is their leader."

Again, Kadorax nodded. He was characteristically silent,

taking every precaution to hide his presence as thoroughly as he could. As the head of the Blackened Blades, he valued stealth and secrecy above all else.

"Shall I take the leader first, my lord?" Syzak asked. He held a small crystal wand between the three fingers of his left hand, clearly eager to cast a spell and begin the fight.

For a moment, Kadorax called his own stat sheet to his vision, flicking his eyes downward to scroll through the myriad of spells and abilities he had mastered over the last decade. He had spent years training both his mind and body, and now he was the highest-level assassin-mystic hybrid in the entire realm of Agglor. Ever wary of traps, he focused his vision on the *Discover Magic* spell and viewed the proper casting procedure from his ability sheet. It had been years since he had needed the spell, and it wasn't one he kept lodged in his brain for quick use.

Kadorax silently mouthed the words to the mundane incantation, having long ago earned the *Silent Casting* talent, and two areas of his vision lit up with brilliant, translucent color. The first had been expected. The humanoid leader—he still wasn't positive what the priests actually *were*—showed a heavy aura of red magic encasing his form, likely a protective ward of some sort. The second area of magic came from a large circular rune inscribed on the wall behind the altar, and Kadorax didn't know what it meant.

"Can you disable the leader?" the assassin whispered so faintly he could barely be heard.

"Of course," Syzak answered with a smile.

Kadorax held up a hand. "He has a red aura around him, probably *Stone Skin* or *Magic Armor*, perhaps of a rank we have not seen before. Can you break it?"

Syzak's serpentine eyes inspected the humanoid once

more, but only for a few seconds. "I have *Strip Enchantment*, though it is a costly spell," he said.

Handing the snake-man a silver shard of reflective metal, Kadorax nodded. "No chances," he breathed. While most of the spells in Agglor could be cast by having them unlocked and either reading or knowing their incantational phrases, certain extremely powerful abilities required specific components which were sometimes incredibly difficult to obtain.

Kadorax's *Discover Magic* casting was about to expire, so he flashed a quick successions of rudimentary hand signals to his companion, and then shimmied over the edge to begin his descent down the nearly sheer rock surface of the temple's interior wall. His gloves, black silk constructions known as *Cat Paws*, silently gripped the flat surface beneath his fingers with all the strength of a well-muscled panther. On the temple's floor, Kadorax melted into the shadows. The place smelled musty and damp, and the flagstones making up the ground were wet with stale rainwater.

Above the assassin's head, a partially concealed flicker of purple light emanated from Syzak's wand, shooting across the temple with blinding speed. The magical glob struck the leader in the chest, and Kadorax saw the humanoid's red aura fade just seconds before his *Discover Magic* spell wore off, unable to be cast again for several hours.

Kadorax sprinted forward on leather boots as silent as the grave. He reached behind his back and grasped the bone handle of a dagger hidden in a sheath under his cloak. The bone was frigid in his grasp, ice cold even through his gloves, and the blade was so dark it actually dripped a steady stream of viscous shadows onto the stone ground between his strides.

He took the first robed priest in the back before any of

them even noticed Kadorax among their ranks. The priest let out a muffled shriek as he crumpled to the ground. When his robe fluttered to the side Kadorax finally saw the head of a jackal underneath, its teeth bared.

Dogheads, Kadorax mused, using the derogatory term for the race. He had killed scores of the jackal-headed beasts throughout the years, and he'd never regret a single strike of his blade.

Another bolt of purple magic sailed over Kadorax toward the doghead leader, catching the jackal fully in the chest. At once, a rigid shell of stone grew up from the temple floor to encase the beast, locking it in place in a dark, constricting prison that was as terrifying as it was effective.

Kadorax didn't waste any time. He spun from target to target, whirling his black blade between the two nearest living enemies and rending them to bloodied bits.

While his compatriots were dying, the final jackal had run a few steps backward and drawn a small crossbow from underneath his dark robe. The weapon clicked and thrummed, and the steel bolt held in its track sprang forward.

Kadorax quickly whispered the words to *Shield Maw*, and a fiery dragon's head sprang to life in front of his body to consume the incoming missile. He didn't need to use such flashy magic—his *Expert Reflexes* would have easily moved him out of the way quickly enough to dodge the bolt—but he *hated* doghead scum. He wanted the remaining jackal to fear him, to contemplate its own death before he gutted it, and the dramatic spell certainly did the trick.

The jackal only spent a few heartbeats trying to reload its crossbow before it gave up and turned to run. Kadorax chased after it, clearing the distance almost instantly and sinking his dagger into the fur-covered doghead. The creature shuddered, but it did not die. It slumped to the ground and mewled, its bounty of experience points flashing in yellow just above its head. Kadorax stepped over, letting the congealed shadows surrounding his blade drip onto the doghead's chest. The shadows themselves were harmless, but the psychological impact they had on a dying foe was certainly palpable.

"P—"

Kadorax stomped down on the creature's throat, silencing it before it could speak a single intelligible syllable.

With a faint rumble, the experience Kadorax gained from the swift battle sifted into his body, adding to his already staggering total. He brought up his sheet again to check his progress toward the next level, but he knew more or less what it would be. The jackals hadn't been worth much. He was still more than fifty percent away from level seventy-three. His next talent, *Exceptional Void Strike - Execution: Rank 7*, was still frustratingly far away. He would have to kill hundreds of dogheads to even make a dent in the total.

Then a rumbling from behind snapped Kadorax's thoughts back to the present, and he dismissed his stat sheet with a thought. The leader was still alive, and he was finally breaking free of Syzak's stone prison.

Seeing his eviscerated companions, the jackal's eyes went wide, but he was still quick on his hairy feet. The jackal rolled left behind the stone altar, drawing a slender sword from his robe and rolling his wrist with practiced ease. Kadorax had never learned the *Detect Strength* ability, but he could tell the jackal leader was far beyond the mere underlings lying dead around the altar. Repeating the words to his most frequently used spell, Kadorax felt the familiar rush of adrenaline brought on by *Slaughtering Surge* filling his veins.

He sprang forward with lightning speed, twirling his lightless dagger downward for a quick killing blow, and met the jackal's adept parry with a ring of steel.

Flurry of Strikes pumped through Kadorax body, moving his right arm as quickly as it could physically go, putting on a dazzling display of violence made possible only by the assassin's maxed out *Agility* stat. Shockingly, the jackal matched his relentless pace.

The jackal leader ducked his shoulder and used a talent, *Armor Break* by the look of the yellow sheen on his weapon, charging forward with power akin to a stone giant fueling his legs.

Kadorax staggered backward. It was the first time in over two years his *Strength* had been matched, and the sheer surprise of it broke his concentration for a split second. The jackal was relentless. The creature's slender blade came in from every angle, slashing at Kadorax's face over and over again.

Growling with sadistic pleasure born from a true challenge, Kadorax summoned his character sheet to the corner of his vision and searched for *Pull from the Void*, repeating the order of the required words several times in his mind before attempting to cast the spell. When he finally let it loose, a shadowy hand of pure magic erupted from his chest and sailed toward the hidden ledge where Syzak waited. The small snake-man latched onto the hand and rode it back down, flinging a rapid barrage of lightning and fire from his wand all the while.

Some of Syzak's magical bolts managed to hit their target, but the jackal leader wasn't particularly fazed. His red aura returned, now visible without magically enhanced vision, and it absorbed the energy of the magical assault almost fully. Kadorax had never seen the defensive enchantment before, and he had seen almost everything, or so he had thought.

Working quickly as he cast, Syzak brought forth a *Wall of Frost* in the narrow gap between Kadorax's boots and the jackal's furry paws. The shaman augmented the spell with another talent activation, one Kadorax had only seen him use a few times, and the wall that erupted from the ground reached far over either combatant's head. Kadorax scampered backward to catch his breath and scour his character sheet for an answer.

"He's fast," Syzak hissed, keeping his wand ready and a spell at the front of his mind.

Kadorax didn't waste his breath on a response. The jackal was quicker than any opponent he had fought before, and he needed something unexpected, something obscure, to turn the tide.

"The wall will not hold much longer," Syzak said. "Should we flee?"

"*Eldritch Fire!*" Kadorax yelled as he completed the spell. A burst of blueish-black flame licked out from the end of his dagger toward the ice wall. A quick activation of *Perfect Timing* let him flawlessly judge the expiration of Syzak's conjuring. Snapping his wrist forward, a burst of black fire cascaded through the falling, dissipating ice, and fully engulfed the howling jackal.

Kadorax lunged forward with his blade, shielding his eyes from the painful mixture of fire and ice raining down on his shoulders. At rank ten, the highest available to any spell, Kadorax's *Eldritch Fire* was nothing short of a cataclysmic conflagration—and it worked. The jackal only avoided part of the blast with his *Improved Reflexes*. His mangy hair danced with flames, and the jackal howled as he spun through the temple, slapping at the licking flames in vain.

"*Coup de Grâce!*" Kadorax yelled, activating his *Assassin's Superior Talent* with a brilliant flourish. His blade danced in his hands, flinging thick globs of shadow to every corner of the room, and the burning jackal could only offer a meager attempt at a parry. In a blur of speed, Kadorax appeared to the jackal's left, then his right, and finally he was behind the beast with his black dagger held high above the creature's spine. He drove it downward with all his strength.

The jackal leader's experience flashed in yellow above his head as he died. The formidable foe had been worth just over three thousand experience, and that brought Kadorax noticeably closer to level seventy-three, though he was still roughly thirty-five percent from leveling again.

Sweat poured down Kadorax's head. Next to him, Syzak tucked his wand back into his belt. "Where's the loot?" the snake-man asked. He nudged the jackal leader's corpse with his boot, pushing aside the front of the robe to inspect the body for treasure. He found nothing.

"Use *Detect Hidden*, Syzak," Kadorax panted, thoroughly exhausted. Part of why he had risen to be Agglor's highest-level assassin had been his choice of battles. He never fought more than one heavy encounter in a day, and he preferred to only test himself once a week if he could, being as frugal as possible with his rewards specifically to allow himself the most meaningful respites. Due to his style, he hadn't taken many of the endurance-related talents, so he had no way of reducing his recovery time with magic.

Syzak uttered the words to the simple spell. "Oh, shit," he said almost at once.

Kadorax skipped backward on the balls of his feet, dagger

at the ready and chest heaving from exertion, scanning the temple for some new threat he had not seen.

"The inscription," Syzak explained, pointing to the magical symbols behind the altar. "There's a door. The jackals were *summoning* something, not imprisoning it . . ."

As if on cue, the wall behind the altar shook forcefully. Something was breaking through it with heavy fists. Something massive and beyond powerful. Something unknown. *Something*.

"Lord Kadorax, I feel it unwise to remain here," Syzak implored, his serpentine eyes full of terror.

"We haven't gotten any loot yet," Kadorax growled. He scanned through his list of abilities, quickly reorganizing them so that his unused spells and talents appeared at the top of his character sheet. "Whatever it is, it's guarding the treasure. We stay."

A few bricks fell out of the wall, and Syzak glimpsed something dark—and enormous—pounding away at the stone on the other side. "Kad! We can come back later!" he screamed. The snake-man turned to run, but Kadorax caught him by the arm.

"We've defeated worse," Kadorax reminded him.

"Have we?"

The wall crumbled inward.

A giant, horned head emerged from the rubble, quickly followed by four muscled arms, each the size of tree trunks. The thing roared, and then it wrenched the rest of its body free, coming to its full height in the high-ceilinged temple.

Lord Kadorax Darkarrow felt his heart catch in his chest. He had fought dragons on several occasions and lived to tell the tales, but those encounters had always been with dozens of other high-level adventurers. With only a single shaman at his side, powerful as they were together, he knew he was outclassed.

The beast, whatever it truly was, stood over twenty feet tall. Its skin looked like rock, but it flowed and moved with such ease that Kadorax knew it was organic—some sort of hardened carapace—and its head was covered in a circular pattern of bulging black eyes that reminded the assassin of a scorpion. It had four arms, each vaguely humanoid and rippling with muscle beneath its thick armor, though it did not wield any weapons in the traditional sense.

"W-what is it?" Kadorax stammered. He tried to access the dungeon boss' character sheet, but all he saw was a series of question marks highlighted in deep crimson floating near the top of his vision.

Before either hero could speak, the boss reared its hideous head. "I am your undoing!" it announced with all the strength of a world-ending earthquake.

Kadorax flew through his list of abilities to find the one that would take him and Syzak farthest from the temple in the least amount of time. "*Teleport!*" he yelled, grabbing his companion with both arms to ensure they traveled together.

Nothing happened.

The four-armed beast laughed, its voice so loud that Kadorax had to cover his ears to keep the pain at bay.

"*Teleport!*" the assassin tried again. Still, his feet remained firmly planted on the temple's stone floor.

"*Shadow Step!*"

Nothing.

"*Fade!*"

Nothing.

Kadorax flew through his list of mystic abilities, searching for something that might work in the boss encounter. He settled on *Smoke Leap*, a low-level ability designed to vault him upward and forward by about thirty feet while leaving behind a decoy made of smoke, but the ability did not function properly. Something blocked it.

"You cannot run, puny human," the massive boss taunted. "No one can escape their own grave."

Kadorax had encountered enemies in the past with similar magic-preventing abilities. Typically, the dampening field was generated by an enchanted ring or amulet worn by the user, but the towering beast featured nothing of the sort.

"S*laughtering Surge!*" Kadorax finally yelled, bringing a fresh wave of adrenaline to his arms and legs.

Syzak summoned forth a shell of protective energy around the assassin, and then a burst of brilliant light shot from the snake-man's wand. The spell landed on the boss' head, but it did not have the intended effect of blinding the creature. In fact, it didn't appear to have any effect whatsoever.

When Kadorax reached the horned beast, it was ready for him. Arm after heavy arm came hammering down into the temple floor like boulders dislodged in a landslide. Each strike was enough to turn Kadorax into dust, and his *Expert Reflexes* were all that kept him alive. Swerving between the arms, the assassin brought his dripping blade of shadows in with all the strength he had left in his body, slashing furiously at the creature's exoskeleton covering its segmented right leg.

Kadorax's blade clicked loudly off the boss' armor. From his position between the beast's legs, he could just barely see into the room from where the horned thing had emerged, and it was full to the ceiling with treasure—more than the assassin had ever seen before. Piles of glittering gold shone in the torchlight, and iron-banded chests were stacked in neat rows as far in as he could see.

Breaking his greed-fueled reverie, a huge hand swept Kadorax up from the ground, crushing all the air from his lungs. On the ground, Syzak used every ounce of obscure arcane knowledge he had to rain blow after blow on the creature, though none of them had any visible effect. Even spells like *Void Prison*, an incredibly high-level magical assault designed to immobilize even the most magic-immune foes, simply did not succeed.

The boss brought Kadorax up to its huge maw. "I am your undoing, human!" it yelled. Its breath smelled rotten and old, like the beast had been chained in its prison for hundreds of years with nothing but dead adventurers to fill its belly.

Kadorax saw a hint of yellow coming down from the top of his vision. It was his experience total—the amount the boss was about to claim for itself. "I'll see you at the spawn, my friend," the assassin called to Syzak, his voice shaking.

The snake-man nodded. "In the next life," he answered. "In the next life . . ."

Laughing all the while, the dungeon boss squeezed. It didn't need to activate any ability, and it didn't even bother to watch. In an instant, Kadorax's chest caved in on his organs, squishing the life from his body like a bug caught beneath the hoof of a horse.

CHAPTER 2

Kadorax awoke with a splitting headache. He was naked, covered by only the barest of roughspun sheets, and he was terribly cold. Somewhere nearby, he heard the sounds of a noisy inn filtering through the poorly constructed walls and door. When he sat up, his head spun like he'd been drinking all night. Kadorax had only died in Agglor one time before, and it had been exactly the same. More than two decades ago, when he had been relatively new to the world, he had been scouting a rocky cliffside in the service of a nobleman, and his foot had slipped, sending him to his death on the ground below. The next day he had awoken in a different town, in a different part of Agglor he had never seen before. For whatever reason, respawning imparted the most brutal of hangovers.

Back on Earth, a place that amounted to little more than a distant memory in Kadorax's mind, he had been someone else. He couldn't remember his family from that time or even what he had looked like, only that he had been an avid gamer, and then one morning had awoken with a splitting migraine—in Agglor. Respawning sent shreds of his old life that still remained locked in his brain flooding back to the forefront. He felt the vague notion that he had been married in his past life, and he wondered if his wife still missed him. After first awakening in Agglor, he had spent several years determined to make it back. And then the memories had begun to fade, and he had given himself fully to the world, embracing its structure and chaos, becoming one of its masters.

Now Kadorax would have to begin anew. Level one. No class. No talents. No specializations. He tested his arms, flexing them in multiple directions, and the muscle felt puny beneath his skin. The same, however, could not be said for the layer of fat ringing his midsection.

"My lord?" a groggy voice broke through Kadorax's contemplation.

"Syzak?"

The snake-man groaned. "It was horrible," he went on. "That thing ate you, and then it trapped me in a corner of the temple . . . Then it squished me under its foot."

Kadorax shook the image from his head. "It's over now, Syzak. And don't call me your lord. I'm just a commoner, a level one like everyone else."

Syzak's head peeked around the corner of the doorway. "Will you choose to be an assassin again?" he asked.

No answer came quickly to Kadorax's lips. In his first life on Agglor, he had been a mystic, using arcane and shamanistic magic to bend the rules of the universe to his bidding. But then something as mundane as a slippery rock had sent him spiraling to his death. That was when he had decided to embrace the life of a sure-footed assassin, and he had excelled in every possible way.

"What do you think that thing was?" he asked, rubbing his temples with his palms. His shaggy hair was in his eyes, something he hadn't experienced in twenty years or more, and he looked around for a blade to shear it away from his head. Of course, he found no such weapon. The room's only furniture other than the straw bed on which he sat was a dresser, and inside he knew he would find a cheap set of clothing wholly inadequate for the elements outside.

Syzak thought a moment before answering. "Some sort of minotaur? It had horns. But all those eyes? And why would the jackals be charged with its defense?" he wondered aloud.

"Damn dogheads . . ." Kadorax muttered. Every spell and ability he had known as a level seventy-two assassin hybrid classed with a mystic had been erased from his memory, but his old habits and thoughts were as strong as ever.

Reading Kadorax's eyes, Syzak felt a queasy lump growing in his own throat. "You aren't thinking of fighting that thing again, are you?" he asked.

"Of course I am!" the former assassin answered. "Did you see that loot? The treasure room? Leagues beyond anything we've ever earned before!"

Syzak let out a pained sigh. His eyes still showed a heavy dose of fear, like memories of the horned jackal beast wouldn't leave him alone.

Kadorax threw off the simple sheet and made his way to the wooden dresser against the near wall. There were pants and a shirt in the uppermost drawer, and the second held a belt with a small leather pouch attached to it by heavy thread. There weren't even any shoes, and by the feel of the room, he had respawned somewhere very cold.

"I don't think I'll go assassin again, Syzak," Kadorax said. "My blade didn't even put a scratch on that thing's armor. I'll need something else."

The snake-man looked genuinely surprised. "You were an assassin for so long. That's all I can think of you as."

Kadorax nodded. "Yeah, but we need something different. And before we figure out any of that, we just need to learn what that stupid thing is. Once we know what can kill it, we can decide on classes."

For a moment, Syzak looked a bit perplexed. "You have no other aspirations?" he asked.

"What else is there? We can't go home. Success in Agglor only comes in two forms: loot and levels," Kadorax answered. "Whatever that boss is, it's the biggest thing we've ever seen, and so is the loot chamber. I'm going after it."

Syzak let out a long exhale, which sounded tiny and almost like a squeal coming from his snake mouth. "I suppose you're right," he said after a while.

"You don't have to follow me," the human reminded him. Kadorax had taken the sheet from his bed and wrapped it around his shoulders like a cape, trying in vain to keep some of the biting cold at bay. Being exothermic, the snake-man was even worse off, shivering uncontrollably in the doorway.

"Please don't abandon me . . ." Syzak whispered out of reflex.

"You were my pet snake back on Earth, Syzak. I'd never abandon you, but you *are* free to choose your own path here. I won't have you as my slave," Kadorax said with the hint of a laugh.

Despite the reassurance, Syzak remained deflated and nervous.

"Let's get some food and find a lord," Kadorax said before

his companion could add anything else. "And we certainly need some more clothes. You look ridiculous."

Downstairs, the inn was only marginally warmer. A low fire burned in one corner with a pot of boiling meat hanging above it, and the front door didn't close very well, so a constant draft came from underneath the wood. A bit of frost clung to the room's only window. The center of the room was filled with small tables, each with two chairs, and each with only one occupant. The people, as far as Kadorax knew, were class trainers that he would only get to see once. He recognized the assassin immediately as a tall woman in all black casually spinning a small dagger on the table in front of her. Some of the others were hard to guess.

Before selecting a class, Kadorax turned to the barkeep, a portly old man with cataracts, few teeth, and even less hair. The last time Kadorax had respawned, the barkeep in that particular establishment had been a real person, and he hoped the same was true of the old man before him now.

"We need some information, if you have it," Kadorax said.

The barkeep looked the poorly clothed pair up and down before replying. "What is it you're after?" he asked with a gruff voice.

"Any news?" Kadorax casually offered.

"Other than the Gar'kesh showing up?"

"Ha," Kadorax laughed. "A Gar'kesh doesn't have four arms, horns, and a huge row of eyes, does it?"

"Aye," the barkeep answered.

Kadorax shook his head with a smile on his face. "Well, that was remarkably easy."

"You met your demise at its hand, didn't you?" the man asked. He grabbed a stone mug from a shelf behind him to pour a beer.

"You're a perceptive one," Kadorax confirmed. He pulled up the barkeep's character sheet and saw the man was a fifth-level bard with inordinately high insight. Kadorax figured the barkeep had some sort of magical item enhancing his abilities, but the classless civilian no longer had any spell capable of detecting it.

"Everyone dying these days has the same story. The Gar'kesh is killing whole villages at a time. A bunch of jackals tried to imprison it, but they never came back. The thing must've killed them when it broke free."

Syzak leaned in close over the bar, his beady eyes nervously shifting side to side. "How long has it been since the Gar'kesh awoke?" he asked.

The barkeep looked away in contemplation. "Two weeks? Three? Maybe a little more, I'm not sure. News travels slowly over the Boneridge Mountains," the barkeep explained.

"*Over* the mountains?" Kadorax asked incredulously. The Boneridge Mountains were huge, beyond imposing, and the only pass was so heavily guarded and taxed that movement from one side of the range to the other was basically impossible.

"Aye, you're on the west," the old man added.

"No wonder it's so cold," Syzak said with a shiver.

"Go on and get your classes sorted out, and I'll let you eat a little before we close." The man took a long swig of the dark beer he had poured, then turned away from the pair to attend to the meat cooking over the fire.

"And what can kill a Gar'kesh?" Kadorax asked after him.

The barkeep shrugged. "The jackals thought they could, or maybe they had been the ones to summon it. Jackal raids have been increasing in frequency, according to the latest rumors," he said. "Apparently the Priorate Knights have allied themselves with the Blackened Blades and the Miners' Union. They're all set to head out in search of Atticus Willowshade, should the old warlock still be alive. The king seems to think he'll have the answer."

"A warlock . . ." Kadorax mused. Warlocks were outcasts by nature, shunned by most civilized societies for a myriad of very valid reasons. Kadorax had only met a handful of warlocks in his previous life, and every one of them had struck him as unnervingly strange. Atticus had a reputation among the warlocks as one of their champions—a god even—though he'd earned his mantle through numerous acts of unspeakable evil. The only reason the king hadn't sent an army to slaughter the man was because he feared it would fail. All the rumors about Atticus varied to some degree, but they all came together on two points—that the warlock was immortal, and that the warlock was never to be trifled with.

Kadorax scanned the room for the warlock trainer, an uneasy knot growing in his stomach, and his eyes settled on the most bizarre humanoid he had ever seen. The trainer was a grotesque amalgamation of a reptile and a skeleton, with bony protrusions breaking forth from scales all over its body.

"No wonder no one ever goes warlock," Syzak said. "Don't tell me that's your plan."

"Um, I think I'll pass," Kadorax answered. The trainers were arranged in a purposeful pattern ranging from magical to martial, and the two trainers nearest the warlock were both clad in dark colors with little bones dangling from their hair. It looked a bit dramatic and overblown, but it definitely reinforced the stereotype that any magic dealing with death or the dead was evil.

"What do you train?" Kadorax asked, dropping himself

into a cold wooden chair opposite a dapper-looking elf in all black with a dark leather top hat, bone earrings dangling on the sides of his face.

The elf beamed at Kadorax. "Hello, traveler! I am Nearblight the Elf, a necromancer. I can teach you to command the dead, shape their bones, and bend the dark essences to your whim." The elf's happy countenance didn't align well with his grim visage.

"Controlling bones? That sounds pretty cool," Kadorax said more to himself than anyone else.

"I don't know," Syzak added. "What are the drawbacks?"

Right on cue, the elf continued, "Disadvantages include weakness to fire, weakness to charm, an inability to take most other classes as a hybrid, and a strong social stigma."

"Well, that might not be too bad. Could I hybrid class as a warlock?" Kadorax asked.

"Yes, adventurer."

"Not bad!"

Syzak didn't look too certain. "Being a social outcast will make everything more difficult," he said. "I don't know . . ."

Kadorax turned to an equally dark-clad woman at the next table. "And your class?"

She turned to meet his gaze, her eyes full of excitement. "Hello, traveler! I am Banemaw the Hungry, a bastion of chaos incarnate. I can teach you to scourge your enemies, lay waste to countless foes with wave after wave of hellfire, and bend lesser creatures to your will with a mere thought."

"Ka—" Syzak started with panic in his voice, but he didn't get more than a single syllable out before he was interrupted.

"Hell yes!" Kadorax shouted, sliding over to the woman's table. "Count me in!"

The woman smiled even more, extending her pale,

dainty hand for Kadorax to shake. When their skin connected, Kadorax felt a surge of energy jolt through his arm toward his heart, and a little bit of blackened mist rose up from their clasped hands like a signature sealing a pact.

"Welcome, fellow bastion of chaos incarnate! It is good to meet another of my kind," the woman went on.

"What would go well with . . . whatever the hell you are?" Syzak asked, his snake eyes wide.

"Another shaman?" Kadorax replied, barely paying him any attention. His full attention was on the woman before him.

"As a bastion of chaos incarnate, you'll need to know just a few things," she continued with a cute little chuckle. "First, you will be able to use abilities and cast spells from the schools of fire, darkness, chaos, and domination. Second, a bastion of chaos incarnate is proficient with either a whip, a greatsword, or a spear. Third, a bastion of chaos incarnate must always wear heavy armor in battle."

"*Must?*" Kadorax asked. He had always preferred light bits of leather and not getting hit over the knights and paladins clanking around in heavy steel plates.

"Yes, adventurer," the woman said with a cheerful nod. "In order to complete the training, a metal soul rod will be implanted in your chest. A bastion of chaos incarnate must protect their soul rod at all costs, for to destroy it would mean death. Is this information useful to you, traveler?"

Kadorax felt his face going white.

"Good luck with that," Syzak sarcastically chided, moving away toward another trainer. The snake-man slapped his human friend on the shoulder as he left.

"In my chest?" he gasped. Kadorax's assassin training had required a bunch of balancing studies and discourses on stealth, along with a lengthy introduction to meditation—which he had never once used. Surgery felt like a bit much.

"To know chaos is to understand pain, adventurer," Banemaw said. "You must become a master of both. Are you ready to begin?"

Kadorax leaned back in his wooden chair. Suddenly, the cold chill in the air didn't seem too bad. "Yeah, I guess I am," he finally said.

The woman rose from her chair and turned, leading Kadorax out of the inn. Or she *should* have led Kadorax outside, but instead she turned before reaching the door, heading for another slab of wood with a heavy lock just to the exit's side.

"Where are we going?" Kadorax asked. It had been quite some time since his first respawn. Perhaps things had changed.

"We must descend into the pit, traveler," she said over her shoulder. Her pale fingers fetched a key from a pocket hidden in her dark clothing, and she slid it into the lock.

Wondering if he had even seen the strange woman during his last time in the inn, Kadorax asked, "So, are you new here?"

"Yes," Banemaw answered, her voice as soft and cheerful as ever. She took the steps on the other side of the door quickly, almost jovially, leading Kadorax deeper and deeper into darkness. "I arrived at the inn only recently, traveler, and my power is reserved solely for those who have proven themselves to be strong. You are my first, and only a small number have gone before you."

"That at least explains why I've never met another bastion of chaos, I suppose."

At the bottom of the staircase, Banemaw whispered a

single word, and a thin line of fire leapt from her hand onto a nearby torch, illuminating the small room.

The inn's basement wasn't even close to what Kadorax had expected. There were no training dummies, only one rack of cruel-looking weapons—sharpened steel, not blunted practice instruments—and the floor was stained dark with blood.

"I'm starting to think I might have made my decision a bit too hastily . . ." he murmured, though he did not turn back. Kadorax knew he could not leave. Once he began the training, there was no escape. The only way to go back was death. Remembering that he hadn't actually exhausted the dialogue options at the table, he asked, "What are the disadvantages?"

"Disadvantages include lowered resistance to charm, higher component costs for advanced and expert spells, and the *Encroaching Insanity* debuff," the woman said as she used a cloth to wipe down the only piece of furniture in the room: a large stone table that reminded Kadorax of a sacrificial altar in an Aztec jungle.

"I've never even heard of *Encroaching Insanity*," Kadorax whispered. Looking at the stone table, he knew it was meant for him. There wouldn't be any formal training involved in the process. There would only be pain.

Resigned, he took off his threadbare shirt and climbed atop the table. "Let's just get it over with."

The woman nodded and smiled, then moved to the rack of weapons on the back wall. "In which weapon class would you prefer expertise, adventurer?" she asked.

"You said I'd be proficient with a whip, greatsword, and spear, right?"

"That is correct, adventurer," she answered. "And you

must select one weapon class to become your expertise. Are you ready?"

Kadorax thought for a moment before answering. He had used swords before, but his strength from his previous life was gone. He didn't know how long it would take him to become fast enough to be considered skilled with either the greatsword or the spear. "How about the whip?" he said.

The woman pulled a silver whip with a long handle from the rack. The entire device was perhaps fourteen feet in length, and the end split into three separate pieces, each adorned with a hollow barb. Kadorax laid down on the stone, and Banemaw began unscrewing the bottom half of the whip's long hilt. When she had finished, she set the main part of the whip aside and held a curious-looking cylinder in her hand. The tip of the object, the end opposite the connection to the rest of the whip, had a gleaming point set with a deep crimson ruby.

"Lie down, adventurer," Banemaw encouraged him. The point of the strange cylinder was hovering dangerously over Kadorax's bare chest.

"And that thing is going to go into my body?" he asked.

The woman smiled gently, and then she plunged the metal rod deep into Kadorax's sternum, eliciting a spray of warm blood all over her face and arms. She pressed down on the rod with all her weight, leaning over the table for leverage, and Kadorax felt his consciousness begin to fade.

The proud man, once the highest-level assassin in all of Agglor, did not scream as he was ritually impaled. He ground his teeth together so hard they hurt, but he did not scream. After several seconds of grunting effort, Banemaw finally pulled back her hands, and the metal rod was seated fully in Kadorax's breastbone, flush with the torn and bloodied skin around it.

"You are now a bastion of chaos incarnate, adventurer," Banemaw said with genuine glee. "To know chaos is to understand pain."

Then, as the woman winked, everything went black.

When Kadorax awoke a split second later, he was no longer cold, though he was still covered in his own blood, and the metal cylinder was still soundly lodged in his body. *This thing should have ripped apart my lungs and diaphragm, maybe my heart. How am I still alive?* Even on Earth, he had never been terribly good with biology or anatomy, but he knew enough to fully understand that he should have died.

The room he was in was not dissimilar to the tavern basement he had somehow left. The room smelled of blood, though it could have just been his own musk filling his nostrils, and all the walls were stone. To either side of his head, torches flickered and gave off plenty of light. Unfortunately, there wasn't much to see.

"Hello?" Kadorax tried. No answer came.

"Is this some kind of character or trait selection process?" he asked the empty room. Again, nothing.

Finally, Kadorax lifted himself up from the stone table and stretched, amazed that his chest did not burn with pain. In fact, he didn't even feel the metal between his ribs. Not internally, at least. He ran a hesitant finger over the end of the cylinder. It was warm to his touch almost as though it was a real part of his body.

"I'll figure that out later," he said.

Focusing on himself, Kadorax summoned his character sheet. At the top in curvy, red lettering, was his class information: *Bastion of Chaos Incarnate - Level Two*.

"Level two?" he wondered. "That's new."

The rest of his stats were displayed under his name and class:

Strength: 15
Agility: 13
Fate: 19
Spirit: 13
Charisma: 14
Bond: 10

Kadorax had to stop when he read his final stat. *Bond* was something he had never seen before—on his sheet or anyone else's. He had never even heard it mentioned. Focusing again, he honed in his thoughts on *Bond* to display the description:

Bond: 10 - Your connection to reality. As the bastion grows in strength and level, the connection weakens. Can be reinforced by various means. When Bond reaches 0, the bastion will return to the chaos.

To the side of the stats, in a small green box for active buffs and debuffs, Kadorax finally saw his ominous disadvantage:

Encroaching Insanity: Rank 1 - The seed of chaos living within your soul rod. As the bastion increases in level, the power of the chaos grows, further weakening Bond. At Rank 10, Encroaching Insanity becomes Living Nightmare.

With a grimace spreading across his face, Kadorax expanded the *Living Nightmare* description.

Living Nightmare - The bastion's mind has been lost to chaos, granting Soul of the Void.

Kadorax tried to expand the description for *Soul of the Void*, but all his sheet would display were question marks. A shiver worked its way up and down his spine.

Thankfully, the rest of Kadorax's sheet appeared to be normal. His experience total flashed, prompting him to select a talent, so he expanded the menu to browse the options.

Torment: Rank 1 - The bastion's weapon becomes encased in shadow, inflicting a lasting mental anguish on the target. Torment has an increased effect when used with a whip. Effort: moderate. Cooldown: 30 minutes.

Sturdy Mind: Rank 1 - The bastion's mental faculties are fortified, raising Spirit by 1 and Bond by 1. Passive.

Nimble Feet: Rank 1 - Chaos begets speed, enhancing the bastion's overland speed and reducing the bastion's reflex time. Passive.

Kadorax dismissed the sheet from his vision and decided to make his selection later, preferably once he had acquired more information. Knowing nothing about the class, he had no way to anticipate what kinds of talents would be available to him at higher levels.

Set into one wall of the strange room was a staircase just like the one he had descended a few minutes before, and Kadorax took it at once. As expected, he found a wooden door at the top. He pushed it open, half expecting some wild ambush, but instead found the tavern more or less as he had left it. The most striking change was the color. Everything was draped in a sepia tone, like he was wearing red-tinted glasses.

Instead of trainers sitting at each table, waiting for him to approach, every chair was empty. All of them were perfectly arranged, flawlessly centered at each table.

"Hello?" Kadorax called.

The inn's front door opened on a gentle breeze. Again,

Kadorax noted that he did not feel the biting cold he knew should have been in the room.

A creature, roughly humanoid in shape, stood in the doorway. "Hello?" Kadorax said once more.

The creature beckoned him outside, and Kadorax followed. The whole world was red, and everything Kadorax could see was ablaze. The nearby trees were enveloped in flame. The buildings lining the road on either side had already been reduced to ashes and charred frames, and more burning pitch continuously fell from the sky as far as the eye could see.

"Welcome to chaos," the creature said.

Standing amidst so much stinging light, Kadorax could just barely make out the being's shape, confusing though it was. It stood roughly as tall as a man, but its edges were hazy. Kadorax got the distinct feeling that whatever it was, it did not fully exist, at least not in any comprehensible sense.

"I am Ligriv, and I shall be your guide through chaos, whenever you shall have need of me," the humanoid said.

"What is this place?" Kadorax asked. His eyes struggled to take in everything.

Ligriv took a step closer. "As a bastion, all of your strength originates here: chaos. You cannot perceive chaos' actual form, so you will see it exactly how your mind *thinks* it should be seen. That means it will change frequently. The lower your *Bond*, the more clearly you will experience the true form of chaos when you visit."

"How often is that going to be?"

"A bastion may find respite from wounds here, but at a cost," Ligriv went on. "To know chaos is to understand pain. Never forget that."

"How could I?" Kadorax said. "No one wants to shut up

about it. But isn't this supposed to be my training? Shouldn't you be teaching me how to use my abilities?"

Ligriv offered something close to a laugh, then took several steps backward into the burning street. "I have already taught you so much!" he taunted with a smile. "Everything left to learn is up to you. The next time you are here, perhaps I will show you more. For now, you have knowledge enough."

Kadorax's eyes fluttered open, and he was back on the stone table beneath the inn, a fiery, splitting pain alive and well in his bloody chest, though his shirt had been replaced.

Banemaw's face quickly filled his vision. "You're ready now, adventurer," she said, beaming as always.

"Uh, thanks."

Ushering him toward the stairs, Banemaw politely urged him to leave.

Though the pain was immense, Kadorax somehow managed to stumble toward the door. He was only a handful of steps closer to the inn when he remembered the whip he was supposed to receive. "Hey, can I get my weapon?" he asked.

Banemaw was already behind him, offering it on her palms like a sacrifice given to a god.

Kadorax took the weapon, and then he saw *Weapon Expertise: Whip* flash on the side of his vision. Shortly after the message faded, several more followed it, conveying his proficiency with greatswords and spears.

"I'm going to need a real weapon," Kadorax mumbled.

He took the whip and tied it to his belt, a dissatisfied frown on his face. He had never used a whip, in combat or otherwise, and it felt unreasonably impractical despite the undeniable intimidation factor that came with it. *You picked it*, he reminded himself. *Have to figure it out sometime.*

When he reached the top of the stairs, Kadorax found Syzak waiting for him, a staff in the serpent-man's hand.

"I went shaman again," Syzak announced before the question could be asked, "though I'll be building down a different path to change it up. I've got *Spike Trap*, *Summon Rain*, and *Cure Minor Ailments*. What'd you get?"

Kadorax shook his head. He wasn't sure where to begin. Wincing, he lifted his shirt to show his companion the soul rod lodged in his flesh. "It hurts like a bitch," he stated. "And Banemaw gave me a whip. But I'm slowly losing my mind, so I've got that going for me."

Syzak laughed as he called the human's character sheet to his vision. "Damn, Kadorax. *Encroaching Insanity* looks terrifying."

"Where to?" Kadorax asked, hoping to change the subject.

Syzak pointed back at the bar. "We need to eat, remember? Let's grab some food and some better clothes, and then we can try to find a lord for our first quest."

CHAPTER 3

The free clothes the two had been given by the barkeep were hardly better than the roughspun items they had looted from the dressers in the rooms. Both Syzak and Kadorax had opted to wear both sets of clothing in a vain attempt to ward off the cold. The town they had spawned in was called Coldport according to the barkeep, and it certainly lived up to its name. South of the inn was a small harbor on a river, but the water was almost frozen over, and little children in heavy parkas were happily playing atop the ice near the shore. To the north, the wind and snow obscured almost everything, and the Boneridge Mountains towered far off on the horizon to the east under the rising sun.

"We have a long way to go to get back to the temple," Kadorax lamented.

Syzak's razor-sharp teeth chattered together violently. "Let's find a lord. I'll take the first job they offer," he said. Typically, the snake-man's voice sounded like a creepy serpentine hiss, but the cold chopped it as he spoke and turned it into something almost comical. "The town hall is just at the end of the road. Let's go." He didn't wait to see if Kadorax would follow before setting off in the hall's direction.

Coldport was a small village, though their town hall was somewhat large and warm, a welcome respite from the elements for what appeared to be at least half the town. There were even a few vendors set up inside, making the building feel more like a market square than a civic construction. On a raised floor a few feet above the rest of the bustle, a lean man in a formal coat and hat was recording figures dictated to him by several others similarly attired.

"Come on, there's the board," Syzak said, pointing a scaly finger at a large panel hanging on the far wall with all sorts of notices pinned to it.

Kadorax scanned the announcements for something that looked interesting. "Pig farming, rat extermination, security for a nobleman's dinner party, healing a team of draft horses, sailing . . ." he read aloud. "Coldport doesn't have anything good."

"Here's one that might work: meeting an emissary on the road and escorting her into town," Syzak said, pointing to the flyer.

Kadorax pulled one of the sheets from the wall. "Here it is, the local blacksmith was captured by a band of thieves!" he read.

Syzak took the quest from his friend's hand and pinned it back on the board where it belonged. "We're way too low level for that, remember?"

"Yeah, maybe. I don't know about being a bastion, though. It feels like I could be crazy strong." Somewhere deep inside, Kadorax felt like the class he had chosen was somehow stronger than other classes of his level, like he had been given some advantage he hadn't yet fully realized.

"You haven't even picked your level two talent!" Syzak reminded him, shaking his head.

"Fine, we'll do the escort quest first, and then we'll rescue the blacksmith. I'm going to need some heavy armor," Kadorax said.

"Heavy armor?" the snake-man questioned. "You've always used light in the past."

Kadorax turned so only his companion could see his front, then lifted his shirt to reveal the soul rod. His chest still throbbed with pain, but he could feel himself slowly growing accustomed to it.

"What the—"

"I'll explain it later," Kadorax cut in as he let his shirt fall. "Once I figure it out for myself. All I know now is that if it gets damaged, I die."

Kadorax took the paper detailing the escort quest and read it over, committing the important parts to memory before stuffing the folded sheet into his belts. His simple clothes didn't even have pockets. Finding the lord who had offered the challenge proved rather simple, as all the town's nobles were already gathered in the warm hall.

"Lady Brinn, Lord of the Frozen Coast," the imposing woman said once Kadorax had made the introductions. She was of average height and build, but her voice was full of confidence, laden with an 'I don't have time for this' kind of attitude. A heavy studded mace hung loosely from her belt, and the callouses on her hands said she'd used it more than once.

"We've come to accept your challenge," Kadorax stated. "We will escort the emissary from Assir safely to the harbor, my lord."

The woman thought it over for only a second before nodding. "Fine," she said, making the deal official. "The reward is forty iron bars, payable upon the emissary's safe arrival."

It was commonplace, especially during the lower levels, to ask for some of the reward up front in order to get properly outfitted for the quest at hand. "It is cold, my lord," Kadorax continued. "We humbly request warmer clothes and proper boots before heading into the wilderness."

Again, Lady Brinn answered quickly, saying, "I can provide it, and you shall receive twenty iron bars as reward, not forty."

"Yes, my lord," Kadorax accepted. The drastic reduction, as opposed to going into debt to acquire the clothing, meant he and Syzak would be able to keep their upfront payment even if they didn't complete the quest, though failure in Agglor often meant death anyways.

"My estate is south along the river," Brinn explained. "Go there, and my bondsman will see to it that you are properly clothed for the journey."

The lady gave them directions to the estate and a map to the meeting point with the emissary, and then Kadorax and Syzak set off toward the river.

"Been a long time since we've done an escort quest, hasn't it?" Kadorax casually asked on the walk.

"Well, there was that dragon egg we guarded through the swamp not long ago," Syzak reminded him. "But I suppose it doesn't count since we killed the owner once he paid us."

Kadorax laughed at the memory. He hadn't been evil in his previous life, not exactly, but he had been far from what most would have considered to be good. Simply put, Kadorax followed no code. There were others who worshipped the gods of Agglor and were voluntarily bound by various creeds or oaths—and Kadorax viewed them all as weak. Any limitation was to be avoided. Still, Kadorax didn't think of himself as an amoral person. He didn't go from village to village wantonly slaughtering. Instead, the former assassin had only killed when it was advantageous—usually in hopes of a huge payoff.

Walking next to him down the street in the center of Coldport, Syzak was of a different mind altogether. The snake-man was loyal only to his former owner, and he understood little of human ethical dilemmas, even after so many years spent in Agglor. Typically, Kadorax had to keep Syzak's propensity to kill somewhat in check, though the shaman at least understood when taking prisoners was in order.

Lady Brinn's estate wasn't nearly as large as the two adventurers had envisioned, but it still towered over the houses nearby. Kadorax knocked on the door with the bottom of his fist. After a few moments, a smartly dressed man open the door and ushered them inside. As was the norm for many quests, Kadorax and Syzak had been expected, so the bondsman took them directly to a parlor room where a large amount of clothing and other equipment had been laid out.

"No dagger or short sword," the bastion said after a quick inspection of the gear. "But having an actual pair of boots will be nice."

Syzak found the heaviest garment present, a thick traveling cloak made of wool and interlocking patches of leather, and wrapped his cold body greedily within its folds. "There we go," he hissed with pleasure.

"You got a staff to cast spells from your training," Kadorax lamented. "I have no idea how to use a whip." He found a pair of leather boots that were pretty close to a decent fit and slipped them on. There were gloves, as well as a knee-length coat, and the whole ensemble made him look more like a street beggar than an adventurer about to set out on a quest.

"If it snows, you'll need a hat," the snake-man said.

Kadorax rummaged through the rest of the clothes and gear, but he didn't find one. "I need some XP even more than a hat," he remarked. "Once we start getting a few survival talents, we won't have to worry about the cold."

"Even a basic escort quest should get us at least one level."

"Yeah, I hope so," Kadorax said. "Let's hit the road. The sooner we get to the emissary, the better. Maybe we can get this all wrapped up before nightfall."

Outside, the wind was relentless. It blew in from the river, carrying crystals of frost and snow that clung to Kadorax's skin wherever it was exposed.

Their map led them north along a road that quickly turned into nothing more than frozen dirt winding through gentle hills and rocky outcroppings. "There should be an outpost a little ways into the foothills," Kadorax said. They found a marker hammered into the road at an intersection, and their map instructed them to take the eastern path, keeping the distant mountains in front of them.

Then, after several uneventful hours of trudging forward and bemoaning the cold, they saw a plume of smoke rising up from a chimney that marked the outpost's location. In the wilderness, the small places were used by anyone who could find them and gather enough fuel to take advantage of the hearth. Travelers of means, or those too slow to make their trips in a single day, often stayed overnight at the various outposts dotting the landscape of Agglor, and that made them prime targets for both low-level adventurers and bandits in search of a quick sack of loot.

"Should be a simple enough quest," Kadorax announced. The two were standing on a low ridge of jagged rock overlooking the outpost. There were several horses and a single wagon, and one man in armor roamed aimlessly around in front of the door. "Looks like the emissary already has guards, and no high-level bandits would bother with such a small caravan. Not unless they're profoundly stupid. It isn't worth the cold."

"Let's not waste any time," Syzak said, moving toward the outpost without hesitation. He kept his eyes on the smoke, clearly eager to be inside, and made sure his staff wasn't visible from under his cloak so he didn't accidentally raise an alarm. Some people were unnerved by snake-men, and Kadorax never knew what reactions they would get, especially when approaching unannounced. He laughed to himself when he realized how little had changed since the shaman had arrived in Agglor and grown legs. Back on Earth, he had elicited even more fearful responses whenever he had escaped his cage.

The guard patrolling the front hailed the two when they were near enough for the wind to not steal their words.

"We're here about the emissary headed to Coldport," Syzak replied with a friendly wave.

"Don't mention our levels or let him see your character sheet," Kadorax added under his breath. "Though I doubt it will matter anyways."

The armored man pushed open the outpost's only door to show them the way inside. The interior room was small, made entirely of stone, and the top reached three stories into the sky with a ladder leading to the uppermost battlements.

On the ground floor, a middle-aged woman sat next to the fire with a distant look in her eyes. Across from her, a sickly looking child rocked back and forth on his heels, his arms wrapped tightly around his knees.

"You're the emissary?" Kadorax asked, stepping to the side of the door and shutting it behind him.

The woman looked up momentarily, then glanced back to the fire. "Lady Brinn is my mother," she began. "I am the mayor of Assir, a town not far to the northeast at the edge of the Boneridge Mountains. I'm en route to Coldport to get on a boat bound for the capital. I suspect my personal guard, Kel, is more than capable of looking after my son and I, but my mother likes to worry. She's always been rather high strung." The woman's hair was long, falling roughly to her elbow in tight brown curls. For a mayor, her appearance was rather disheveled, like she hadn't slept in days.

Kadorax summoned her character sheet to his vision. Not everyone in Agglor even had a sheet; some, especially lifelong farmers and others who lived in the peaceful countryside, did not complete their training. The emissary's sheet took Kadorax a bit by surprise.

Brinna of Assir, Human, Mayor of Assir Village
Rogue - Level Five
Strength: 13
Agility: 17
Fate: 10
Spirit: 11
Charisma: 9

Active Conditions: Wasting Sickness: Rank 1 - Brinna has been afflicted with a magical disease, and her organs are beginning to suffer. Without treatment, ranks will increase. At rank 4, Brinna will likely perish. Penalties to Strength, Fate, and Charisma increase with each rank.

The emissary's sheet had a moderate list of rogue abilities under the *Wasting Sickness*, but Kadorax knew them all by heart. Rogues and assassins were very much alike, and many of their talents and abilities were identical. Glancing at the list sent a bit of melancholy through Kadorax's mind. He could recognize every ability on the list, and he knew he had been able to use some of them in the past, but the specific memories of how they worked were lost.

"You're sick," Kadorax stated without any tact whatsoever. "Your son looks even worse."

Brinna stared at the man, her eyes hollow. "He has *Wasting Sickness: Rank 3*," she explained. "That's why I'm going to the capital. They were supposed to send a cure, but it never arrived. So, for the next few weeks, I have set aside my duties as mayor and taken up the mantle of an emissary on behalf of the people. It is not just my village which suffers. Everyone who lives in the western foothills of the Boneridge Mountains will be afflicted before long. We can't contain the plague."

Despite his heavy clothes and proximity to the fire, the boy shivered. A bit of drool escaped the corner of his mouth.

"You should get moving at once," Kel said. His voice was just a bit too loud to be comfortable in the small outpost.

"You aren't joining us?" Syzak asked.

The man shook his head. "I must return to Assir and care for those that remain. With everyone so sick, the villagers are ripe for an attack. It is only a matter of time before a bandit lord or even a pack of wolves overruns the streets."

Kadorax began to wonder if the *Wasting Sickness* was contagious, and he took a small step backward. "Then let's hit the road, Lady Brinna," he said quickly. "No use staying here."

The woman stood, and Kadorax realized how tall she was. Her body looked toned, though the muscle of her arms and legs was only barely visible beneath the leather and fur she wore, and Kadorax knew she would cut an imposing image as a both a mayor and a rogue when healthy.

Brinna lifted her sickly son from the floor of the outpost, then used her boot to push a pile of sand onto the fire in the hearth.

Outside and in the cold once more, Brinna offered her guard a weak farewell before turning south. "Several hours of daylight remain. We should not waste it," she said.

Kadorax took a minute to introduce himself and Syzak, and then the four began back toward Coldport, though Brinna could not move quickly with her son bound up in her arms.

"You've seen some combat, then?" the bastion asked. A level five rogue was an odd candidate for a mayor, though Kadorax had known of dozens of government officials back on Earth who he would have described by the same moniker.

Brinna nodded. "My twin sister was the mayor of Assir before me, a bard like most government types, and I ran our ragtag village guard. There wasn't much crime, just the usual drunken ruffians every now and then, but I did see some action against a band of jackals harrying our farmers last year."

"Damned dogheads," Kadorax muttered. "Filthy beasts can't leave us humans alone, can they?"

"Ha, they aren't so bad when they stick to their caves and their dens," the mayor said.

The four trekked slowly through the rocky foothills, stopping frequently to allow Brinna to rest her arms from the weight of her son. Sometime before nightfall, Kadorax caught the scent of a charcoal fire lingering in the air.

"Someone was nearby recently," he said, holding up his hand to stop the group.

Syzak's tongue flicked to either side of his mouth. "They're still here," the snake-man said in a low whisper. "There was a campfire, cooked meat, and humans."

Kadorax's right arm drifted near to the whip at his belt, but he had yet to try and practice with it, so he knew he wouldn't have the slightest idea what to do with it in his hands. "Do you know which direction?" he whispered.

Clutching her son tightly to her chest, Brinna fell back a few steps to crouch next to a boulder that was almost large enough to offer adequate cover. "We should just keep going. There isn't much time," she urged.

"You're right," Kadorax said after a moment of consideration. He took a few steps forward, and then he saw a flicker of firelight reflected off a nearby patch of stone that caught his eye.

Syzak hushed the mayor with a scaly finger held to his mouth, but the woman did not need encouragement to remain silent. Under normal circumstances, she looked like she would not have shied from a fight. As she hid with her sick son, Brinna's hand drifted down to one of the daggers in her boots. Carefully, she set her son down—his head lolling awkwardly to the side—and watched the two adventurers.

"Let's go," Kadorax whispered. He brought up his character sheet and scrolled through the abilities he had available to him as a level two bastion. He focused on the *Nimble Feet* talent, keeping it visible while the rest of his sheet vanished, just in case he needed to purchase it quickly.

The two crept along the side of the barely visible path toward the fire. Ahead, perhaps a hundred feet from the trail toward Coldport, three humanoid figures sat around a dwindling fire, the smell of poorly prepared meat lingering heavily in the air. Behind the three figures, far enough from the cookfire to not benefit from its heat, was a bearded human with his hands tied behind his back.

"The blacksmith?" Syzak wondered under his breath.

Kadorax nodded. "Two quests at once?" He felt a wave of adrenaline enter his bloodstream at the prospect of a battle.

"I don't know," Syzak quietly hissed. "Three against two, and I don't think I need to remind you what levels we are."

Kadorax barely processed his companion's words. "You have *Spike Trap*, right?" he asked.

Staff in hand, Syzak had started to scamper forward when Kadorax caught him by the forearm. "I'll get their attention, then you'll need to make the trap at their feet," the human said.

"It's only rank 1, so—"

Kadorax unhooked his whip and stepped a few paces toward the campfire. He threw his arm through the air in what he thought would produce a huge crack from the unorthodox weapon, then frowned when the end quietly thudded into the ground at his feet. "Well . . ." He tossed the whip aside and picked up a rock, hurling it as hard as he could toward the figures.

Luckily, the rock achieved the intended result.

"Hey!" called one of the men seated around the fire. All three of them stood. Behind the trio, the bound captive's eyes went wide in surprise.

"We've come to rescue him!" Kadorax shouted, pointing a finger toward the prisoner. Without a proper weapon, he didn't feel intimidating at all, but the bandits weren't particularly difficult to goad.

They charged right toward Kadorax and Syzak, rusty and

dented swords in their hands. The ground between the two groups wasn't terribly expansive, and most of it was strewn with uneven patches of exposed rock breaking through the topsoil, causing one of the bandits to trip over his own feet and be left behind by his companions.

"*Spike Trap!*" Syzak yelled, moving his staff to cast the spell. At once, a small, radial pit no more than three feet deep appeared right in the path of the oncoming brigands. The bottom of the pit was lined with wooden spikes, though they weren't particularly secure or terribly sharp. Still, falling three feet onto spikes certainly had a very specific effect on the charging bandits, and their screams soon filled the air. One of them was badly hurt, perhaps even mortally wounded. The second had used the first as a squishy bit of cushion and had emerged from the pit almost entirely unscathed. A ragged cut oozing blood through the man's right pant leg appeared to be his only injury.

The third bandit, slowed by the uneven ground, easily avoided the *Spike Trap* altogether.

"That didn't go quite as well as planned," Kadorax said under his breath. He had enough of his own knowledge left from his previous life to be able to read the movements of the bandits and determined that they were relatively untrained, but the information wasn't helpful. He had no weapon, no easy route of escape, and no chance of negotiation.

Time to pick a talent, he thought, quickly calling up his available skills.

Nimble Feet would mean abandoning the emissary and her son to die. He pushed it aside to view *Torment*, then quickly selected it and rolled backward to recover his whip from the ground.

"*Torment!*" he yelled, striking toward the bandit. A tendril of darkness wrapped itself around the whip, and the weapon rocketed forward with magical guidance. It slashed down the side of the nearest bandit's neck, leaving an angry streak of blood in its wake.

Throwing down his sword, the bandit reached up to his neck with a look of horror plastered to his face. Kadorax knew he hadn't inflicted much damage—the whip hadn't done more than scratch the surface of the man's skin. Still, the man's advance came to a halt.

He had no way of knowing what was going on inside the bandit's head, but Kadorax could tell it was extreme. The man's eyes darted from side to side. His mouth was frozen in a soundless scream, and his hands trembled as he gripped his neck.

Not wasting any time, Kadorax pounced on the bandit's discarded weapon and came up in a roll. He slashed to his right, and the pitted steel bit into the man's thigh, rewarding him with a gout of warm blood. The bandit fell backward, fully engulfed in his own screaming, and then there was only one.

The bandit hesitated, squaring his feet and preparing for battle. His sword was almost identical to the one in Kadorax's hands, but looked stronger and more fit for combat. Kadorax pegged him for level three or higher.

"There's two of us," the bastion stated, summoning all the confidence he could find. He pointed to Syzak, and the snake-man bared his rows of jagged teeth.

"Take your wounded," Syzak hissed, "and run. Save yourself while you can."

Kadorax swung his stolen sword casually by his side like he was some renowned fighter able to kill scores of men without breaking a sweat. In reality, he was terrified. He knew he didn't have the skills he needed, and his base stats were pathetic.

Syzak took two steps forward and began chanting as though he was going to cast a high-level spell, exuding confidence.

"*Sweeping Strike!*" the bandit yelled, slashing horizontally for Kadorax's chest.

Kadorax skipped backward, and the front of his shirt was caught in the blade's path. The material parted easily under the magical attack, and then the bandit was rolling through the swing with impossible speed to where Syzak stood. Luckily, the shaman had his staff on his left, and the bandit's weapon crashed into it with a loud crack. Kadorax dashed forward, stolen blade held low and tight to his body. He didn't dare to try anything fancy, especially because he could already feel the effects of so much combat at such a low level, and he didn't have any endurance talents. Regardless of Kadorax's exhaustion, the bandit couldn't possibly attend to the half-snake shaman in front of him and the human behind, and he was skewered where he stood.

Kadorax drove the blade into the man's lower torso until the handguard hit cloth, and then he ripped it out, dropping the dead bandit to the ground like a heap of discarded bricks. Not far off, the wounded and terrified bandit cried into his hands on the ground, though Kadorax suspected the effect of his *Torment* ability had long since worn off.

"We're lucky these idiots weren't too bright," Kadorax said, flicking some of the gore from the sword in his hand as he moved to the last bandit.

"Just finish him quickly—I can't stand when they scream like that," Syzak added. He panted from the effort of the

Spike Trap he had cast. Being only level one, the spell had consumed a huge amount of his energy for the day.

Kadorax leveled his blade above the wounded bandit's neck, then leaned on the hilt to drive it home. The man's screams quickly died in his ruined throat. "You there," he called to the captive, "you're the kidnapped blacksmith from Coldport, yes?"

The burly man, bound at the wrists and gagged, nodded.

When he was freed, he took a few moments to stretch and walk a bit before introducing himself. "I'm Ayers," he said, his voice gruff with age. "Thanks for coming to my rescue."

Syzak was busy rooting through the dead men's belongings, stacking a neat pile of useful items next to one of the bodies. When the *Spike Trap* had run out of sustaining magic, the bloodied spikes had vanished altogether, leaving nothing but a torn bandit on the flat ground.

"I'm glad we found you, Ayers," Kadorax said. In the bottom right corner of his vision, three numbers flashed by in bright colors. They showed his experience, and he was surprised to find that he had gained enough to reach level three, though killing three bandits of higher level certainly warranted a high reward.

"Are you on the road back to—"

A deep wail interrupted the blacksmith's sentence, and all three of them turned back toward the rocks with a start. "What was that?" Ayers asked.

"Brinna," Kadorax solemnly stated. In the heat of the battle, he had forgotten her. Pushing aside his next tier of available talents, he darted back to the road, but Brinna did not appear in trouble. She was hunched over her son near a large boulder, and her sobs told everyone that the boy had died.

RESPAWN

"What happened?" Syzak asked. He tried to sound gentle, that much was obvious, but his serpentine head and jaw made his soft words sound more sinister than anything else.

The woman looked briefly over her shoulder, then turned her gaze back to the body in her arms. "There," she said, pointing down the road.

There was a fourth bandit, lying face down on the stone and dirt. One of Brinna's daggers protruded from the top of his spine.

"He came from the other direction . . . just after you two charged in like idiots," the woman explained between sobs.

Kadorax lifted her off the ground with an arm. She let the boy fall from her grasp, and his lifeless body strangely did not show any signs of physical harm.

"He doesn't look injured," Kadorax said quietly after a few moments of letting Brinna exhaust her emotions. "How did it happen?"

She shook her head against his chest. "It was just the fright," she wept. "He was too weak, and his heart couldn't take the stress."

For some reason, that made Kadorax feel at least a little better about the situation, though he couldn't help but attach the majority of the blame to himself. Attacking the bandits *had* been reckless. There wasn't any way to really justify it other than to say Kadorax was typically reckless at a low level. After all, he and Syzak would respawn if they died. It wouldn't be ideal, but it wouldn't mean the absolute end for them. The boy, less than twenty years of age, was not afforded the same luxury. His death would be permanent.

"I'm so sorry," was all Kadorax could think to say. He had been in his early twenties when he had arrived in Agglor, and he had been to a handful of funerals back on Earth. Back then, just the same as now, he had no idea what to say. There was nothing that would bring the boy back short of finding a powerful necromancer to reanimate his corpse, but that wouldn't restore his mind anyways.

"He was going to die soon, I know that," Brinna stated, brushing some of the tears from her face and regaining a measure of composure. "The cure would come too late for him. I just . . . I didn't want it to end this way. Not here. Not like this."

"We'll bury him, if it makes you feel better," Kadorax added. "Or we can bring the body to Coldport for a proper funeral."

Brinna turned to look once more at her dead son. "There are enough rocks. We can make a cairn, and then we should leave. I can come back later on my return trip to the villages. If there's time then, I can give him a proper burial."

Leaning against the rock where her son had died, Brinna watched the other three place stones on top of her son's body. There wasn't any great place for the cairn to be constructed, so they made their rock pile near the bandits' campfire, as that was at least a decent ways from the road.

When the four were finally underway once more toward Coldport, the sky was dark with night. The blacksmith didn't say much beyond offering his thanks, and the two adventurers let Brinna walk in silence amongst her thoughts.

Level three, Kadorax thought to himself with half a smile. Taking risks meant advancing quickly, and he was more than eager to be strong enough to face the Gar'kesh once more. Before he got to his newly available talents, he had three stat points to distribute, and those were a relatively easy decision. Especially in the beginning, he preferred a balanced build, especially until he could figure out exactly what it was he was supposed to do as a bastion. At level three, his sheet read:

Strength: 15
Agility: 14
Fate: 20
Spirit: 14
Charisma: 14
Bond: 10

Satisfied with his decision to raise *Agility*, *Spirit*, and *Fate*, he expanded the available talents to take up the majority of his vision, trusting Syzak in front of him to warn of any oncoming treacherous footing.

Torment: Rank 2 - The bastion's weapon magically extends to a second target beyond the first, and Torment inflicts slightly more damage than rank 1. Torment has an increased effect when used with a whip. Effect: moderate. Cooldown: 28 minutes.

Improved Perception: Rank 1 - The bastion sees more in the distance, especially foes and dangerous traps. Improved Perception allows the bastion to see magically hidden objects at rank 6. Passive.

Bastion Weapon Proficiency: Rank 1 - Chaos bring fluidity, and the bastion becomes proficient in all weapon types, allowing weapon-specific talents for those types to be earned. Passive.

Fortune Teller (Fate: 20): Rank 1 - The bastion can mold Chaos itself into visions of the future, sometimes predicting events yet to come. Effect: minor. Cooldown: 1 day.

Immediately, Kadorax liked the look of *Bastion Weapon Proficiency* and the rather mysterious *Fortune Teller* talent. He had never heard of anyone else being able to accurately predict the future, but he also had no idea how useful it would. He imagined a bright yellow warning flashing up in his vision the split second before he was impaled on some minotaur's spear or eaten by a dragon. It probably wouldn't be useful without higher ranks, and that would mean forgoing a lot of other talents that were certain to be equally as interesting.

Thinking of the stolen bandit sword tucked into his belt and hitting his thigh with every step, he focused on *Bastion Weapon Proficiency* and locked in his choice. As far as he knew, every class in Agglor had a similar talent that unlocked all sorts of weapon choices, but he hadn't thought any classes other than warriors and fighters were able to gain access to all weapon types. As an assassin, he had taken a similar talent, though that one had only applied to unorthodox implements such as wire of all varieties, shuriken, razors, caltrops, certain types of gas bombs, and blowguns. Having proficiency with the short sword meant he could use his whip to initiate combat if he needed to, and then he could revert to something more familiar and still earn relevant experience points and talents.

"Hey, Syzak, did you level from that fight?" he asked his companion.

The snake-man nodded in the darkness. "Yeah, level two. I took *Improved Traps: Rank 1*," he said. "It increases the size of *Spike Trap* and any other traps I learn later on. My other options were a new healing spell or a weird passive that would let me interact better with animals."

"Ha, a snake going full beastmaster would be cool, though!" Kadorax replied.

"As one who used to live in a small glass cage, I don't think I would feel right keeping wild animals as my slaves," Syzak said, only half joking.

"Yeah, you're right," Kadorax said. "I think *Improved Traps* was the right choice. That *Spike Trap* was really effective."

Syzak had one of the bandits' swords on his own belt

as well, though he'd probably never need to use it—at least not before getting something of higher quality. In his past life, the snake-man had wielded a staff to cast his spells and had a pair of short sickles for anything that wandered too close, though they had been more objects of appearance in the long run. The way the two worked so well in tandem, not much ever got close enough to Syzak to engage him in melee combat.

"We'll have plenty of iron when we get our reward, any idea what you'll want?" Kadorax asked. Iron ingots were a staple among low-level quests, as everyone needed gear, and small villages often operated more on bartering than currency anyways.

"I wouldn't mind iron-shod boots," he answered.

"Good idea," Kadorax agreed. "Walking on dirt and gravel is terrible in cloth."

CHAPTER 4

The four traveling companions reached Coldport a few hours after dawn. They were quite hungry, tired, and more than a little cold. Brinna still hadn't spoken a word since they had built a cairn for her son.

At Lady Brinn's estate, they were treated to a warm welcome complete with a warm meal. Kadorax and Syzak collected their reward of iron bars on a small wooden cart. As mother and daughter took some time to reconnect after breakfast, Kadorax and Syzak went to visit their new friend at the forge.

"Good to see you again," Ayers beamed when the two walked through the door of his forge. "I have your reward, even though you didn't formally accept the quest that was posted."

The man brought out an oilcloth and unrolled it on a wooden desk a few feet away from his anvil. Inside were two proper belts and scabbards. "Carrying those swords out in the open has to be a pain. These should help," he said.

Kadorax and Syzak both accepted their reward without complaint. Sword belts weren't expensive by any means, but they were certainly useful.

"We need some boots," Kadorax said once his new belt was secured around his waist. He guessed his midsection had at least four inches of fat that hadn't been there in his previous life. He hated feeling so soft.

Ayers wheeled the little cart full of iron to the other side of his furnace. "A good pair of leather for the both of you?" he asked.

"Iron-shod leather, if you can," Syzak corrected.

The blacksmith looked over the ingots once more and counted them. "They won't be the prettiest boots in Agglor, but I can make them," he said. "Good leather is expensive, you know?"

Kadorax extended his hand to finalize the agreement. "Can you have them ready tomorrow?"

"Aye," he answered with a smile. "Since you saved my life, anything you need I'll work on right away, whenever you want. Just keep bringing me more materials."

The two thanked Ayers and then left, heading back in the direction of the town hall. "Well, we've got ourselves a blacksmith now," Kadorax said. "Lady Brinn will let us stay one night at her estate, so we'll need to do something for whoever runs the inn to secure food and a room. After that, all we'll have left to do is establish a fiefdom for some steady tax income."

Syzak laughed and slapped him on the back. "You can't seriously be planning a fiefdom already, can you? You're at least ten or twelve levels from completing a quest with that kind of reward," he said.

"Ah, but a man can dream, can he not?" Kadorax sighed.

"I still have no idea what that means," the snake-man replied. "I'm not even sure I believe that these dreams you speak of are real. It sounds insane."

"It really is all darkness when you sleep?" Kadorax asked. When the two had first arrived in Agglor, Kadorax's dreams had been relentless, like his body had taken to dreaming as a way of coping with the sudden change in everything else. He had dreamt of Earth, of all the things he had loved to do, but as he had advanced through Agglor, the dreams had slowed. For whatever reason, Syzak did not experience any dreams whatsoever, and he had no memories of experiencing them on Earth, either.

"Yes," the snake-man answered. "Perhaps animals do not dream at all. Or perhaps you've been putting me on for twenty years as some elaborate joke only you will find humorous."

Kadorax shook his head. "But the dog dreamed all the time, right? At least it looked like she did. Animals have to dream."

"And yet I do not."

"Whatever," Kadorax concluded. "Let's get another quest so we can figure out where we'll get to eat and sleep in Coldport, shall we?"

Bustling as ever, the town hall was loud and noisy. Several groups of petitioners were anxiously awaiting their turn before the mayor, and a group of well-dressed nobles were conducting a tea ceremony of sorts in one of the more lavishly appointed rooms.

Kadorax and Syzak went straight for the quest board. A dozen or so leaflets were tacked to the board in no particular order.

"Here's one that might be our level," Syzak pointed out.

"Undead have been seen in the local copper mine, and the foreman wants help exterminating them."

"What's the pay?" Kadorax asked.

"Only ten iron ingots, but five copper ones as well," answered the shaman.

Kadorax thought it over for a moment. "Not bad, but experience from killing undead is always pathetic. We need to power level if we're going to have a chance at killing the Gar'kesh."

Syzak looked them over again, but he didn't see anything terribly promising. "Coldport is too small to have really lucrative quests," he said. The most efficient way to acquire experience in Agglor was through grouping together to take down larger enemies, and those types of quests were typically found at military outposts, large mercenary encampments, and other official locations, not backwoods villages along frozen rivers.

"New quest incoming! Make way at the board!" a voice called from the town hall's door. A man in a green tabard bearing an unfamiliar crest marched toward the board, a scroll in his hands. Whenever someone posted a job, there was always a bit of formalism surrounding the event—as though it was something far grander than a man nailing a piece of paper to a piece of wood.

"Adventurers wanted for lycanthrope removal," Kadorax read aloud as the man posted the notice. "Contact Lord Percival by the docks for more information."

"A lycan? That would give a ton of experience," Syzak noted with a serpentine smile.

The two shared a knowing look, each fully aware of the other's thoughts regarding boss-style quests—and lycanthropes in general. "That's our quest," Kadorax stated.

They left the town hall quickly, heading toward the

chilly river that gave Coldport its name. "And what about food and a place to stay?" Syzak asked, remembering their original intention.

"We'll make plenty," Kadorax told him. "The reward was in gold, not raw materials. We can just buy a room."

Coldport's docks were small by comparison to just about any other city or village in all of Agglor, and there were only a couple modest warehouses. A single-room structure that housed the harbormaster's offices stood in front of them all, and that was where Kadorax and Syzak began their search.

"We're looking for Lord Percival," the man began when they had entered and approached the large desk that dominated the space.

The attendant glanced up from a ledger where he was transcribing numbers from one piece of parchment to another. "Second wharf. By the red ship," the man said without much enthusiasm.

Kadorax thanked the attendant, and the two went back outside, easily spotting the red ship since it was the only one in port. The vessel was somewhat large, perhaps a bit too large for the size of the river in which it sat, and there were a handful of sailors moving about on its top deck. Curiously, the ship's figurehead was not the typical mermaid or seafaring god that most sailors of Agglor preferred, but instead the wooden sculpture was of a shackled child—probably a boy, though the details of the features had been worn smooth by the ocean—with a twisted expression full of pain, and a blade sticking out of his chest.

"That's a pretty messed-up ship," Kadorax remarked, leading the way down the wharf.

Syzak nodded in agreement. "Makes me wonder what Lord Percival is going to be like," he said.

As it turned out, Lord Percival was quite easy to spot. The captain was resplendently dressed, pacing back and forth on the dock next to a ramp, and shouting orders to his crew all around. They were hard at work unloading crates onto the pier, and several muscled dockhands strained under the weight of each crate as they moved them toward one of the nearby warehouses. A gaudy feather bounced to and fro as the captain gestured.

"Lord Percival?" Kadorax inquired from a few paces away. He didn't want to get too close to the lively captain for fear of being accidentally hit by a pointing hand.

"Yes?" the man quickly answered, turning with a flourish of his embroidered coat. He was about a foot taller than Kadorax, with a bit of deranged mania glinting in his deep blue eyes.

Kadorax wasn't exactly sure where to begin. "You posted a quest in town?" he started. "About a lycanthrope?"

"Yes," the captain confirmed, "so I have indeed. And I am to assume you two have come for details, hoping to collect?"

The two had to wait for a moment as the captain directed more of his underlings in the unloading process. "Well, do you have any more details? We'd like to take the quest."

Percival dug in one of his elaborate pockets for a moment before producing a tightly bound scroll of parchment and handing it over to the adventurers. "The *Grim Sleeper* has been lawfully commissioned to pursue a foul beast, and her last known whereabouts place the lycanthrope here in Coldport," he explained. "I'm always looking to augment the *Grim Sleeper's* forces with an additional mercenary or two such as yourselves, preferably on the front lines."

Kadorax unfurled the scroll and held it so the snake-man at his side could read as well. "A woman, middle-aged, from

Assir village, seen multiple times in and around Coldport. She's to be considered extremely dangerous, with unknown allies, advanced levels of illusion magic, and shapeshifting magic usable for limited periods, though the parameters are unknown. The lycanthrope's last known aliases: Brinn, Brinna, Brianna, Briar, and other derivatives thereof," the man said, his voice quieting as he read the names at the end of the parchment.

"What say you, fine adventurers?" Percival carried on. "Fancy a werewolf hunt? A little fur to darken your blades?"

"We've met that woman," Syzak hissed. Perhaps it was a product of his former life as a house pet, but whatever the reason, the snake-man *hated* dishonesty. He had no issue with murder—especially not with murder for hire—but for whatever reason, Syzak loathed dishonesty. He stomped one of his boots on the wooden deck beneath his feet and spat.

"Oh?" Percival raised an eyebrow. "And this were-beast, did you engage her in combat?"

Sighing, Kadorax shook his head. "I saw her stats," he said. "She was a level five rogue. I recognized her skills as well. I don't think she's the target."

"Illusion magic can be a fickle entity," the captain said with an almost whimsical air.

Kadorax rubbed a hand on his chin. "Altering her sheet?"

"Is that possible?" Syzak asked.

"I'm not entirely sure . . ." the other adventurer said.

"Perhaps there is another stealing the name, and you two happened upon the real woman?" the captain suggested while directing one of his crew with a wave.

"The older noblewoman?" Syzak wondered aloud.

Kadorax rolled the scroll and handed it back. "Could be either," he stated, "or it could be someone else entirely."

"We'll root out the werewolf," Syzak declared with finality. "When is your crew planning to set out?"

Lord Percival issued a sharp whistle, and a person appeared at the nearby railing a moment later. The captain waved, and the figure began slowly walking down the gangplank, though not with the urgency that any of the other crew had shown. When the person reached the dock, she removed her dark hood, revealing a pale, tattooed face belonging to a withered husk of a woman who could only be referred to as human in the most basic possible sense.

"Gentleman, I'd like to introduce the Grim Sleeper, my personal little death artist who happens to lend her name to my ship as well." Lord Percival placed a hand on the woman's back, eliciting a slight bow from the seemingly ancient woman, and smiled brightly like he was showing off a prized treasure to an interested buyer.

Kadorax tried to access the woman's stats, but she clearly didn't consider him friendly, so her information was hidden. "What a lovely acquaintance," he said under his breath. The Grim Sleeper's tattered robe hung loosely from her body. The stillness of it said she wasn't breathing.

"I bought her for fourteen thousand bars of silver," the captain boasted. "A rather reasonable price for such a powerful warlock, don't you think?"

The Grim Sleeper inched forward, and the two adventurers got a strong waft of the grave emanating from her corpse-like body. The woman was like a plague, a moving blight upon the sunny day that doused everything she came near in gloom. The buying and selling of a warlock's soul, while technically illegal, was something a fair number of the mercenary captains of Agglor practiced. When warlocks became powerful enough, they learned how to place their soul in an enchanted object—a phylactery—and the people who controlled those objects received absolute obedience from their charges.

Aura of Despair: Rank 3 flashed in Kadorax's vision, listing the effects he was already more than aware of feeling. He took a few steps backward, and the aura vanished from his sheet, sending a palpable wave of relief through his mind.

"If you don't mind the Grim Sleeper's company, you may depart with her at once in search of the werewolf," the captain informed them with a smile. As the warlock's master, he was clearly unaffected by her aura.

"Actually," Kadorax said, "we have some gear being made in town. It should be ready tomorrow, then we can leave. Do you have room on your ship for us to stay the night?"

Lord Percival offered an over-exaggerated bow. "By all means! There are bunks on the second deck. You shall find more than enough space near the back, and my crew will give you plenty of privacy, or as much as can be afforded on a ship."

Syzak hadn't taken his eyes from the warlock. "She doesn't stay in the bunk room, right?" he asked, tongue flicking over his scaled lips. Kadorax shared the sentiment.

"I have no need of rest," the woman spoke. Her voice was icy, fogging the air, and deeper than it should have been, coming from a woman of her frail stature.

"Yes," Percival added. "She prefers to patrol the top deck at night when we are in port, and woe to any witless thief who tries to break in and steal from the ship's hold."

Kadorax didn't want to think of the horror that would befall some hapless idiot or drunken sailor who happened to stumble onto the wrong ship completely out of innocent mistake. He got the idea the Grim Sleeper wouldn't offer much mercy on account of circumstance. "Right," he said, leery as the warlock inched forward. "If there's anything you need from us this afternoon, my friend and I are eager to get as much experience as we can. We'd gladly carry shipments or help with the rigging so long as the work yields some reward."

Percival thought for a moment, but it was clear by his expression that he had something in mind. "You two are from the east, yes?" he asked.

Syzak answered in the affirmative.

"I have a collection of star maps—intriguing, really—and they were all compiled in the east. Though my own adventures have taken me far, I simply am not as familiar with the landmarks on that side of the mountains as I am with those on the fairer side. If you two would be willing to take a look at the maps and offer some guidance, I'm sure they would be of some benefit to your *Fate* scores, yes?" the captain explained.

"Maps?" Kadorax repeated to himself. "We've been almost everywhere in the east. I'm sure we could lend a hand."

The two adventurers spent the afternoon hunched over a cluttered deck with a measuring tape, a rusted goniometer, and more candles illuminating the room than either of them cared to count. As it turned out, the maps Percival had collected correlated to much more than just the stars: they were also oriented toward multiple ancient ruins, sites that Kadorax knew well from his life as an assassin roaming through all of Agglor's buried places. With the help of the ship's navigator, a portly elf of at least a hundred years with a beard down to his belly, the maps were finished not long after midnight, and both Kadorax and Syzak were too tired to pay much attention to the terrifying warlock prowling the deck as they made their way to the bunk house.

When dawn broke, the ship was buzzing with activity

once more. The smell of frying pork and seafood filled the oily air, and sailors spared no volume as they shouted to one another over the din of commerce. On the top deck, the glare of the early morning sun off a fresh layer of snow coating Coldport was nearly blinding, especially after being indoors for so long. Near the wheelhouse, Lord Percival had established a breakfast table where sailors came and went as they pleased between their duties. To the starboard side of the wheel, the ship's cook worked over a grill bolted directly to the railing, allowing the coals beneath the cooking surface to be easily dumped right into the ocean.

Kadorax and Syzak ate their fill with the captain looking dutifully after his underlings from the head of the table. When they were close to finished, the Grim Sleeper ascended the stairs next to the wheelhouse like a wraith stalking a victim. Her feet didn't seem to move, and her bedraggled, wispy hair flew in odd directions contrary to the wind.

"We must stage our onslaught soon," she announced with enough force to draw the attention of the three nearest crewmen as well as her intended audience.

Everyone at the breakfast table stood. "Well, you heard it, gentleman," the captain said, rubbing his hands in front of his chest to ward off the cold sting in the air. "We do have a brig here aboard the *Grim Sleeper* which you're more than welcome to use, though the contract does require me to produce a werewolf's head, so I'm not positive how exactly you might come to need such a space."

"We'll take care of it in town, hopefully quietly," Kadorax answered. He had a strong stomach for torture, of that there was no doubt, but the prospect of being in a confined space below deck with the Grim Sleeper was something he wanted to avoid if at all possible.

"Excellent," the captain said with a smile.

"To the wolf," the warlock groaned, turning her back and gliding down the stairs. Kadorax and Syzak followed her—though not very closely—all the way to the edge of downtown Coldport, if the village could be said to have such divisions. With the driving cold, there weren't many villagers about in the streets. Those who caught more than a passing glimpse of the warlock hurried their steps, suddenly aware of a new chill in the air that was a bit too much for their taste, sending them running for the refuge of the indoors.

"Lady Brinna's estate isn't far," Kadorax stated. He felt a twinge of guilt for going after his recent employer, but he held no love for werewolves either. Such shapeshifters were somewhat rare in Agglor, though all of them—at least all that were known to the public—were violent beasts deserving of death.

Moving quickly, the two adventurers took the lead, though they headed toward Ayers' smithy before the estate.

Kadorax made the warlock wait outside in the cold. It didn't appear as though she minded.

"Your boots are ready," the smith said upon recognizing Kadorax and Syzak. He lifted two pairs of heavy boots, leather shod with iron, and dropped them onto the counter.

Even before picking them up, Kadorax could tell they had been enchanted. "You've put a bit of magic in them?" he asked. As an assassin, he had always been wary around things that looked too much like gifts. Those gifts had more often than not turned out to be traps.

Ayers came around the counter and slapped the smaller man on the back. "You saved my life," he reminded Kadorax. "I had some extra runic thread in the back, and I figured you could use it. But don't get too excited. I'm not some master-level enchanter from the king's court. I'm just a blacksmith from a small village who likes to dabble."

Kadorax focused in on the boots, and their magical properties displayed in his vision:

Steady Boots - Increases the wearer's Agility score by 2. Passive while worn.

"Hey, those aren't bad," Kadorax remarked with sincerity. "Thanks a lot."

When the two of them had ditched their shoddy cloth boots and secured the enchanted footwear to their feet, they thanked the smith once more and returned to the blustery cold.

"To the estate," Syzak said with dark determination. "How will we know the woman is the wolf?"

The Grim Sleeper turned her hideous visage upon the adventurers, stepping too close for a moment and affecting them with her powerful aura. "I can taste fear," she declared. Her voice rattled in her dry throat. "The lycanthrope will show herself through her terror."

Kadorax tried to think of a spell or ability that would allow the warlock to literally taste fear, but he didn't know any off the top of his head. He also wasn't sure if the strange woman was even capable of hyperbole, or if perhaps she held some magical item that augmented her perception. "I'm pretty sure both of them will be terrified," he finally stated.

The group moved stoically through Coldport's streets. When they reached the estate, the Grim Sleeper wisely stepped back and around a corner, remaining just barely out of view. Kadorax could only hope her aura didn't extend too far through the walls of the house to reach anyone inside.

The door opened, and the younger Brinna was there to greet them. She wore a grey cotton tunic and matching pants, looking sleek and rogue-like in the early morning sun. "Gentleman," she said with a bit of surprise. "Please, come in out of the cold." She held the door open just enough for the two adventurers to walk past into the opulent foyer.

"We have some grim news," Kadorax said once the door was shut to the blustery air outside. Without any magically enhanced method of detection, he had no other way to root out the lycanthrope, so he figured throwing it out in the open and judging the woman's reaction would have to be good enough.

Brinna looked curious, though she did not respond.

"We were just hired to find a werewolf hiding in the city," Kadorax went on. "Do you know anything?"

The woman placed a hand over her chest in surprise, and her eyes became large, a reaction that appeared genuine. "You're serious?" she almost gasped.

Kadorax nodded.

"In Assir, some of the villagers claimed they had seen such a creature, but I never believed their stories. Some of the older folk liked their ale a bit too much, you know? If it is true . . ."

"We'll find the beast," Kadorax told her. "But there's something else." He stepped close enough to hear her breathing, listening for any signs of authentic fear or surprise. "The shapeshifter has been using your name, or that's what the report claims. What do you know?"

Brinna's breath hitched in her throat for a split second, and that was enough of a reaction for Kadorax to believe the woman was not their target. "My *name?*" she said. "You're positive?"

Kadorax ushered her closer with a hand. "I believe it isn't you," he said, eliciting a nod of agreement from the snake-man at his side. The two had carried out enough interrogations together, albeit usually with the aid of magic, to have come to the same conclusion. "Exactly how much do you know about your mother? That's our next best lead."

"No! Sh—" Brinna gasped, but she cut off her own words before they became loud enough to alert whoever else was in the estate. Her eyes darted to the door on her right.

Silently, Kadorax motioned for Syzak to peer through the crack in the door. When the shaman confirmed the other room to hold no danger, all attention turned back to Brinna.

"She would never . . ." the woman whispered.

Kadorax wanted to believe her—the woman had lost so much recently that the death of her mother would probably be impossible to bear—but he trusted the report from Lord Percival more than the words of a distraught daughter. "She's in the house?" he asked quietly.

Brinna nodded. She pointed to the door on her right. "The room beyond the parlor, through there," she said.

"Good," Kadorax replied with a nod. "First, we need to figure out if she's actually a lycanthrope. Have you noticed anything strange? Anything strange—"

"Like killing villagers and eating them raw?" Syzak interjected, his scaled mouth curling into a snarl.

The woman shook her head. Her eyes didn't leave the floorboards under their feet. "I've only been here a day, and I'm scheduled to leave this afternoon. I have to get to the capital before Assir is lost to the *Wasting Sickness*. If my mother is a werewolf, I . . . I don't know."

"A house like this, few visitors, a remote village; she could be killing people here and hiding the evidence in this very estate. We should investigate," Kadorax stated. It had been several years, but he and Syzak had completed very similar quests in the past—hunting humans who had appeared completely normal but were suspected of harboring dark secrets.

"Where would she hide something she wanted absolutely no one to find?" Syzak whispered.

Brinna turned and led them to another room deeper into the estate. The second area was a kitchen larger than most houses, and a few loaves of baking bread filled it with a sweet and savory aroma. "There's a basement," Brinna said, her eyes watching the doorway. "Perhaps you'll find evidence there."

"And her personal room?" Syzak asked.

"On the second floor. I can show you," she answered.

Kadorax had the higher *Spirit* score of the two, so his perception would naturally be better, though not by much. "I'll take the basement, you take the room," he said.

"Be quick," the snake-man agreed. "I don't want our friend waiting too long and getting bored. Meet here or out front as soon as you can."

Brinna pointed Kadorax in the direction of the basement staircase, and he darted for it at once.

The cellar beneath the estate was dark and wet, full of wooden crates, shelves stacked with food and other mundane items, and a handful of dangling spider webs. Using what meager light drifted down from the kitchen above, Kadorax found a candle mounted to a metal tray on one of the nearby shelves. It took him a few moments longer to find the firesteel resting nearby, and then another minute or so to finally get the candle to light.

The candle didn't help much, but the cellar was also somewhat small, and Kadorax could see most of it from where he stood at the bottom of the stairs. Everything was just as he had expected it to be. There were no overt signs of a werewolf: no bloody paw prints, no tufts of hair wedged in the sides of boxes, and no carcasses from recent feedings. Still, Kadorax moved slowly between the rows of dry goods, taking his time to inspect everything. When he reached the end of the cellar, he looked around for some sort of hidden door or magically concealed alcove cut into the wall. Without any perception talents, he knew he'd never find the evidence he sought if it had been hidden with anything other than mundane efforts.

As Kadorax was about to head back for the stairs, a new idea sank through his mind to settle in the bottom of his thoughts: if Brinna *was* the lycanthrope, the basement was the last place he wanted to be. She could have tricked him, played him for a fool, and separated the two adventurers to make Syzak easier to kill, and he'd be trapped in an underground room with a single exit. *Stupid*, he silently chastised himself. With a higher *Spirit* score, he would have never been so careless.

Kadorax ran toward the staircase, throwing the candle down on the shelf where he had found it, hesitating for only the briefest moment to see that it had extinguished. Nothing unusual could be heard from the top of the stairs. Kadorax pushed open the door and left the cellar behind, searching the next room for the upper floor. He half expected to hear his companion's screams coming from somewhere overhead, but again, nothing besides silence greeted his ears.

It didn't take more than another half minute to find the staircase. Kadorax had no idea where anyone else in the estate was, and he couldn't shake the feeling that he was charging headlong into a trap, or perhaps a grisly scene involving his best friend being torn apart by wolf claws.

The stairs only ascended a single floor, and they creaked

under Kadorax's new boots, groaning from his weight. Whatever awaited him at the top, it would certainly be well aware that he was coming. Somewhere down below, he thought he heard Lady Brinn's voice, though he couldn't be sure. *If she's still down below*, he thought, *maybe nothing has happened.*

On the landing, Kadorax faced a narrow hallway with two doors on his right and only one on his left. Three options. The door on the left was open, so he went there first. It was a bedroom, sparsely appointed for such a nice estate, and no one was inside. Turning back to the hallway, Kadorax finally heard a yelp from a voice he recognized. Syzak was in trouble.

"Wha—" the snake-man's voice sounded before it was quickly cut off.

Kadorax burst through the door farthest from the stairs.

Syzak and Brinna both turned to regard him with bewildered expressions on their faces. "What's wrong?" the shaman immediately asked. His muscles tensed, and his tongue flicked out to taste the air.

As far as Kadorax could tell, no one in the room was injured or in any way distressed. "What happened?" he asked, shutting the room's door behind him.

Syzak still looked confused. "We found something behind the bureau." He held up a clump of hair from a torn pelt. It looked like it had once been an animal, and bits of sinew still hung from the edges. "What's going on?"

"Shit," Kadorax spat with a stomp of his foot. "Well she knows I'm here, at least. I wasn't exactly quiet."

"Brinna?" the old woman called from the first floor.

There was a thin locking bar on the door, and Kadorax slid it quickly into place. "This could end poorly," he said under his breath. "If she's really a lycanthrope, she'll smell us in here."

Footsteps made their way down the hall, and then a knock sounded on the door. "Brinna? What are you doing in my room?"

The young woman's face was a mask of sheer panic. Despite having a fairly decent amount of combat experience for someone living in a remote part of Agglor, she clearly did not have the nerve of a seasoned warrior. And beyond that, she wasn't wearing any weapons at her sides.

"Yes, Mother," she called, stalling for time. "Just . . . one moment."

Another knock, louder than the first, sounded against the door. "Open the door!" The woman was done asking—the tone of her voice made that quite clear.

Brinna shot the two adventurers a worried glance, then slid the locking bar back to the open position and pulled in the door. "Yes?" she asked, her soft voice quaking just enough to give away her fear.

Lady Brinn's eyes scanned the room, and they settled on the shredded carcass still dangling from Syzak's fingertips. "Oh," she stated flatly.

"Ma'am—"

The older woman cut him off. "I suppose you adventurers are here about a quest, then, yes?" she announced.

Kadorax figured it was useless to lie. His *Charisma* score was still low, and it would take a legendary amount of the stat to talk his way out of the situation. Clearly, the lycanthrope had read his intentions without issue. "We're bringing you in," Kadorax said with as much confidence as he could.

The woman's flesh began to shift and stretch. It peeled away at her wrists, giving air to her more sinister lupine form. "You will? Is that right?" she cooed. The skin around her neck and face began to transform as well, and then her shoulder jutted upward, adding at least two feet to her height all at once.

Back on Earth, Kadorax had known all the standard werewolf stories. He had watched them transform in movies and howl at the full moon dozens of times, usually only a moment or so before they were cut down by some badass gun-wielding hero. On Agglor, werewolves were a little different. They didn't need the full moon—not even night or dusk—to transform, and they were closer to Mister Hyde or the Hulk than anything from the softer movies.

"*Spike Trap!*" Syzak called, channeling the spell through his staff. A circular pit appeared directly beneath the werewolf, but there wasn't enough wooden flooring between the first and second floors of the estate for the trap to fully form. Instead, the floor simply vanished, and the spikes all clattered harmlessly down into the foyer below.

"Shit," Kadorax muttered as he drew his whip. With enough distance, perhaps it would be useful. As he brought his arm back and prepared to use *Torment*, the werewolf leapt across the hole in floor.

Lady Brinn landed next to Kadorax with a fierce roar. Her claws, each digit at least half a foot in length, swiped at the man's chest with enough force to rend him in two.

Kadorax dodged backward, his shirt torn to ribbons, and barely escaped a quick and painful death. The claws had still hit him, though, and he spun from the momentum.

"Mother! No!" Brinna screamed. She had her back pressed tightly against the far wall, her palms flat as though if she only pushed hard enough it would give and release her from the estate.

Now standing on top of the room's bed and ducking to not bash his head on the ceiling, Syzak cast *Cure Minor*

Ailments with his staff aimed at Kadorax's bloodied chest. The spell was quick and landed without issue, knitting back most of the flesh the werewolf had torn.

Using the heightened *Agility* from his boots, Kadorax sidestepped the flailing lycanthrope and drew his stolen bandit sword from his hip. "*Torment!*" he yelled, bringing the blade down hard on the creature's exposed back. He got lucky, but not lucky enough. The blade only scored a glancing hit, and then Kadorax was out of talents. He would have to wait half an hour to use *Torment* again, and the fight would be long concluded by then, of that he had no doubt.

Still, *Torment* was a powerful ability. The werewolf staggered, her ferocious roaring culled to a momentary whimper, and she stepped away from the three.

"*Summon Rain!*" Syzak called, casting from the bed. An almost comically small rain cloud suddenly formed in the room, centered directly on the beast's beady black eyes.

Kadorax didn't waste any time. He lowered his shoulder and charged forward, keeping his sword held close to his side so he wouldn't have to waste time swinging it. The combination worked, and the rain-slicked, confused werewolf stumbled backward another step where she lost her footing beyond the gap in the floor. One final shove, and Kadorax sent the creature tumbling to the floor below only an instant before the *Spike Trap* faded and made the floor whole once again. With the werewolf below, Kadorax, Syzak, and Brinna were alone, almost safe, though none of them felt like heading for the stairs.

"*Blood Fury!*" came a husky, animalistic voice from below, muffled by the floorboards and mixed with the sound of something heavy hitting the floor.

"That can't be good," Syzak stated flatly.

Hands on his thighs and doubled over to recover his breath, Kadorax agreed. "If her *Blood Fury* is above rank one, we're all dead. The talent will drain her life force, but she'll be so much stronger it won't matter. We have to run."

Syzak had completely drained his entire stock of spells, and his eyes showed his weariness.

"I don't get it," Brinna said to no one in particular. "She . . . she's a . . . a werewolf?"

"Figure it out later," Kadorax told her, grabbing her roughly by the shoulder.

"But she's my own mother . . ."

"Right now, all that matters is getting out of here," the bastion yelled. He dragged Brinna toward the door, Syzak pulling up the rear of the sorry-looking trio.

Another crash sounded down below, far larger than the first one. "*Rend!*" the monster shouted, but another voice overlapped it at the end.

"*Pyre!*"

Kadorax's heart leapt in his chest. For a split second, he thought the werewolf had somehow summoned enemies, magic-wielding enemies, and was about to raze the estate.

Then he remembered the Grim Sleeper stationed outside in the cold and the wind.

The Grim Sleeper cast another spell as the three rounded a corner to enter the foyer, but the words were so horridly pronounced that none of them had any idea what it was. In front of them, right inside the estate's main entrance, was a gruesome scene. The werewolf bled profusely from its leg, probably from one of Syzak's ill-fated spikes, and the creature was on all fours.

The Grim Sleeper towered above Lady Brinn. Her mouth was open, *unhinged*, and a dark stream of thick, purple magic rolled out of it. The lavender vomit enveloped the werewolf's torso, and everywhere it touched began to smolder, filling the room with an indescribably acrid stench. The werewolf convulsed, sending sickening pops and cracks through its own spine, and then it was fully engulfed in flame.

Brinna wailed at the top of her lungs. Kadorax held her back, but that was all he could do. The Grim Sleeper's work was complete, and the only thing left was to watch the werewolf slowly turn to blackened ash.

"Don't look," Kadorax whispered, turning the woman's head into his chest. In all reality he didn't want to see it, either, but he couldn't look away. As the lycanthrope burned and her screams subsided, the Grim Sleeper remained motionless.

"What is it?" Syzak wondered aloud, his own mouth agape.

Kadorax shook his head. "Just be glad she's on our side," he replied.

When the spell finally concluded a minute or two later, there wasn't much left of Lady Brinn—but that didn't stop the warlock from immediately kneeling down with a small knife to claim her prize.

Ignoring his substantial experience gain, Kadorax led the shaken woman outside to the street. Brinna sobbed into the man's chest, her hands in small fists, but all the fight and terror had left her—replaced by nothing but horror. Assuming her mind survived the ordeal, grief would come later.

"Come with us," Kadorax told her. "We have a ship, and we can see what's been holding up that cure you need in Assir. Just put everything out of your mind." He knew he was terrible when it came to women—always had been—but at least he had the wisdom to leave out the part where Brinna's mother's killer would be staying on the same ship.

Though she barely calmed, the woman allowed herself to be led away. Kadorax and Syzak hurried her along toward the docks, both grateful to be as far from the Grim Sleeper as possible.

CHAPTER 5

Back aboard the ship in Coldport's small, icy harbor, Lord Percival had shown enough mercy to make the Grim Sleeper retreat below decks as Brinna attempted to recover up above by the wheelhouse. The woman had refused to go below to the bunks, preferring the open space and bright sunshine to the dank and cramped crew quarters.

"Well," Syzak said, the word sounding a bit muddled from his serpentine mouth. "That was the kind of quest we had been after, right?"

Kadorax nodded. He felt horrible and more than a little sick to his stomach when he thought of the damage done to Brinna's mind, but he couldn't deny the huge amount of experience points he had scooped up for his part in the fight. Based on his own gain, he guessed the werewolf had been at least level ten, maybe twelve, and he shuddered to think what level he would see if he ever got a glance at the Grim Sleeper's stats. The warlock was nothing compared to the assassin he had formerly been, but those days were behind him. Kadorax was just glad he was firmly in the captain's good graces.

"You're level five now?" Kadorax asked his companion.

The snake-man happily nodded. His dark eyes were a thousand miles away, scanning page after page of options on his character sheet.

Kadorax had also reached level five, though perhaps the most profound result of the battle had been the loss of a single rank of *Bond*, bringing his total in that category to nine.

The rest of his stats hadn't changed, though he had gotten the customary level five boost to two selections:

Strength: 16
Agility: 15 (+2; Steady Boots)
Fate: 20
Spirit: 13
Charisma: 14
Bond: 9

Kadorax didn't like seeing his *Bond* in the single digits. With no prior knowledge of the stat's existence, he had no clue what to really expect. Thankfully, his *Encroaching Insanity* debuff hadn't gotten worse—it was still in the first rank.

When he had memorized his new stats and taken a moment to relish in the advancement, Kadorax finally began to scroll through the various talents and passives available to him as a level five bastion of chaos incarnate.

Torment: Rank 2 - The bastion's weapon magically extends to a second target beyond the first, and Torment inflicts slightly more damage than rank 1. Torment has an increased effect when used with a whip. Effect: moderate. Cooldown: 28 minutes.

Blade Training (Light): Rank 1 - Showing affinity for the short sword, the bastion unlocks the ability to earn several fighter talents related to one-handed swords, daggers, and knives. Blade Training (Light): Rank 1 also grants Riposte: Rank 1. Passive.

Conjure Darkness: Rank 1 - A sphere of utter darkness escapes the chaos and seeps into reality, blocking all mundane forms of vision. Effect: minor. Cooldown: 15 minutes.

Chaos Shock: Rank 1 - The bastion pulls a sliver of chaotic energy into the world and thrusts it forward, creating a random magical effect. Effect: minor. Cooldown: 30 minutes.

Bringer of Pain: Rank 1 - Sacrificing some of the bastion's own health, the user creates a small portal at the target location to siphon pain directly from the chaos into the physical realm. Effect: moderate. Cooldown: 1 day.

Cage of Chaos: Rank 1 - The bastion is surrounded by a subtle layer of swirling elements emanating from the soul rod. The armor reacts violently to several strikes, especially elementally imbued attacks, before dissipating, requiring a day to regenerate. Passive.

Fleet Footed: Rank 1 - A burst of speed carries the bastion to a target location in a blur. Early ranks of Fleet Footed have a chance of unusual side effects. Effect: minor. Cooldown: 30 minutes.

Silver Tongue: Rank 1 - The bastion's ability to converse is enhanced by an element of unpredictability, raising Spirit and Charisma each by 1. Passive.

Sleight of Hand: Rank 1 - Hiding objects comes naturally to one possessed by chaos. The bastion can use misdirection and minor sleights to conceal small objects from view. Higher ranks allow more complex sleights and for larger, louder objects to also be hidden. Passive.

Kadorax had three selections awaiting him, one for level four and two for level five. All things considered, he was progressing through levels faster than he would have thought possible, though at great risk to his own body, of course. The fight with the werewolf could have easily gone downhill, and Kadorax had to laugh when he considered the very real chance that he and Syzak could have woken up in a tavern in a different village again instead of Lord Percival's ship.

His first instinct led Kadorax toward *Cage of Chaos*, as he often favored passive abilities that couldn't miss or be deflected. Investing in attacks with long cooldowns meant there was always a chance the target would be unaffected for some reason or another, and the entire talent would be a waste. Without giving it much thought, Kadorax focused his vision on *Cage of Chaos* and unlocked the talent. He felt the effects of the talent begin at once, and the new sensation made his skin crawl. Little bits of what felt like metal shavings wormed over his skin beneath his torn shirt. They circled in a continuous pattern from right to left. Kadorax knew it would take some time to get used to.

With two more selections remaining, Kadorax wasn't exactly sure what he needed. "What are you getting for level five?" he asked, breaking Syzak's own concentration for a moment.

The snake-man's eyes were glazed over. He blinked away his contemplation, and a smile spread across his scaled mouth. "I get three new talent options," he said happily. "I've never gotten so much all at once before. Kind of overwhelming, in a way."

"Yeah, I agree," Kadorax replied.

"I already took *Silent Casting*," the shaman stated. "That's still the best passive any spell caster can take. Honestly, it should be a requirement in every adventurer's build as soon as they hit level five."

Kadorax couldn't agree more. Though he did wonder if playing a bastion would frequently require the use of stealth since the trainer had mentioned heavy armor. He knew he wouldn't do nearly as much skullduggery as when he had been an assassin, but still, not having to announce a spell was invaluable. Should they be captured, Syzak would still be able to cast even when gagged, assuming the captors didn't prevent his magic through other means.

"What are you thinking for the other two?" Kadorax asked.

Syzak mulled it over for a moment. "There's another rank of *Improved Traps* which feels pretty useful, but I need another trap first before the passive will actually make it worth it. There are some really cool ones. *Frost Rune* might combo well with *Summon Rain*, and *Poison Cloud Trap* could be really useful."

"Do you have any defensive options? If we're going to be taking on quests way beyond our level range, we need to make sure we at least survive," Kadorax said.

"I have some choices from being a snake," Syzak explained. "*Paralytic Envenomation*, *Two-Claw Defense*, and *Hardened Scales*. What do you think?"

Kadorax accessed his friend's character sheet to read the details of each. "They all look good," he said after a moment. "Maybe hold off on *Two-Claw Defense* since you might get some cool staff defenses later. I'd take *Hardened Scales* for sure."

"That's exactly what I was thinking," Syzak said. He focused on *Hardened Scales*, and then his shimmering green body took on a slightly deeper hue, and his *Strength* increased by one. He then unlocked *Paralytic Envenomation: Rank 1* as well before scrolling back to the offensive talents.

"Definitely get another trap when you can," Kadorax told him.

"Hopefully I'll get some more trap options in the next level or two," he said. "Now we just need better gear. Some gloves would be excellent. We should at least be wearing decent armor by level five, right?"

"Yeah, we need to talk to Ayers. And we still haven't gotten our reward from Percival, either. Let me get my next two talents, then we'll go see about some gear." Kadorax ran through his available choices once more. *Blade Training* certainly appealed to him, but some of the other talents were simply too interesting to pass by. Since he didn't know anything about a bastion's talent progression, he had no clue if the skills he passed by would ever come around again. Finally, he settled on *Blade Training (Light): Rank 1* and *Chaos Shock: Rank 1* to round out his limited offensive abilities.

After he had learned his talents, another choice appeared before his vision, one he hadn't quite expected. Sometimes certain abilities led to others, though the new options didn't usually appear until the next level was attained. Underneath *Blade Training (Light): Rank 1*, Kadorax had to decide between two different skill paths:

Bloodletting: Rank 1 - The bastion deals extra damage while wielding any blade with a fuller. Higher ranks of Bloodletting allow various poisons and barbs to be applied to the fuller. Passive.

Torture: Rank 1 - Using a light blade for torture rather than killing, the bastion becomes more proficient at targeting specific organs to inflict the most pain possible. Higher ranks of Torture allow for more advanced techniques. Passive.

It didn't take long for Kadorax to focus on *Bloodletting* and unlock it. He had never considered himself a 'hero' or even a stereotypical 'good guy,' but he didn't want to be plucking out eyeballs and slicing off ears in a fight. He preferred his combat to be as quick as possible, giving him the least amount of time in which to be killed.

Before he closed his sheet, he read the details on the

new *Riposte* ability he had learned as a result of taking *Blade Training*:

Riposte: Rank 1 - If the bastion's Agility score is higher than an attacker's, the bastion may attempt to riposte the opponent. Effect: moderate. Cooldown: 1 day.

Overall, Kadorax was more than pleased with his progress. He had completed only three quests since respawning in Coldport, and he reckoned he and Syzak were already the two strongest people in the town . . . if the Grim Sleeper didn't figure into the calculation.

"Alright, ready to get some new gear?" Kadorax asked. He gave Brinna one last glance, but the woman only stared out to the water like she was waiting for something to come into the harbor, her eyes a thousand miles from the present. For a moment, Kadorax thought about inviting the woman along, but he shook the notion out of his head. She would be better off if she had some time to grieve by herself.

Lord Percival was easy enough to find with his outlandish clothing and ostentatious hat waving about the cold breeze. The crew of the *Grim Sleeper* had more or less finished their tasks from the day before, so the captain didn't have much to do in the way of leadership. Instead, he stood at the bow smoking a carved wooden pipe and looking longingly out at the town.

"We'll depart from Coldport soon," the captain said without turning to greet the two adventurers. "I have a bounty to collect in the capital, and there are more rumors—more monsters—left to track down all over Agglor. A pair like the two of you, I could put you to good work, you know. Though I'm sure you have other pressing matters to attend to here in Coldport."

Kadorax had to stifle a laugh. "No, sir. We're just as eager to leave Coldport behind as you. If you'll have us, we'd love to stay aboard your ship, at least until you reach the capital."

Finally, the captain turned. He leaned against the railing behind him, his pipe dangling precariously from the corner of his mouth. With a quick flourish, Lord Percival produced a small leather bag full of coins. He opened the top and took a single golden disc from the rest, then tossed the bag to Kadorax. "I'll keep one coin as payment for your room and meals aboard the *Grim Sleeper*," he said happily. "Though the accommodations aren't the most spacious or forgiving, especially during rough seas, you're both welcome here anytime you like."

"Perfect!" Kadorax replied. He handed the bag of coins to Syzak for safe keeping. Perhaps it had something to do with the shaman's former life on Earth as a pet snake—for he was always a bit of a miser—but no one ever attempted to pickpocket him, even in large cities and crowds, making him the natural choice to carry the coin purse.

"If you have any pressing business in town, I suggest you attend to it at once," the captain said after taking a drag on his pipe. "I intend to leave by nightfall, perhaps sooner if my crew is agreeable."

Kadorax and Syzak both thanked the captain and turned for the gangplank.

"Let's get what we can from Ayers, then be off," Syzak said.

"Yeah," Kadorax agreed. "The capital isn't far from Darkarrow. I wouldn't mind paying my old fief a visit, either. Lady Astrella should hold it now. I hope she isn't making a mess of things. I fully intend to reclaim my seat as Lord of Darkarrow at some point, and I'd hate to come back to ruins."

The snake-man laughed in his weird, serpentine way. "Yes, I had a few magical pendants stowed away in my room as well. If anything, they would fetch a fair price to buy us some different gear."

As they made their way back through the streets of Coldport, Kadorax and Syzak noticed more than a handful of guarded whispers aimed their way. Apparently, word had gotten out that they had killed a noblewoman in her own estate, and the citizens weren't terribly happy about it.

They reached Ayers' shop without any of the commoners saying a single word directly to them, which made Kadorax think his reputation in Coldport had also grown a few notches. "How many coins do we have?" he asked.

Syzak counted them without removing the money from its pouch. "Twelve gold," he answered. "Not too bad."

"Let's see what Ayers has in stock."

They opened the door, and a wash of heat came at them from the fires of the forge. The blacksmith was busy hammering a length of steel against one of his anvils.

"Ayers!" Kadorax called between hammer strikes, catching the man's attention.

"Welcome!" he called back. The smith took a few more swings at whatever he was making, inspected it for a moment, then set down his tools to approach the counter. "What can I do for you?"

"We're heading out of Coldport, probably for good, and we could use some new gear," Kadorax told him.

The smith rubbed his chin, an inquisitive look on his face. "You two were behind that werewolf business, weren't you?" he asked. He didn't sound afraid or accusatory, just curious.

"She had been preying on villagers for some time," the snake-man said proudly. "We put an end to it."

"I take it you'll be leaving on that ship?" the smith asked.

Kadorax nodded. "By tonight."

"A group like you two," Ayers went on, "could use a blacksmith to mend your armor and fashion new implements. I'm not a fighter, never have been, and one monster living in Coldport means there will probably be more that no one knows of yet. I'd like to come along, if you'd have me."

"Well, I can't lift your anvil, and a forge on a wooden boat feels like a bad idea . . ."

Ayers waved away the concerns. "Ah, a boat that size is bound to have something on board already. They'd need a place to mend their chains, fix the rudders, and reinforce the mast after a battle, don't you think? If I lined the room with a bit of wax sealant and made sure the chimney was properly secure, I could have a floating forge up and running in no time. Of course, all that would take a bit of money, and there's the matter of paying the captain for my stay . . ."

Kadorax saw the whole thing coming together nicely in his head. Having his own blacksmith aboard a floating headquarters guarded by a warlock powerful enough to solo a werewolf without taking so much as a scratch—*that* was almost as good as having his own fiefdom, maybe even better.

"Would ten gold get you set up with plenty of materials and tools for the foreseeable future?" he asked.

The smith nodded at once. "I'm in," he beamed.

"Good to have you along!" Kadorax said. He motioned for Syzak to give the man the promised gold, then moved his gaze to the finished products behind the counter. There wasn't much that would be useful for adventuring, sadly. "Can you be at the ship by dusk?"

Ayers agreed. The man was already moving quickly through the small shop as he packaged various tools and components into several wooden crates.

"And do you have any chest armor? I'm plenty warm in cloth, but I'm tired of nearly getting gutted in every fight," the bastion said. He poked a finger through one of the tears in his clothing.

Ayers rooted through a short barrel next to his anvil and pulled out a few scraps of leather that looked large enough for rudimentary armor. "If I have the time, I'll put together two chest pieces before I come down to the docks," he said.

Kadorax and Syzak let him take a few quick measurements before departing for the harbor, eager to get out of the town before any of the glowering villagers gave them trouble.

Back in sight of the *Grim Sleeper* towering over the pier, they knew at once that something had happened. The upper deck was awash with activity.

The two adventurers ran up the gangplank, and they found Lord Percival kneeling over a humanoid shape in a pool of cold water. They couldn't tell if the captain had been injured, or if anyone had been injured, but they saw two crew members rush up from below with a cloth stretcher stacked with blankets between them. Not far off, the Grim Sleeper prowled back and forth with her dark cowl pulled low over her eyes to block the sun.

"What happened?" Kadorax asked. He got a little closer, and he saw Brinna lying on the deck, her clothes soaked, her body shivering but otherwise still. At least shivering meant she was still alive.

"She jumped overboard by my guess," Lord Percival announced. "My crew didn't see her do it. One of them just saw her down in the water bumping up against the hull. There's no telling how long she had been under."

The captain worked quickly over her still form, ensuring

the woman's mouth was fully opened, but nothing came out, water or air.

"I can bring her back," the strange warlock said after another round of pacing. "She isn't lost entirely."

All eyes on the deck turned to the Grim Sleeper.

"And turn her into . . . what?" Lord Percival asked. It was clear from his voice that he was just as terrified as everyone else.

Kadorax wondered if the woman had taken an even darker path as a multiclass option. If she began raising an army of the dead onboard the ship, things were going to get a lot more complicated.

The Grim Sleeper shook her head. "Not turned, just brought back," she said. "I'm not a necromancer." Her last words sounded vile, like the mere act of explaining herself was a grave inconvenience.

Lord Percival and several of the others on the top deck turned to look expectantly at Kadorax. "You don't need my permission," the man said, backing away from the still body.

Finally, the captain nodded to his warlock slave, and the spellcasting began.

"*Capture Essence!*" she called into the frosty air with a screech. At once, Brinna's soul—or at least that was what Kadorax thought it was—materialized in the air just inches above her flesh. It shimmered, reflecting the light in unusual patterns, and waited. The Grim Sleeper then began moving her hands like she was pulling an invisible rope. Ever so slowly, the soul drifted toward the warlock, and all the sailors scattered to the railings in fear.

Kadorax wasn't sure if the warlock was about to devour the soul or help it. Both possibilities terrified him.

When the soul reached its destination—the outstretched, rotted fingertips of the Grim Sleeper—it crumpled in on itself into the shape of a ball. The woman then whispered incomprehensibly into the soul before throwing it back in the direction whence it came. Lazily, the balled-up soul drifted through the air. It landed on Brinna's forehead, and there it perched seemingly forever, like a single raindrop caught suspended in a cloud.

"*Banish!*"

And the soul was gone.

Kadorax thought that he should have screamed. A thousand thoughts raced through his mind, but not a single one was strong enough to break through the wall of fear that had risen between his brain and his tongue.

"What—" the captain started. His words died in his throat.

Brinna's body stirred, and her lung function seemed to return as she coughed and coughed, her hands slowly drifting toward her own neck.

"Is she alive?" Syzak wondered with a whisper quickly stolen by the wind.

Percival rushed to Brinna's side and propped up her head, angling her mouth away right as she began to push the water from her body. A few tense moments later, it became apparent that Brinna would survive, though everyone on the deck worried for her sanity.

"How do you feel?" Kadorax finally asked when he found the words to speak.

Brinna shook her head. Her eyes were still closed, and they moved like a drunk only half-awake from last night's blackout. "I . . . W-where am I?" she stammered.

Bond minus 1.

Bond: 8

Kadorax blinked the message away from his visual field. He would deal with that later.

"You took a tumble from my ship," the captain gently explained.

"I remember that, I think . . . What happened after?"

Percival looked over his shoulder to ask the Grim Sleeper to explain it herself, but the strange warlock was nowhere in sight. "My associate brought you back. For a second there, we thought you'd died!" Kadorax wasn't sure if levity was the right choice, but the statement had been made.

"That thing?" the woman's eyes opened and darted around, panicked. "You let that thing touch me?"

"Well," Lord Percival said with a sigh, "no, not exactly. She did not touch you. She merely helped with a bit of magic."

Brinna got to her knees, coughed up another glob of phlegm mixed with river water, and met Kadorax's gaze. "What did she do to me?"

Kadorax put his hands up as though the woman might take to her feet and charge him. "Honestly, I have no idea," he told her. "She cast a spell, and then you woke up. I don't really understand what I saw."

The response was enough to at least temporarily placate Brinna, so she crossed her arms and sat back on her ankles, seemingly trying to collect her scattered thoughts. "I'm . . . I'm hungry," she stated.

"Is that so?" Percival asked, clearly surprised by the sentiment. "There's food below deck, if you'd like. Is there something you might prefer?"

The woman shook her head, then made for the nearby trapdoor on very shaky legs.

Still more confused than anything, Kadorax asked Syzak for a gold coin, then handed it to the captain. "That's for saving her and letting her stay on board," he said. "And we also have a blacksmith joining us, if there's room."

Silently, Percival nodded as he slipped the coin into a pocket. His eyes wide, he never took his gaze from the hatch where Brinna had disappeared.

Ayers arrived on the *Grim Sleeper* an hour or so before sunset, and then it took the crew only a few more minutes to make the ship ready for departure. Despite the hours that had passed, Brinna hadn't spoken much. She sat in the dark of the bunk room by herself. As they started to move away from Coldport, away from everything and everyone the woman had ever known in her entire life, Kadorax tried to figure out if the warlock's spell had actually damaged her mind.

"How do you feel?" he asked, taking a seat on the swaying hammock next to her. A single candle burned on a low table nearby. The flickering light added an eerie glow to the room that only made the woman's melancholy more palpable.

Brinna met his eyes with a vacant stare. "Everyone is dead," she whispered.

Kadorax wasn't sure if he should try to put his arm around her once again to let her cry or not. He decided that less contact would probably be best. "We'll get the cure from Kingsgate," he reassured her. "We'll be able to save Assir in time."

"If the cure even exists," she answered.

Kadorax looked again at her character sheet and found the *Wasting Sickness* was still only in the first rank. "If one exists, we'll find it in the capital. Kingsgate has the best mages and researchers in Agglor."

The woman's eyes returned to the creaking floorboards beneath them. "It won't bring them back," she said.

"Your mother will respawn somewhere," Kadorax reminded her.

Brinna's voice took on a hardened edge. "She was a monster. She killed people, and she lied to me. Maybe for my entire life. She's no mother of mine."

Kadorax understood the sentiment. Werewolves were a scourge meant to be eradicated. When they transformed, they lost whatever moral guide had kept them sane as humans. They would kill indiscriminately, and that often meant their own family members, especially in small towns where hunting was limited.

"Did you know your father?" the man asked.

Brinna nodded. "Mother said he died three years ago from fever, but now I'm not so sure," she said.

The boat swayed as it made a gentle turn through a bend in the river that would take them out to sea. "And . . . falling over the rail this afternoon?" Kadorax quietly pried.

"I jumped," Brinna said with half of a laugh. "I just wanted to start over, you know? To find a new village, new people to occupy my time."

"And when the Grim Sleeper brought you back, what did you feel?" Kadorax went on.

Heaving a heavy sigh, the woman stood and used one of the taut ends of the hammock to steady herself. "I saw bits and pieces of what she was doing, that vile creature. I saw, but I couldn't stop her."

Suddenly, Kadorax's mind was filled with images of the woman jumping again from the railing, doing it every night, day after day, until she got her wish. He wasn't too sure he'd even try to stop her. If she would just respawn, what was the point? Who was he to keep her from starting life anew?

"Well," Kadorax finally said, standing as well. "If you decide to stick around, I'm sure we could use your help. You're a level five rogue. I used to be a level seventy-two assassin, the Lord of Darkarrow. You might have even heard of my exploits. I could teach you a great rogue build, help you along the way. What do you say?"

She mulled over his words, then turned away, gazing out a small, frosted porthole at the waves gently lapping against the side of the ship. "Maybe," she answered after a moment. "For now, I just want to sleep."

Kadorax left her to her own thoughts. He had never been great at consoling people. Perhaps with more points in *Spirit* and *Charisma*, he would be able to better understand her thoughts and empathize. As a bastion, he didn't think he'd be earning too many increases in those departments. If he ever wanted to learn how to be at better listening, or whatever the skill was that he lacked, he would have to learn the old-fashioned way.

In the room beneath the wheelhouse, Kadorax found Ayers hard at work establishing his seafaring blacksmith's shop. He had been right, and there was a small anvil on the *Grim Sleeper* already, but there was no one skilled enough to use it efficiently. Minor repairs to the ship had been carried out by a man named Nathan, who quickly attached himself to Ayers as an apprentice. In the back of the room, two heavy black chains moved up and down as the wheel was turned, and a small grease box located near the top of the assembly kept them moving smoothly.

"I see you've settled in nicely," Kadorax said.

Ayers and Nathan were busy organizing a new tool bench

and several tall cylinders full of raw materials. "Ah," the old man replied. "Not quite yet! There's still the matter of establishing a forge, or at least a crucible, otherwise I won't be melting anything without going to port."

"Just don't burn down the whole damn ship," Kadorax joked, though he still didn't really understand how the whole setup *wouldn't* burn it down.

"And I've got leather vests for you and the snake. They aren't much to look at, but they'll do until I get some finer materials." Ayers fetched two dark chest pieces from a crate near his feet and handed them over. "Just the most basic enchantment I have. I need the good magic to keep the heat contained, plus I never got that many talents related to adventuring in Coldport, but damn, I can churn out a barrel of nails in no time at all with *Advanced Carpentry: Rank 7.*"

Kadorax grinned from ear to ear. "At Darkarrow, my former estate, we employed two different master smiths. One kept the house and grounds in working order, and the other was forbidden from learning a single talent unrelated to magically enchanted gear. I would have killed him if he had spent seven ranks on *Advanced Carpentry!*"

"I'll be getting some more interesting talents, don't worry about that," the man said with a smile. "Coming up next I'll get to decide between *Minor Runecrafting: Rank 2* and *Enchanting Hammers: Rank 3*. They're still low-rank talents, but they're better than nothing. Just keep bringing me raw materials, and my level will continue to grow!"

Kadorax had every intention of doing just that. Employing a good smith was paramount to a life of success in the dungeons and forsaken temples of Agglor. Eventually, he would need to find a skilled mage to hire as well if he wanted any spell scrolls made, but that could wait.

Focusing his vision, Kadorax accessed the details of the new leather vest the smith had given him:

Toughened Leather Vest - Empty rune slots: 2. Reduces incoming concussive damage. Effect: minor. Passive while worn.

"Thanks for the vest," Kadorax said. "What kind of materials would you need to make some runes for it?"

With a sigh, the smith shook his head. "You wouldn't want either of the runes I know how to make. What I need most are schematics. Find me a few diagrams for adventuring runes, and then I'll make you something useful. Right now, all the runes I know enhance talents in commerce and craftsmanship builds."

Kadorax thanked him again and left, searching out Syzak to give him his vest. He found the snake-man sitting at a table near the wheelhouse on the top deck, enjoying a drink with Lord Percival and one of the deckhands as the sun finished its journey beyond the horizon, leaving the *Grim Sleeper* in blueish darkness.

"Come, take a seat," the captain bade. "We were just talking with Syzak about your previous life. I'd heard about you two, you know? The Lord of Darkarrow is quite a lofty title."

"And we had earned the fiefdom a dozen times over," Kadorax agreed. "More than two decades without a respawn. That's a feat not many adventurers can boast."

Syzak took a long swig of whatever sweet drink he was enjoying. The liquid was dark green, the color of wet leaves, with the syrupy scent of sugar. "What's even more interesting was life before Agglor. You should hear about that," he said. He wasn't drunk, not yet, but his words were starting to slur, and his serpentine hiss was becoming more prominent with each drink.

"We're both Earth-born," Kadorax said. As it always did, the revelation garnered raised eyebrows from both the sailors seated at the table.

"I met an Earth-born woman once," the captain said. His eyes lifted up to the sky as he remembered. "She was beautiful, so full of life and energy, curiosity and excitement. But alas, she lives somewhere east of the mountains, and I have not seen her in many years."

"And what did you lot do on Earth? I've heard all sorts of crazy stories," the sailor said with a noticeable slur, "but I don't believe most of them. And I've never heard of snake-men being Earth-born. How'd that happen?"

"*How* it happened, I doubt we'll ever learn," Kadorax told him honestly. "And you're right, there were only humans on Earth, no snake-men. No jackals, elves, dwarves, gnomes, or any of the other non-human races that exist on Agglor. Just humans, at least for the intelligent species."

"Ha," the sailor snorted. "Jackals aren't intelligent here, either."

"Right you are, my friend," Kadorax said. "And it wasn't interesting, but I wrote titles back on Earth. I just sat at a desk and filled out paperwork all day, letting the government know when people bought vehicles." He had once tried to explain the concept of a car to someone from Agglor, and it had not gone well. From then he had learned to just say vehicle instead, though that always provoked a bunch of weird responses as well.

"The king wanted to know when someone bought or sold a wagon?" the sailor asked.

"Yeah, basically. I think you've got the idea," Kadorax replied.

"Bullshit!" the sailor drunkenly announced. "Earth-born are full of tall tales! Liars, the lot of you!"

RESPAWN

The man stumbled, spilling a bit of drink over the side of his cup.

Ignoring his drunken underling, Lord Percival had a few questions of his own. "When did you arrive in Agglor?" he asked.

Kadorax had to think back on it. Time didn't operate *exactly* as it had on Earth, and without a phone in his pocket to constantly remind him of the date and time, he'd let such trivial things as those frequently slip from his attention. "Well, it's a bit murky there, but sometime around thirty years ago, I think," he answered. "Quite some time. I barely remember much of those first couple years. And other than being terrified and confused all the time, there isn't much *to* remember. Agglor is a lot different than Earth. Namely, this place is far more dangerous."

The captain nodded, sipping his drink like a gentleman. "Would you go back if you could?" he wanted to know. There was a bit of longing in his eyes that hinted at a larger story.

"Not at all," Kadorax said definitively. "Life on Earth wasn't bad, but it certainly wasn't great. I never would have had the chance to become a lord of a fiefdom, that's for sure. And besides, everyone back home probably thinks I've been dead for three decades. Trying to start over there would be a lot more challenging than respawning here."

The captain's eyes drifted among the stars. Behind the table, the helmsman moved the wheel a quarter turn, and the ship responded by rocking gently to starboard. "The woman I had known . . . that's all she ever talked about: going back to Earth. She wanted so desperately to return to her home, but she never did figure it out."

Kadorax had done the same thing when he had first awoken in a dingy, stuffy inn above a bunch of class trainers.

Thoughts of escaping Agglor and getting back to Earth had consumed his first two years, maybe even more, until he had finally broken down one night in one of Kingsgate's many alleyways, weeping in self-pity until dawn. That had been the first night he had ever killed a man. The morning after, he had changed his name, accepted a low-level quest to earn some food for himself and Syzak, and decided to never feel sorry for himself again. If he was stuck on another planet, he would make the best of it.

The three managed to drain an entire bottle of the captain's expensive, sickly sweet booze as they reminisced and told jokes until well after midnight, eventually heading below a few moments after a new helmsman replaced the previous one at the wheel. The ship was sailing steadily south along the center of the river, and they didn't pass much in the way of civilization. There were a few villages, some roughly the size of Coldport, though most were smaller, and they only saw two other boats the entire night.

When dawn broke, the *Grim Sleeper* was close enough to the open ocean for the lookout stationed above in the crow's nest to see the masts of the larger ships at sea. Unlike all the smaller villages and ports along the way, the mouth of the river was guarded by a sprawling city built from stone and fine craftsmanship, flanked on either side by huge, monolithic statues that rose up from the shoreline like the sharpened fingertips of some ancient, buried god grasping at the sun. Legend said that during certain times of the year, the sun and moon would align perfectly between the pillars—that was when the world's magic was always at its height.

Kadorax awoke some time before noon with the smell of salted pork filling his nostrils. Not far from the bunk room was the main galley, and there was no door to keep the two distinct aromas from intermingling. Above it all, the strong smell of the sea dominated every inch of the ship.

It took a moment for him to get his bearing, and Kadorax realized he was alone. Everyone else who slept in the hammocks was gone, including Syzak and Brinna. When Kadorax tried to stand, he felt a jolt of pain accompanied by a splitting headache lodged directly behind his right eye, and he had to flop back into his hammock all at once, trying in vain to shut out the world.

After ten minutes of struggling not to puke onto the floor, Kadorax got to his feet and shuffled toward the galley in search of fresh water and something bland to settle his stomach. Food and drink in hand, he climbed to the top deck, eager to take in some fresh air and find his friends. The view, even from a distance, was enough to make him stop in his tracks. He had seen Oscine City before—even a few times from a ship not unlike the *Grim Sleeper*—but the sheer magnificence of it all still caught him off guard. Earth's cities simply could not compare.

Oscine City, or Songbird Harbor as it was known to the locals and most of Agglor's more romantic types, stretched for several miles down the golden coastline, its waters a deep azure shade that glittered in the sunlight. Overhead, a flock of gulls and other marine birds cut noisily through the air. Life was always plentiful in Oscine City, especially compared to the frigid temperatures brought on by Coldport's high elevation.

Then slowly, like a sheet being pulled in front of the world, another ship passed between the *Grim Sleeper* and the bay, plucking Kadorax from his thoughts. Lord Percival's vessel continued further out to sea, beyond the reach of the longest wharfs and past the larger ships anchored further yet.

"How long until we reach Kingsgate?" he asked as he approached the captain. The capital was located on a somewhat remote island not terribly far from Oscine City, but otherwise isolated from the rest of Agglor. Dozens of different stories circulated as to how the city came to be on an island and why the various monarchs had not moved it to the mainland. Despite the plethora of more outlandish tales, most of Agglor's residents knew the truth. Kingsgate had been built over a huge iron mine, the largest in the known world, and the people who controlled the production of steel controlled everything.

Not much was known about the royals themselves, and by Earth standards, Kingsgate employed a very strange form of government. Most of the important decisions were handled by the heads of the various guilds and associations throughout Agglor, and the king focused most of his attention on ensuring the continual squabbling of the groups so that no one organization ever gained too much power over the others. Still, the mines under Kingsgate paid for roads through Agglor, kept the city guards fed and stocked, and allowed the royal family the luxury of unlimited privacy.

Kadorax had seen the king—Lord Bennington was his name—only once. He had been in the castle fulfilling a contract at the time, and he hoped the chance encounter had gone unnoticed due to the nature of the work the assassin had been carrying out. By all accounts, Bennington was a fair ruler, uninvolved as he was.

The captain checked one of his instruments. "We should arrive by tomorrow morning, assuming the wind stays as it is," he said.

"Any chance we could make a stop in Darkarrow on the way back?" Kadorax's estate was on just the other side of the Boneridge Mountains, only fifty or so miles from Oscine City, but completely unreachable by land. Stopping there would likely add an extra two days to the *Grim Sleeper's* voyage.

"I've always had a bit of a soft spot for plucky villages in their time of need, and I don't think the medicine for Assir can afford to wait," Percival said with a shake of his head. He turned to look at Brinna, who was leaning against the back railing, facing forward.

"After will be fine," Kadorax agreed. He left the captain and headed in Brinna's direction, trying to hide his nervousness that the woman would jump to her death.

"Feeling better?" Kadorax asked.

She nodded, though it was clear she wasn't really paying much attention.

"Have you ever been beyond Oscine City before?" he went on.

"Not that I can recall," Brinna answered. Her voice was still distant.

Kadorax decided to just get right to the point. "So is there someone we're supposed to meet to get Assir's cure? Somewhere we need to go?"

"The Royal Alchemy Guild was supposed to deliver the serum directly to Coldport, and then a quest would have been posted by my mother to escort the serum to Assir. We can start by talking to the guild and the harbormaster. I don't know if the shipment ever left the docks," she explained.

"Well, at least we have a plan," Kadorax said. "I never had too many dealings with the alchemists of Kingsgate, but I do still have some contacts within the city, especially the shadier parts. We'll find your cure."

Brinna nodded, still looking away into the distance at nothing.

CHAPTER 6

The rest of the journey into Kingsgate went without incident, and the *Grim Sleeper* pulled into the wharf an hour after sunrise. The island itself wasn't terribly wide, but it towered over the ocean. Every layer of the city had been built higher in elevation compared to the one below, leaving the magnificent castle of Raven's Peak at the top to oversee the world. Raven's Peak had been built from stone plated with renowned Kingsgate steel, though all the shine and luster of the metal had been worn dull by centuries of heavy rains, relentless winds, and the constant briny attack of the sea. At one point, legend said that the sun reflecting off the steel had been so bright that no man could bear to look at the castle. Now, the structure was dark and foreboding, like a jagged chunk of obsidian broken from a spear tip.

The crew made fast the ship, and Lord Percival was the first to disembark, wearing a lavish coat and a plumed hat like the first day Kadorax had met him. Behind him, Ayers carried a sack of materials he planned to trade in town, and Kadorax, Syzak, and Brinna took up the rear.

"It's been a few years, but I'm pretty sure I still remember where the Royal Alchemy Guild is," Syzak stated. As a shaman, he'd had some cursory dealings with alchemists from all over Agglor, especially at higher levels when he'd needed components to be able to cast his spells. At level five, he was still a long way from requiring anything more than a word.

Syzak led the group through a winding series of roads, each one bustling with activity, until they ascended two sets of staircases leading to an inner section of the mountain away from the din of the outer harbor. The courtyard before the actual guildhall was sprawling, filled with well-manicured shrubs, flowers of every color, and a quaint fountain made from bronze, trickling a stream of water into a series of cascading metal buckets.

Two people were busy tending to the horticulture, one an older human male with a wispy beard and the other a snake-man like Syzak, covered in scales from head to tail.

"What was the name of your contact?" Kadorax asked.

Brinna didn't slow down to ask either of the guild members in the courtyard any questions—she just marched right up to the door. "The serum was to be made by a woman called Jorn, but that's just what the messages said. We had paid a courier from Assir to communicate the village's needs. I never thought that the courier might have been compromised."

"That might be exactly what happened," Syzak said. "When was the last time you saw the courier?"

Brinna knocked on the door. "He was still in Assir when I left with my son, recently returned from a trip to this very building, or so he had said."

As a class, couriers didn't have much in the way of deception talents like rogues, fences, or assassins, but that wouldn't stop anyone from either multiclassing or being an outright liar. Kadorax didn't bother to ask how much Brinna had paid.

The door opened a moment after Brinna's knock, and another half-serpent greeted them. The female was smaller than Syzak and clothed with a colorful robe lined with many pockets. The tops of various alchemical implements could be seen at her waist. "Yes?" she asked.

"Do you know anything about a serum, an antidote, scheduled to be delivered to the village of Assir?" Brinna started right away, nearly knocking the snake-woman back with her gusto.

"Y-yes," she answered, making all three stop at once.

"You have?"

The snake-woman stepped backward to let the newcomers enter the guildhall. "We sent the shipment out a week ago, I think. It was a just a box of potions containing *Cure Minor Disease*, right? One of our newly recruited members took the box himself."

"Has he returned? Did you get any news?" Kadorax asked. Next to him, Brinna was speechless.

"I'm sorry, but I wasn't involved. You'll have to ask the Potion Master. He's downstairs," she explained, pointing toward a nearby staircase with a scaled claw.

Brinna didn't wait for any more directions. She took the steps two at a time, a dangerous feat considering she was descending, and barged onto the lower floor with all the decorum of a wild animal.

The potion room, illuminated brightly by magical lanterns anchored into the ceiling, was full of guild members, and every bit of conversation in the laboratory came to a halt the moment Brinna entered. Several large desks full of implements dominated the center of the room, and a few racks of completed potions hung on the walls to her left.

"The Potion Master," Brinna demanded. Behind her, Kadorax, Syzak, and the snake-woman from foyer awkwardly tried to defuse the situation by looking as normal and calm as possible.

One of the alchemists holding a small vial of purple liquid motioned to another room at the end of the lab. "He's that way . . ." the man said.

A little more reserved, Brinna walked briskly to the indicated door and knocked. A voice from the other side told her to enter, and Brinna pushed open the door.

The Potion Master's office was brimming with activity. Several large cauldrons simmered over a low fire against one wall, and almost every inch of open space was crowded by scrolls, books, alembics, beakers, and all manner of other alchemical items. In the midst of them all was a tall human man. Half of the Potion Master's facial features were obscured by an extensive pattern of scarring that began at the corner of his mouth and carried up through the rest of his forehead and scalp.

Again, Brinna didn't wait to begin her interrogation. "You sent a shipment of cures to Assir?" she shouted over the noise of the bubbling cauldrons.

The Potion Master looked up from a scroll he was reading, furrowed his brow, then returned to his reading as though nothing had happened.

Brinna gave the man a few more seconds before repeating her question slightly louder.

At the same time, Kadorax brought up the Potion Master's character sheet, or at least what little he could read from it without them being on better terms. The man was a level forty-one alchemist multiclassed as a wizard as well. If he wanted to, it wouldn't take him much more than a thought to kill all three of them.

Luckily, the Potion Master wasn't in the mood for a slaughter inside his own office. "Are you always so loud, or are you simply deaf and cannot hear yourself speak?" he said flatly.

Blushing, Brinna offered a weak bow of her head as her only apology. "The shipment—" she went on, but the Potion Master began to speak again before she could finish.

"Yes, yes, I heard you the first two times," he replied. He set his scroll down on a nearby table and removed the monocle he wore on the unscarred side of his face. When he had sufficiently polished the lens on a bit of his cloth apron, he looked Brinna up and down, no doubt scrutinizing her by magical means as well as mundane. "I sent the cures last week with one of our initiates. Did it not work?"

Brinna's hands were clenched into fists. All the sorrow she felt at the loss of her son and mother had been channeled into the only thing she had left to occupy her mind, and more and more of the grief turned into anger every time she hit a snag in her quest. "Has the initiate returned?" she asked.

The man shrugged. "Tal!" he called to the main area of the lab. "Tal? Have you returned?"

"He's not back yet, sir," one of the other researchers responded.

"There you have it. He has not yet returned." The Potion Master thought for a moment, then plucked a thin glass vial from one of the wooden racks in front of him and moved to add its contents to a large beaker.

"The potions never arrived in Coldport!"

Studiously taking notes on the swirling admixture he had just created, the Potion Master didn't bother to look up from his paper as he replied, saying, "Then you are welcome to stay in Kingsgate until Tal returns here, and I will notify you once he does. Just tell someone upstairs where you are staying."

Brinna stomped her foot on the floor. Kadorax held his breath as a few of the nearby vials clinked together from the vibration. He was ready to make a run for it if any of them broke or fell. "Can you locate him?" the woman demanded.

The Potion Master let out a long sigh. "I can, but I do not have the time. And frankly, I do not think I have the patience, either," he stated.

"What would it take for you to scry him now?" Kadorax ventured to ask.

Looking directly at Brinna, he smirked. "A thousand gold. If it's that important to you, you must've brought ample payment, right?"

Kadorax placed a hand on Brinna's shoulder and leaned close to whisper in her ear. "Go wait upstairs in the garden," he told her. "I don't think he likes you. We won't make any progress with you yelling at him."

Though her eyes shot daggers at everyone else still in the room, Brinna left.

"My apologies," Kadorax began. "She just lost someone, well, two someones. She's in a bit of a hurry to get back to Assir with a cure. If I still had my fief, I'd pay your thousand gold. But you've probably seen our sheets—we just respawned not long ago. I'm Kadorax, the former Lord of Darkarrow. Perhaps you previously dealt with the alchemist from my estate, a gnome by the name of Cassi. Is there any chance you knew her?"

Intrigued, the Potion Master thought for a moment with a hand on his chin. "Cassi . . . Cassi . . . Actually, yes, I do believe I remember her. Everyone who's been around Kingsgate for any real length of time would know Darkarrow. What happened?"

Kadorax laughed at the thought of his previous life's reputation. He felt utterly helpless in comparison. "Jackals," he said with a bit of disgust. "Damned doghead temple in the north, east of the mountains. But trust me, I'll get my revenge."

"I hate those filthy dogheaded scum," the Potion Master sneered. "They're always going on about summoning their gods to Agglor, setting up temples all over the place, sacrificing virgins and the like. Bunch of bastard lunatics, if you ask me."

"I cannot tell you how many times I've said those exact words," Kadorax added.

The Potion Master came around from his table to shake Kadorax's and Syzak's hands. "If it helps you get back at a pack of those filthy beasts, count me in. I'll find Tal and let you know what happened. A simple scrying like that should be easy, especially to find someone I've known for a good bit of time. Wait in the garden, and I'll be up before long," he said.

"Glad to hear it," Kadorax said.

The two adventurers thanked the Potion Master, then went back up to the first floor, careful not to interrupt any of the other alchemists more than they already had.

In the garden, Brinna was busy pacing back and forth, her knuckles white at her sides.

"Calm down," Syzak told her. "He's going to find Tal, and then we'll know what happened to the shipment."

"Really?" Brinna gasped.

They explained what had happened below, and then all there was left to do was wait. Thankfully, the garden was a beautiful place to spend the morning, and they weren't there for very long—half an hour at the most—before the Potion Master emerged. He carried with him several different vials in leather pouches that could be attached to belts—they were the same kind of pouches Kadorax and Syzak had both used countless times before in the midst of combat to gain all sorts of alchemical benefits.

"It seems your fear was well placed, my lady, and I do apologize," the Potion Master began. "Tal was killed. I was able to scry his body in one of the warehouses by the docks. He never made it aboard his ship."

"And the cure?" Brinna pressed.

The Potion Master shook his head. "I didn't see it. I'd bet Tal was murdered for the vials, and whoever did the killing didn't realize exactly what they were. So now you have two options: I can set a pair of my apprentices toward synthesizing a new batch for you to take back to Assir, but that will require time, or you can try to find the original shipment. I doubt the thieves would have been able to find a fence for *Cure Minor Disease* potions, and they're too useful to just dump them into the sea, though you never know."

"We'll take the quest!" Kadorax announced before any of the others could say anything different. "Killing lowly cutthroats is kind of our specialty right now, and we can all use the experience we can get. Where should we start the search?"

The Potion Master chuckled and handed one of the elixirs he had brought to Brinna. "Here, this is the last *Cure Minor Disease* I had in the storehouse. I saw your sheet. You might as well be the first test subject, right?" he said.

Brinna removed the stopper from the potion and held it to her lips. It smelled like blueberries and jasmine. Tipping it back, her expression contorted as she drank. When the vial was empty, *Wasting Sickness: Rank 1* disappeared from her character sheet. She also regained one point each in *Strength*, *Fate*, and *Charisma*.

"Here," the man went on, offering a vial to each of them, "these should help. It doesn't seem right to have the Lord of Darkarrow running around with almost no gear. The potions are old, so the taste has probably gone sour, but they're the least I can do."

"Healing?" Syzak asked. He swished the liquid side to side in the glass.

"*Minor Healing Potion: Rank 4*," the alchemist confirmed. "It'll patch up some pretty nasty wounds." He turned to Kadorax, whose potion looked nothing like the others. "That one's a special, homemade brew. It'll let you find dogheads from quite some distance, though you probably won't need it considering their perpetual stench. And when you drink it, save a little bit to douse your weapon. That stuff's like liquid fire to a doghead. One hit and they'll turn tail."

Kadorax hooked the pouch onto the side of his belt with a huge smile. "How long will it last?" he asked.

"Only an hour. I'm still working on a more potent version, and then hopefully a permanent brew later on."

"Let me know when you get it figured out," Kadorax told him. "I'll be your first customer."

Once Brinna and Syzak had their healing potions secured, the alchemist explained where he had seen Tal's body, drawing a crude map of Kingsgate's docks in the garden soil. He had some suspicions, and he was able to narrow down the warehouse selection to three that each bordered the waterfront. One of them was rather close to where the *Grim Sleeper* was moored, so that was the direction in which Kadorax led the others.

"None of us have any talents related to investigation," Kadorax said. They stood outside the first warehouse, completely unsure what their next step would need to be.

"All we really need to do is find the body—at least for now," Brinna reminded him. "The Potion Master didn't say it was hidden or had been removed."

"Right," Kadorax agreed. "Now how do we get inside?"

Each of the warehouses along the waterfront was privately owned, and the different companies made sure to protect their goods from trespassers, often touting their level of security as a point of marketing to potential renters. The warehouse before the group had several guards: two dwarves, short warriors with nasty-looking spears, watched the front, and another pair continuously patrolled around the perimeter of the building with their weapons on their backs.

"Just a month ago, I could've broken into a compound guarded by forty dwarves, all expecting my arrival," Kadorax lamented. Most of his assassin talents had been geared toward the actual act of assassination, but almost every piece of gear he had owned in that previous life had been to get him in and out of various places undetected.

"I'll do it," Brinna said calmly, an air of determination coming over her features. "If I see the body, I'll find a way to signal you from inside. If not, I'll just sneak out."

"Do you think *Sneak: Rank 1* is going to be enough?" Syzak asked.

Brinna nodded. "Those guards aren't very attentive. They probably don't see much action here anyway, and I think I can climb the supports on the side without them noticing. As long as I can climb faster than they can circle the building, I can drop in through the roof before they have a chance to see me."

Brinna did have the *Surefooted: Rank 1* talent, but Kadorax wasn't confident that it would be enough. The sides of the warehouse were climbable, anyone could see that, though the task would be difficult—and falling would alert all four dwarves. A risky task indeed. "Be careful," Kadorax said.

The rogue nodded and slunk away at an angle that kept her a good distance away from the warehouse, but brought her to a better vantage point from the side of another building. When the guards were just making the turn out of her view, she sprinted for the warehouse, vaulting over a short span of ocean where the decking had rotted through and not been replaced. She grabbed one of the support beams that extended maybe eight inches beyond the rest of the walls, then began to climb.

Kadorax had to admit he was impressed. He hadn't considered the backwoods mayor as anything more than a politician with a few combat skills, but Brinna was quickly starting to prove her worth. The woman only slipped once, and then she was on the roof searching for an easy access point.

Before long, Brinna dropped into the warehouse and out of view.

"If this all goes to hell," Syzak said a moment later, "do we try to save her, or do we make a run for it?"

"You can't see the guards' stats from here, can you?"

Kadorax asked. He had been pondering the same question ever since Brinna had left.

"Not from this distance, but I doubt they'd be friendly anyway," the snake-man answered, shaking his head.

"The Kingsgate docks aren't as heavily guarded as other cities since they have the royal guard here, but that doesn't mean the company employing those dwarves went cheap," Kadorax said. "I've at least got them beat for reach if I use my whip, and dwarves can't really jump over your traps, but that's it."

Syzak's tongue nervously darted out over his lips. "A distraction, then?"

"It is the best we could offer."

"We need the Grim Sleeper here. She could take on all four dwarves without a problem," Syzak continued.

"And get the whole royal guard called in!" Kadorax laughed. "She's an abomination—a monster. Kingsgate wouldn't let her live if the leaders knew she was openly stalking the streets and killing warehouse guards."

"Brinna better pull it off," Syzak agreed.

The two waited in their hiding place behind a few barrels and discarded fishing nets next to a market building for a few more minutes before movement in the water caught their eye. It was Brinna, and she surfaced about fifty yards south of Kadorax and Syzak, pulling herself onto a dock. She wore a smile that said she'd found something.

"There wasn't an easy way back to the roof," the woman explained as the other two met her on the dock, "but the floorboards were pretty old, so I just wrenched one of them up and slipped through."

"I take it the body wasn't inside?" Kadorax asked.

Brinna shook her head. "No corpse, but it had been so

long since I'd snuck past anyone that I actually ranked up in *Sneak!* I forgot what it was like to actually adventure and use my talents. Being a mayor . . . that's boring." She was sopping wet and probably cold, but her expression showed nothing beyond her excitement.

"Good to hear it!" Kadorax said. "Now let's get to the second warehouse before anyone wonders why you took a swim while fully clothed."

In truth, a few of the nearby sailors had looked a little curiously at the woman already. Their stares were probably more related to the way her wet shirt clung to her chest than anything else, so Kadorax didn't see much reason to be alarmed.

The second warehouse was a good bit from where the *Grim Sleeper* was moored. In appearances, it was almost indistinguishable from the previous warehouse Brinna had infiltrated, but the guard presence was significantly higher. Humans patrolled the grounds, and there were a lot of them. A trio of guards stood watch at the front, and more were stationed at each corner, even on the end that stuck out over the water.

"Remember that distraction we talked about?" Kadorax said.

Syzak knew exactly what to do. In his previous life, distracting enemy mobs so the assassin could infiltrate all manner of buildings had been one of his specialties, and it was a job he enjoyed doing. It usually meant it was Kadorax's neck on the line as opposed to his own.

"Start getting closer," Kadorax told the dripping wet rogue on his left. "When Syzak pulls the guards with a trap, make a run for it."

"Got it," Brinna confirmed. Her eyes gleamed, and her

jaw was set like a fighter about to enter the ring for a bout she knew she would easily win. The woman had a hunger to her.

Silently—thanks to his level five talent—Syzak cast *Spike Trap* directly in front of the set of guards watching the warehouse door. The wooden decking vanished, and the spikes fell harmlessly into the water below, but the distraction was perfect.

Shouts of alarm rose up from every corner of the building. The guards rushed to the front with their weapons drawn, all eyes on the street. One of them began casting a series of buffs on the other guards. Kadorax hoped the enhancements weren't perception related, but he knew they probably were. He wished he'd had enough *Fate* to have taken the *Fortune Teller* talent and see what was going to happen next, even if it was only a few seconds in the future.

Brinna ran on the balls of her feet, never waiting long enough to let the dock boards beneath her feet make a noise. She was halfway to the warehouse, still undetected, when a woman walking along the road at a higher elevation than the docks began to point and shout.

"Damn *Spirit* score's too low," Kadorax grumbled. "None of us thought to check the streets above."

Both Kadorax and Syzak scrambled from their hiding place to the nearest staircase that would take them to the street on the next level.

"Hey!" Kadorax yelled, cutting off the woman at the top of the staircase right as she was about to ruin the entire plan. The problem was, he hadn't thought any further ahead than simply getting her attention.

"What?" the woman exclaimed. She stepped back defensively, and her eyes were still following Brinna down below.

"Run!" Kadorax finally shouted at her. He kept running as

well, pushing past her and sort of gathering the woman up in his wake. The ploy worked, and the three carried on around the next bend in the street, out of view of the dock.

Syzak pulled on Kadorax's shoulder to slow him down. "Go get the guards!" the snake-man commanded the civilian. "Dock nineteen! Get them quick!"

The woman kept on going, huffing and puffing up the incline and shouting for the city guards all the way.

"Dock nineteen?" Kadorax asked when the woman was out of earshot.

The two turned back toward Brinna, but she was out of sight. "I just made it up. Hopefully it exists, and she ends up leading the guards to the other side of the island. Either way, Brinna better be quick."

They ran back to the harbor level, eyes darting around the docks for any more alerted workers or passersby, and one of the warehouse guards spotted them.

"You there!" the lead guard shouted. "Stop!"

"Now we're screwed," Kadorax said under his breath.

"Maybe buy Brinna some more time?"

"Hide your character sheet. Don't let them see the trap skill."

"Where are you going?" the guard demanded. His voice carried weight and authority bolstered by his status as a twelfth-level watchman. The man had certainly caught a few thieves and miscreants in his day.

"We heard a bit of commotion," Kadorax tried to explain. His *Charisma* score wasn't high enough to lie outright, especially to a skilled watchman, so he had to rely on organizing the truths he spoke in a logical manner.

Behind the watchman, Syzak's *Spike Trap* faded, and the dock went back to normal.

"And you thought what?" the guard shouted. "That you'd come down here? The two of you happen to be walking by and just think you're going to help a professional crew? I'm not buying it." The man turned back to the others gathered before the door. "You two, sweep the interior. Something's not right."

Kadorax's heart sank. Judging by the size of the warehouse, Brinna had about thirty seconds, maybe a minute, before the guards would find her.

The guard brandished a heavy club in his hands. "One more time. Tell me what you're doing."

"Hey, come on, man. We were just around the corner and saw some magic, that's all. Just curious to see what was going on," Kadorax said.

"Not good enough," the watchman concluded. "Apprehend these trespassers!"

The watchman swung his club for Kadorax's head. Syzak jumped forward to intercept the hit, taking the club squarely on his shoulder. What normally would have been enough force to send the shaman sprawling was reduced by his *Hardened Scales* talent to merely a glance, and Syzak landed with both arms wrapped around the watchman's waist. Too close for the man to defend, Syzak sank his fangs into the watchman's flesh, puncturing his armor and envenomating him with a full dose of paralyzing toxin.

"Stay back!" Syzak yelled to the other watchmen. He held their leader's paralyzed body in his claws, and Kadorax had a dagger at the man's throat.

"We didn't come here looking for trouble," Kadorax stated.

One of the other watchmen held his arms out to keep the rest from charging in. "Why were you here?" he asked.

The man wasn't nearly as confident as the leader had been, and his focus was squarely on Syzak, obviously figuring him for the stronger of the pair.

The leader started groaning as the effects of the toxin quickly left his body. At the first rank, the talent just didn't pack much of a punch.

"Look," Kadorax began, fishing for a way out, "we came here to look for something, but that doesn't matter now. We don't want to kill this man, but we're not going to jail, either. Make your decision."

Behind the watchmen—none of whom were actually looking at the actual warehouse they had been hired to guard—Brinna slipped out of a second-story window. She made eye contact with Kadorax for barely a second, shook her head, then slithered down to the dock and slipped into the water. Kadorax watched her silently swim in the direction of the *Grim Sleeper*.

The leader was coming around a lot faster than Kadorax had imagined. The bastion put on his most intimidating snarl. "I'll kill—"

"Alright, alright!" the closest guard interrupted. He sheathed his short sword and held up his palms. "Let him go, then get out of here. You didn't even manage to break in, and the arrest wouldn't be worth it. We don't have to kill each other."

Kadorax didn't wait for them to change their minds. He dumped the leader over the side of the dock opposite the direction he planned to run, then took off at a full sprint with Syzak not far behind.

The two continued on the docks, easily outpacing Brinna in the water not far to their left, until they had rounded not one but two turns in the circular harbor to put them sufficiently out of sight. The handful of workers nearby gave them a few inquisitive looks, but they all had other things occupying their time, so none of them bothered to ask any questions. Only a few piers down, the *Grim Sleeper* was still peacefully moored, giving Kadorax and Syzak a bit of comfort.

Sitting down on the edge of the dock, they waited for the rogue to catch up.

"That was a close one," Syzak breathed. Above them, on the first tier beyond the harbor, they could hear a troop of soldiers marching by at a quick pace.

"Glad we got new armor," Kadorax replied. "You could've taken some serious damage. There's no way we would have gotten through all those watchmen."

"And I don't want to get thrown in jail, and I *certainly* don't want a bounty on my head in Kingsgate," the shaman added.

Brinna found a ladder two piers away and climbed up, then set about wringing her hair dry for the second time that day.

"Glad you know how to swim," Kadorax said once she rejoined the group.

Brinna grinned. "I grew up on a river. Everyone in Coldport and Assir knows how to swim."

The three decided to return to their ship before they brought any more attention on themselves, and Brinna needed to dry off before she got sick from the cold permeating her body. Unfortunately, she didn't have any extra clothes onboard. There was, however, a clothesline that the long-term crew used whenever they needed to dry their own attire, so Brinna had to settle for going barefoot in ill-fitting borrowed clothes while hers hung to dry.

"So, what was in the warehouse?" Kadorax asked. Other

than the helmsman taking watch, they were alone on the top deck.

"Found Tal's corpse in there, but the crate of potions wasn't with him." Her voice became low and somber. "There was a lot of broken glass near his body. He probably just dropped the crate when he died, and they all shattered. We'll have to get the potions somewhere else."

"Who would want to kill a courier for the alchemists?" Syzak wondered.

Kadorax was trying to figure out the exact same thing. None of it really added up, but he also wasn't privy to any of the Royal Alchemy Guild's politics or intrigue. There could be hundreds of other groups with scores to settle, for all they knew. "Probably best to keep our necks out of it, whatever it is," he said.

"We need more potions for my village," Brinna stated.

"Do we check Oscine City on the way back? See if someone has a huge supply of *Cure Minor Disease* for sale?" Kadorax asked, clearly at a loss.

"No, we just need money. If we can find a skilled priest with tons of ranks in *Cure Disease*, they might be able to cast it enough times per day to cure the village. How many people are sick?" Syzak asked.

Brinna's head slumped downward an inch in defeat. It was a subtle movement, but summed up the situation perfectly. "Assir isn't a big village, but there were more than a hundred infected when I left. That's probably tripled by now. We would need an army of priests to get enough cooldowns of *Cure Disease* to save everyone. I don't have the thousands of gold it would cost to hire them, either. Do you?"

For a long time, no one spoke. A gentle breeze came in from the north, bringing a bit of warmth to the air. Sailors came and went, tending to the ship or going about their own business, and the three adventurers sat in painful silence.

"We could wait here and see if the guild will make more potions," Kadorax finally said to break the silence. "It shouldn't take them more than a week, right?"

Brinna's gaze was fixed on the distance. "That would be too late," she said.

"I know..."

"At the very least I would like to eulogize my village, if Lord Percival doesn't mind taking me back to Coldport. Maybe we could burn the town to contain the disease and keep it from reaching the other villages," the woman continued. A few stray tears made their way down her cheeks.

"I'll talk to him," Kadorax said. "I'm sure he wouldn't mind dropping us off. If the plague gets beyond the villages, all of Agglor could be at risk. If he wants to preserve Oscine City as a valuable port, we'll need to stop the sickness before it reaches their harbor."

In the back of Kadorax's mind, another plan was taking root. Where there was widespread death—especially slow, painful death—other types of magic tended to congregate. Several years ago after a large forest fire had devastated a town east of Darkarrow and killed hundreds of humans and other intelligent races, a wraith had taken up residence to feed off the energy the death had left behind. Undead creatures like wraiths weren't intelligent themselves, just beings of pure magic that drifted from wasteland to wasteland, consuming all the rot, decay, and sorrow they could find. Taking down a mature wraith was a job for a dozen adventurers with specialized gear and potions, but a newly formed wraith... Kadorax grinned as he stood to find the captain. A young wraith was a goldmine. It would be easy to kill, and the experience points would get him well on his way toward hunting the wretched jackals and the Gar'kesh.

The *Grim Sleeper* sailed past Oscine City once more, its huge mast and yards creaking in the steady wind. Lord Percival had collected a rather significant bounty for the werewolf's demise, and he had spent a small fraction of it re-outfitting the ship. The resupply also meant a couple fresh barrels of liquor and food for the crew, so everyone on board was in high spirits. Everyone except the warlock.

The ship's namesake prowled the stern, pacing back and forth and muttering incoherently to herself. Lord Percival explained that she became agitated whenever confronted with the possibility of facing off against an undead. Warlocks, especially ones as deeply overcome by dark magic as the Grim Sleeper, often viewed the wild, undead beasts of Agglor not as evil, but as neutral beings, and sometimes even as friends. Kadorax had no idea what went through the Grim Sleeper's mind, if anything was truly there at all, and it unnerved him. As far as he knew, 'agitated' could mean one tenuous step from sinking the ship and killing them all.

Sailing against the wind, it took the ship two days to pass Oscine City and reach the river that would take them to Coldport. The waters were choked with significantly more ice than had been present when they'd left. Careful not to damage the ship, Lord Percival took over the helm to navigate the slow and treacherous trip. During the coldest winters, the ice and snow from the Boneridge Mountains were known to drift down the river into the sea and freeze Oscine City's harbor, and such weather had been the cause of hundreds of shipwrecks throughout the years. For enough gold, a captain could hire a talented fire mage to burn a path through the water should the need arise. The frugal captain preferred to make use of his extensive sailing talents, though he warned Kadorax of waiting too long in Coldport. If the river froze completely, he would have to beach the *Grim Sleeper* and wait out the winter.

Three days after leaving Kingsgate, the *Grim Sleeper* alighted once again in Coldport with frost clinging to its rails and rigging. Lord Percival paid the harbormaster for his stay, and then the ragtag group of adventurers assembled at the waterline to make the journey to Assir.

For combat, Lord Percival's captain class did not offer much. He was proficient with his cutlass, could dodge several times in an encounter, and had a single rank in an aura he had never found a reason to use: *Batten the Hatches*. When activated, the aura increased the speed at which all of Lord Percival's allies could barricade a ship for heavy weather. According to the captain, he had taken the talent merely because he enjoyed the name. Sailing mostly in waters around Oscine City and Kingsgate meant he always had a safe harbor if the storms ever got too bad, so the talent had so far gone to waste.

The warlock, still in her 'agitated' mood, shuffled in tight circles several paces from the others, her cowl pulled so low she was effectively blind. *Good*, Kadorax thought as he observed the decrepit woman's odd behavior. *The farther she is from us, the less damage she's likely to do.*

The villagers of Coldport gave them a wide berth as the band marched through. They passed Ayers' old shop, now owned by one of his former apprentices, and were only stopped once before traversing the town altogether.

One of the nobles came out from the town hall to greet them. It was early afternoon, and the sun created a horrible glare when it hit the lazy cloud of frost hanging on the wind. "You there, adventurers," the woman called. She had a scroll clutched tightly in her hand.

"Another quest?" Kadorax thought aloud with a bit of hopefulness.

The captain being the most obvious choice for the leader of the band, the woman handed her scroll to him. "We're in need of people like you," she said. "You lot look like you'd know your way around a fight." She looked the warlock up and down and shuddered.

"Aye, what've you got for us?" Lord Percival responded.

"All the details are in there," the woman answered. "An elf who goes by the name of Santo was seen by a few villagers who came here from Assir to escape the plague. We've had about enough of that damned elf, so we put a bounty on his head. It isn't much, but there's fifty gold pieces for his death."

"I know Santo," Brinna growled. "That bastard has been a thorn in my side for years. He fancies himself a necromancer. Maybe he's behind the plague . . ."

Kadorax barely even paid attention as Lord Percival accepted the quest. All of the pieces had fallen into place. He silently chastised himself for not putting it together before, or even asking the questions that would have set him down the right line of thinking. Of course an upstart necromancer had been behind the *Wasting Sickness*. Killing an entire village would provide Santo with all the fuel he could possibly need.

"You didn't think to hunt down the necromancer before

going out and searching for a cure?" he asked, a bit more incredulity in his voice than he had intended.

Brinna looked at him, clearly aghast. "When my son contracted the illness, all I wanted to do was find his cure," she snapped. "Santo was an eccentric living on the outskirts of Assir. He paid his yearly tax—begrudgingly, but he paid. Sure, he was a nuisance, constantly pestering villagers about one thing or another, getting piss drunk and starting fights, and he did a single stint in the jail for grave robbing, but I never suspected..."

Completely ignoring the brief altercation, Lord Percival was busy giving the noblewoman instructions. "If any of the refugees have the infection, they must be quarantined. Read everyone's sheet. Don't let a single person into Coldport without making sure," he explained.

The woman nodded, then hurried back into the townhall, and the quest was accepted.

"What level was Santo last time you saw him?" Kadorax asked. He didn't mean to interrogate the woman, especially considering what she'd been through, but he knew that trying to sound concerned would only come off as condescending.

"I don't know," Brinna said flatly. "I didn't keep a roster of everyone in the town."

"It doesn't matter," the captain mercifully cut in. "We'll bring him down just the same. I'm sure an upstart necromancer is well within the Grim Sleeper's abilities. And there's bound to be some good experience in it for all of us."

Kadorax let the issue drop, content with the promise of quick leveling, and the group set out from Coldport with a bit of hurry in their steps.

RESPAWN

They didn't have to reach the village to know they were too late—far too late. The stench of death clung to the air, and several of the buildings farthest from the village center had been burned. Most of them looked like farms, now just skeletal husks of charred support beams, fallen roofs, and corpses.

"There, the windmill," Brinna said as she pointed to a tall structure in the distance. "That's the heart of Assir. If Santo is still here, that's where we'll find him."

It was just after dusk, and four of them were tired from the trek. The fifth, the Grim Sleeper, didn't show any signs of physical fatigue at all. Instead, she continued her relentless pacing and muttering.

"Will she be alright?" Kadorax asked.

Lord Percival considered his withered charge for a moment, his fingers lingering around a silvery necklace tucked under his shirt. Kadorax filed the bit of information away in the back of his mind in case the Grim Sleeper ever turned on him. Destroying the phylactery, assuming his guess at the necklace was indeed correct, would be the only way to stop her permanently.

"We should camp here for the night," Percival said, pointedly avoiding the question at hand. "I don't want to run into a necromancer's domain in the middle of the night. That feels . . . unwise."

When he looked closely, Kadorax could see a bit of greenish-grey fog drifting up from the vanes of the windmill. A handful of second thoughts crept into the back of his mind.

"Good idea," Brinna agreed. "There are some hunting lodges farther to the west. We can stay in one of those for the night." She looked at the warlock, ever distrustful. "I'd prefer if she . . . that thing . . . stayed outside."

Lord Percival stifled an awkward laugh. "Yes, well," he said, "she does not sleep. Not that I've ever seen. She shall stand guard outside. Now, take us to these hunting lodges."

The lodges turned out to be little more than a collection of wood and thatch huts with cots, some hunting trophies, and doors that didn't lock. Still, it was better than sleeping on the ground in the elements.

When dawn broke, the Grim Sleeper had worn a bare line into the weeds outside the hut's door. From left to right and back again, always jabbering to herself, the warlock had spent the entire night without complaint. A few black splotches—perhaps blood, though it was impossible to know—dotted the trail she had made.

Lord Percival sorted out a cold breakfast of rations from the ship.

"What does she eat?" Kadorax asked when the captain failed to give the warlock any hardtack.

"By the gods, you do not want to know the answer to that question," came the reply.

Kadorax couldn't even begin to imagine what horrors the well-to-do captain had witnessed in the warlock's presence. He thought to his own *Bond* score resting at eight and wondered if it was a smart idea to stay with the Grim Sleeper. Thankfully, his *Encroaching Insanity* debuff had still not progressed beyond the first rank.

"Well," Syzak began when they had finished their rations. "We should get moving."

They approached Assir from the northwest, staying low

to the ground and using what remained of the buildings to hide their advance. Everywhere, covering almost every single inch of Assir, was a blanket of torn, mangled corpses.

"Something else was here," Kadorax whispered.

Brinna visibly shook in her boots. The bodies they passed were her friends, citizens of Assir she had grown up with and known most of her life—people she had been elected to protect.

"A plague doesn't rip bodies apart and throw the entrails all over the village," Syzak observed. He had a bit of his shirt from under his leather vest pulled up to cover his mouth. "This isn't right."

At the end of the short column, the Grim Sleeper was barely trying to hide her presence. She walked nearly upright, and she didn't give a second thought to cover. If Santo was looking for their approach, the elf wouldn't have a hard time spotting her.

"Oh, shit . . ." Kadorax said under his breath. The group crouched next to a ruined wall two streets from the center of town and the windmill. On one of the vanes, slowly going round and round in the gentle, cold breeze, was half of an elf.

"How many other elves lived in Assir, Brinna?" Lord Percival asked.

"None," she muttered, standing upright. "That's him. That's Santo. He was the only elf."

"Whatever he summoned did all of this," Syzak said. The snake-man's voice wavered as he spoke. "I'm not ready to respawn again. We need to go."

Four of them—all but the Grim Sleeper—took a few steps back toward the way they had come. The ground beneath their feet shifted. It jolted to the side like an earthquake, then lurched back and settled, and a few pillars of steam broke free from the newly created fissures all over Assir. Except the steam wasn't grey or even black—it was a putrid green color, and it smelled like an open sewer of death and disease.

"Run!" Kadorax shouted. He broke toward the west, vaulting over bodies as he moved. Behind him, Syzak and the two humans followed suit.

The Grim Sleeper remained standing in the center of the street like she was in some sort of a daze. Lord Percival turned to call to her, halfway between the warlock and the other three. "Come on!" he shouted. "We can't stay!"

The Grim Sleeper started to cast a spell. Her mouth made no sound, but her hands moved in deliberate, rapid motions. From a deep pocket within her tattered robe, she produced a small wooden charm, a talisman carved into the shape of an oval with cryptic writings covering its surface. Grinning, the warlock turned. Her eyes were ablaze with magic and fury. Then she ate the wooden relic, and her grin grew wider.

Assir rumbled once more. The tremors didn't subside after one or two waves. They kept going, only gradually fading, and a new noise joined the tumult: groans.

Throughout the entire village, the bits of strewn people began to animate. Arms and legs climbed together and melded to form all manner of hideous amalgamations, each one scrambling toward the windmill at the center of it all.

"Are those ... things ... Are they friendly?" Kadorax asked. He jumped out of the way of a skittering *monster* that he could barely describe. The reanimated collection of bones and meat had once been a person, probably someone tall, but it had been reduced to nothing more than a spine, ribs, and enough muscle to propel the corpse along the ground like a misshapen spider.

No one had an answer. Brinna shrieked as one of the creatures brushed her legs, and Syzak swatted them with his staff when they got too close. Unaffected by it all, the warlock remained vigilant in the middle of the street, facing away from the insidious windmill.

None of the bone horde went within three feet of the woman as they progressed into the city. Kadorax knew their avoidance was significant, though he didn't have the time or the intellect to figure out exactly why. Stranger yet, the windmill seemed to be gaining speed. Before long, the creatures were scaling the stone walls of the mill and ascending to the top of the highest vane. As the vanes turned, the creatures continued to pile on, riding it around like a giant, sickening festival attraction.

"Seriously, we have to leave," Kadorax urged.

"What is it?" Lord Percival muttered.

Before he even finished his question, the answer started to emerge. The windmill broke apart under the weight of the grotesquery hanging from it, revealing an undead creature within. The whole scene reminded Kadorax of watching a chick hatch from an egg, except the egg was forty feet high, dripping human gore, and the chick was actually an enormous centipede made from tombstones held together by strands of human innards.

Kadorax had heard of grave golems before. They were constructions formed by powerful necromancers, held together by magic and armored in an entire cemetery's worth of headstones. The thing that emerged from the fallen windmill was similar to a grave golem, but it was distinctly biological.

"A grave . . . centipede? Gods, we have to run!" Kadorax said again. That time, everyone agreed.

Everyone except the Grim Sleeper.

The warlock still stood transfixed, her gaze vacant beneath her dark cowl.

"Did you do this?" Lord Percival demanded of the woman. "What did you summon?" If the creations had been demonic in nature rather than undead, a warlock certainly could have been their overlord.

Until that moment, Kadorax hadn't thought it possible for the captain to lose his composure. The captain raved at his slave, yelling and screaming at the warlock, who simply refused to answer or even acknowledge the verbal assault. Finally, Percival pulled the silver phylactery from under his shirt.

The centipede noticed them.

Percival held the phylactery aloft in the warlock's direction. His knuckles were white. Kadorax didn't know exactly what it was made of, or if the man would be strong enough to crush it in his palm, but that was certainly the threat Percival conveyed.

The centipede crawled over a building, its hundred legs carrying it closer to the group.

"Come on! We hav—"

"I'll kill you!" Percival yelled at his slave. "Tell me what you did, or I'll shatter your soul right here! By the gods, I'll do it!"

The centipede scurried around the base of another building. It was close enough for Kadorax to make out some of the details of its carapace.

"Tell me!" the captain screamed. His voice was starting to go hoarse.

The centipede reared back on half its legs, bringing its head roughly in line with the center of the second floor of the nearest building.

"*Pyre!*" the Grim Sleeper bellowed, spinning and falling backward all at once to align herself with the oncoming centipede which was only a few paces from devouring her where she stood. A gout of magical flame burst from the warlock's hands. It shot toward the undead creature, engulfed it, and staggered it for a few moments.

Then the flames subsided, and the centipede raged onward, only marginally burned.

The warlock began casting again, not that Kadorax and the others waited to see what would happen. They ran, abandoning the Grim Sleeper to her fate. At the end of the street, they had two options: either jump a gaping chasm rent in the street, or make their way through the ruins to escape.

"I won't make it," Syzak was quick to point out. He turned first for the ruined building on his left, and the others didn't hesitate to follow him. The gravestone centipede wasn't large enough to topple the house with its body, but they all knew it would easily be strong enough to batter down the door without any trouble.

"*Batten the Hatches!*" Lord Percival called, activating his talent.

"We're not on a boat!" Brinna yelled back at him. Thankfully, the spell didn't appear to care. The aura became active, and all four of them felt a sudden, overwhelming urge to start piling up debris against the door.

As they threw all manner of furniture in front of it, Kadorax honestly couldn't tell if he was actually moving faster or not. Regardless, he was happy for whatever boons he could get. When everything heavy was heaped in the same general space, they turned and resume their run, heading down a narrow, smoke-filled hallway to a door they all hoped would take them outside.

Sadly, they were wrong.

The door led to a badly crumbling staircase. Brinna was in the front, and she didn't slow down on account of the unexpected direction. Instead, she led the group to the building's second floor, most of which had already been destroyed.

The top of the building was strewn with broken boards, the last warm remnants of a recent fire, and more than a few bloody body parts. In the center of the street, the Grim Sleeper squared off against the gravestone-armored centipede with spell after spell. The warlock released fire, darkness, and something that looked like lightning in the centipede's directions.

Twisting and turning, the undead creature dodged almost all of the assault. It took most of the dark-based attack on its armored shoulder, and one of the gravestones covering its body fell to the ground, shattering against the cobblestone street. The creature roared and bent back its head. When it came forward, it spewed a heavy stream of dark green ooze from its maw.

The Grim Sleeper was far from quick. She didn't even try to dodge the oncoming acid that melted her clothing and sizzled her flesh. When the attack subsided, she was still standing. The woman let loose a stream of curses, pointing a boney, emaciated finger at the centipede.

Dark runes skittered across the centipede's armor. They glowed bright purple in the morning light, reflecting the sun in a crisscross pattern that almost made the hideous creature hard to see. Kadorax didn't recognize the curse. Focusing on the centipede's head, he brought up its stat sheet. Without magically augmented vision, he couldn't read most of the stats, talents, and conditions, but he could at least see what the warlock had done to it:

Curse of Vulnerability (Dark): Rank 4 - The target's ability to resist dark, fear, and damage-over-time effects is greatly diminished to be that of a similar creature eight levels lower.

Gibbering Runes: Rank 5 - Runes of confusion whisper vile secrets and profane bits of misinformation directly into the target's mind, interrupting casting and causing erratic behavior. The effect is more profound on unintelligent targets.

Kadorax drew his whip and crept toward the edge of the second floor, where the wall had crumbled into the street below. He didn't have any athletic talents to let him jump the entire distance to the centipede, but he hoped he wouldn't need to make such a leap. The undead creature snapped forward at the warlock with its huge mandibles, catching the Grim Sleeper's shoulder. Bones crunched, and the arm dropped a sickening few inches downward as the shoulder came loose.

Scrambling down the slanted ruins, Kadorax reeled his arm back and let his whip fly. "*Torment!*" he yelled. The corded leather came alive with shadowy energy. The weapon connected with the centipede's side, issuing a loud crack.

Kadorax didn't let up the onslaught. He discarded his whip back over his shoulder and drew his sword, twisting his shoulders to put all of his weight behind a more direct strike. The stolen bandit blade found a soft, gooey section of the centipede unarmored by its gravestone carapace, and Kadorax's *Bloodletting* talent went to work. Though the blade's fuller was shallow and pitted, insect blood flowed down its length in hot spurts.

The creature reeled. Its mandibles clicked together in the air, and its feet thrashed out wildly. Some of them, maybe even a dozen or more, managed to hit Kadorax in the chest and arms. The bastion's *Cage of Chaos* reacted violently to the strikes, shooting four shots of magical ice directly back at the flailing legs.

Behind him, the Grim Sleeper had stumbled down to the ground. She was heavily wounded, but the pain didn't seem to slow her casting. Another burst of fire erupted from her fingertips and engulfed the centipede.

The undead backed away, its head swiveling quickly from Kadorax to the warlock, completely unsure where to send its next attack. Confusion created delay, and Kadorax didn't waste a moment of it. He dove forward with his blood-soaked blade in one hand and his fingers outstretched on the other. "*Chaos Shock!*" he yelled. His mind flashed for a split second, showing him visions of Ligriv and the chaos where he drew his strength, and then a small, almost incandescent fragment of metal was in his left hand. Kadorax drove the metal forward with all his strength.

A shower of lightning erupted from the point of contact, boring a fist-sized hole into the insect's abdomen. Unfortunately, Kadorax felt the full effects of the electricity as well. The magical force rattled up his arm and into his jaw, making his muscles contract and his teeth clack painfully together. Somewhere in the wild cacophony of the centipede's unhallowed screams, Kadorax lost his sword. He clutched at his head to try and make the pain go away, stumbling backward into the rubble below the others at the same time.

The centipede recovered faster than Kadorax or the Grim Sleeper could respond. It slithered forward, legs clicking against the stone, and fell right into Syzak's *Spike Trap*. Though the magical spikes weren't large, they were certainly plentiful, and the centipede had not seen the trap at all. It was completely stuck, impaled dozens of times, its blood filling the fresh indentation in the ground.

RESPAWN

Brinna and Percival jumped down next to Kadorax. They moved in tandem, advancing to the left of Kadorax and the right of the warlock, staying far enough from the wounded woman to be out of her debilitating aura.

With the centipede held in place on the spikes, unable to focus and rapidly leaking blood, Brinna was able to deliver two solid strikes to the beast with her daggers without taking so much as a scratch in return. The beast roared and spewed green acid indiscriminately into the air above its head. A good bit of the toxin fell on Kadorax and Percival, spattering them with sizzling globs of pain.

"There's still the . . . the things!" Kadorax shouted. Behind the centipede, from the direction of the ruined mill, a horde of amalgamated body parts began marching toward the fight, as if commanded by some unseen force.

"The centipede controls them!" Syzak called back, though it was obvious from his voice that it was just a guess. "Kill it! They'll die!"

"Give me the necklace!" the warlock growled to her master. The animated body parts were rushing forward, almost upon them.

Lord Percival hesitated. His eyes were wide with fear, and his hands trembled around the necklace between his fingers. Giving the warlock her phylactery meant she instantly became mortal, but it also allowed her to push more and more magic into her spells, chipping off pieces of her soul to consume as fuel.

The darkest legends of Agglor told of warlocks who became so powerful that even being in the same room as their phylacteries—such enigmatic sources of energy—brought about destruction upon everything around them. Many warlocks chose to imprison their souls in phylacteries specifically to tone down their own abilities, letting them cast the strongest spells in all Agglor without fear of annihilation. To give a phylactery back to the physical body was an immense risk—one that could easily mean the death of everyone in Assir.

"Run!" the warlock cried. She still faced the centipede, but everyone else understood the message had been meant for them.

Kadorax, Brinna, and Percival scrambled up the ruins back to the second floor of the building they had come from. They made slow progress on the crumbling stones and shattered wooden planks. At the top, Syzak struggled to heft them over the last bit of wall. With the building in such a state of destruction, there wasn't anywhere to hide.

They ran for the stairs, hoping to put something between themselves and whatever the Grim Sleeper was about to unleash, however insubstantial the walls were. Lord Percival was last down the staircase—and he was too slow.

A spell ripped out from the warlock with incredible force. Between her and the fallen windmill, all the buildings caught in the spell's path crumbled to the ground. A tremor emanated outward from her feet, followed by two quick aftershocks, and then a blast of heat strong enough to curl the centipede's chitinous segments rolled across Assir.

The building Kadorax was running through fell apart. The heat was too much for the already unstable structure to handle, and the beams tenuously holding up the second floor began falling.

Lord Percival's back and legs blocked most of the fire from getting down the staircase and engulfing the others. He screamed, and Brinna grabbed him by the collar to drag him along. The group emerged in the next street just as the building behind them completely collapsed on itself. Again, Percival caught the brunt of the destruction. Two big crossbeams, one of which was on fire, slammed into the back of his legs on their quick journey to the ground, eliciting further screams from the unfortunate captain.

Brinna pulled him just far enough from the wreckage of the building so that he wouldn't get hit by any more falling debris, then used her body to smother the lingering flames on his clothes. "He's hurt badly," she said frantically, though there was no need.

With a wave of his hand, Syzak cast *Cure Minor Ailments* on the man's legs. The spell didn't fix the majority of the captain's wounds, but it did manage to knit together most of the small gashes, scrapes, and burns.

Brinna opened her potion and held it to his lips, tilting his head to get it to flow down his throat. When the healing potion had run its course, Percival's legs were still clearly broken. His femurs had cracked just above his knees—it would have taken several high-level healing potions to mend that kind of wound.

"I don't know if he'll make it," Brinna said.

Syzak fumbled with the healing potion on his own belt, but Kadorax stopped him.

"Don't waste it," the bastion said. "We don't know if the fight's over. We might need the last potion for ourselves, and it won't help him much anyway."

Hesitating for a moment with his scaled hand hovering over the potion, he finally left it where it was on his belt. On the ground, Percival writhed in pain. "We should make a stretcher," the snake-man said.

Kadorax, missing both his whip and his short sword, grabbed a piece of splintered wood and stepped forward to make sure none of the swarming bits of dead humans were coming their way. As far as he could tell, their street was devoid of threats. He couldn't see over to the other street where the Grim Sleeper and centipede were, and the lack of knowledge made him quiver with fear.

"Stay here," Kadorax commanded. "If anything happens... just leave him and run for it. He'll respawn somewhere else."

He didn't wait for the others to acknowledge what he'd said. Kadorax dashed into another building, hoping it would have an exit on the opposite street so he could figure out what had happened. Immediately upon opening the door, he felt a wave of heat pushing him back. He turned a corner and saw fire climbing up the main interior wall, licking at the floor above.

There wasn't a door leading to the next street, but the wall was weak enough around one of the small windows for Kadorax to force himself through. A thick blanket of smoke and dust blinded him on the other side. He could only see a few feet in front of him, and the particulate in the air stung his throat and eyes. Slowly, Kadorax made his way through the soupy air, testing each step before taking it.

The noise of the battle was gone. In its place, all Kadorax could hear was the sound of fires burning all over Assir, occasionally accented by the distinct rumble of a building's collapse.

He reached a gaping, blackened hole in the street that was far larger than the magical depression Syzak had made with his *Spike Trap*. Scattered all over the hole were pieces of burnt, pungent centipede. Some of the legs still twitched, making Kadorax fear the creature's potential reconstitution. He saw his whip and sword not far away. The blade reflected one of the nearby fires, making it easier to find.

Only a few feet from his weapons, Kadorax saw the charred remnants of a robe clinging to the jagged, broken ground. The warlock's body, reduced to a withered and blackened collection of old bones, poked through the shredded fabric at odd angles. As Kadorax moved closer, the stench became nearly unbearable. Using his boot to move some of the fabric to the side, he searched for any sign of the phylactery that might have meant the woman's spirit had survived. All he found was death.

Behind him, the building he had come through succumbed to the flames eating at its base, and it joined its neighbors as it tumbled onto the ground like a handful of bricks dropped by a giant.

Kadorax didn't feel like waiting to see what else the rotten wasteland of Assir had to offer. He scanned the street as best he could through the thick haze in the air, moved several plots closer to the windmill's ruins, then found an alleyway that connected him back to his party.

"They're both dead," he said quickly, rejoining the group. "Let's get out of here."

Syzak and Brinna had Percival, now unconscious, balanced on a crudely made litter between them. They lifted the captain from the ground, shifted him in their grip a few times, and then the trio started to move, leaving Assir behind them as quickly as they could manage.

About half a mile away from the epicenter of the destruction, Kadorax finally saw a notification of experience points flash in front of his vision. "The battle is over," he told himself. Though it wasn't much relief, he made a conscious effort to let down his guard and relax his muscles, trying to get his heart rate to return to a normal pace.

The group made for the hunting lodges outside the

village. They arrived just before dusk, moving painfully slow on account of the captain weighing them down. Luckily, no undead abominations followed them out of the village.

Sitting around a meager campfire with a box of seafarer's rations open on a roughly hewn log, the three conscious people took a moment to silently collect their thoughts and take stock of what had happened.

Kadorax's entire body ached. His shoulders had been hit by falling debris more times than he had originally thought. A circle of dark bruises had bloomed across the top of his back, and his neck flashed with pain every time he looked too far to his left. Eyeing the sleeping captain, he considered his own injuries basically trivial. At least he could walk and move—even run if the situation called for it. On his stat sheet, he scrolled to the bottom to see the new possibilities available to him as a level six bastion of chaos incarnate. The centipede had yielded a monstrous amount of experience, but it had been split between five of them, presumably indicating that the Grim Sleeper had perished after the undead had been destroyed and not a moment before.

Level six didn't afford him many new talent options:

Torment: Rank 2 - The bastion's weapon magically extends to a second target beyond the first, and Torment inflicts slightly more damage than rank 1. Torment has an increased effect when used with a whip. Effect: moderate. Cooldown: 28 minutes.

Blade Training (Light): Rank 2 - The bastion is faster and stronger while wielding a light blade. Rank 2 allows the bastion to learn complex techniques through combat and training. Passive.

Chaos Shock: Rank 2 - The bastion pulls two slivers of chaotic energy into the world and thrusts them forward, creating a random magical effect augmented by a second impact quickly following the first. Effect: minor. Cooldown: 28 minutes.

RESPAWN

The prospect of being able to learn new techniques without spending valuable talents selecting them with each level made *Blade Training* an easy choice. Kadorax focused on the talent, unlocked it, and then decided he was going to need a better sword. Sadly, not having Santo's body as proof of the elf's demise meant there would be no reward, and a new sword would have to wait until another day.

Across from him, Syzak increased his *Cure Minor Ailments* ability to the second rank.

To Kadorax's right, Brinna made her selection as well. She had a choice between increasing her *Sneak* by a rank or getting a new defensive talent that allowed her block incoming ranged and magical attacks when wielding two weapons. She thought over the two choices for only a moment before settling on *Dual Wielding Block: Rank 1*.

Kadorax had to wonder what level the Grim Sleeper had been and where the woman had learned such dark magic. With an ally like her, he would have been a few steps closer to assembling the right party to slay the Gar'kesh. Now, with the Grim Sleeper obliterated, he needed to find the Priorate Knights and the Blackened Blades if he was going to be strong enough to exact his revenge.

Lord Percival groaned as his eyes fluttered open. Brinna, the closest one to him, tried to comfort the man as he wallowed in pain, but it was no use. Two broken legs was more than the captain had ever experienced before, and he didn't possess the mental fortitude needed to stave off his own screams.

"Anything lurking out here won't take long to find us," Kadorax said grimly. He thought about slitting the man's throat to put him out of his misery, but shook the notion from his mind. He needed the ship back in Coldport, and ships needed their captains.

"Let's wait until morning, and then we need to head back to Coldport as quickly as we can," Syzak said. "We can put him in one of the huts and try to muffle his screams, I guess."

With a grim nod, Kadorax and Brinna set about making the injured man as comfortable and quiet as possible.

CHAPTER 7

It took two days for the group to drag and carry Lord Percival back to Coldport. The man's injuries had thankfully not festered, probably due to the potion's effects at sealing the wounds. They had set both of his legs with scavenged wooden planks and a few bits of rope. Kadorax knew that if Lord Percival didn't get to a proper healer, a cleric with seriously high-level talents, the captain would never walk again, assuming he lived at all.

Coldport was too small to have a powerful cleric, so the group didn't even bother stopping in the town for more than enough time to catch their breath. Sailors from the *Grim Sleeper* came out to the docks to help their captain up the gangway. The galley chef and one of the crewmen took him to the bunk room where they could help keep him stable, as the ship was bound to rock back and forth when it got underway. To that end, the first mate cast off from Coldport as soon as everyone was on board. The *Grim Sleeper* headed south once more, keeping to the very center of the river to avoid the ice along the edges and setting their sights on Oscine City.

Only a few other ships were in the harbor when the *Grim Sleeper* arrived a day later. Some of the ice flowing from the high elevations of the Boneridge Mountains had made it to Oscine City's port, and most of the smaller ships had sailed for warmer destinations to avoid being potentially trapped when the deepest cold of winter set in, whenever that would be. The *Grim Sleeper* moored at one of the nicer, more protected wharves along the city's western coastline, paying a bit more for the slip than if they'd docked elsewhere simply to have an easier time unloading the captain to take him to one of the temples.

Kadorax, Brinna, and Syzak watched from the railing as the crew used an actual stretcher to move Percival into the harbormaster's office. The crewmen planned to wait there while two others found a suitable cleric and paid a sizeable amount for a few spells, giving the adventurers a day or two on their own.

"There's a branch of the Priorate Knights here in Oscine City," Syzak began. "We should find them and see what we can do to join their effort."

Killing whatever it was the jackals had summoned would take a coordinated group, especially if the thing was rampaging through the countryside and getting stronger and stronger with every day that passed. Though he was loath to do anything alongside the knights, he understood their usefulness. "Lead on, my friend. Let's see what the Knights have to offer."

"Are we even strong enough to join the Priorate Knights?" Brinna asked. As a rogue, she'd never be accepted into the order anyways, but that didn't mean they wouldn't consider hiring her for the covert kind of work they could not complete on their own.

"You're right," Kadorax answered. "The Knights won't take anyone below level ten. I'm not hoping to join them outright. We need information, and if we can help procure some resources or track down something that will help the effort, we have to try."

Unlike Kingsgate, Oscine City was low and flat, hugging the coastline and rarely jutting inward. It was idyllic in almost every regard, from the paved, well-maintained streets to the polished and painted spires of the towering cathedrals lining the waterfront—everything was dripping in opulence. The headquarters of the Priorate Knights two miles from the *Grim Sleeper* was no exception. The building was seven stories tall, made from huge marble blocks, and it overlooked the rolling ocean waves from a perch on a crag some hundred feet over the shore.

The climb to the veritable castle was an exhausting one. No road led to the Knights' doorstep—not in a traditional sense. The only guidance given to those wishing to ascend from below was a series of unlit torches hammered into the side of the rocks. The group never had to climb, but several places along the trail were so steep that they couldn't help but wonder if climbing had been the original intention.

Covered in sweat but standing triumphantly at the top, the group marveled in front of the Priorate Knights' doorway. The arched entry was made from bleached driftwood, and it towered over their heads, gilded in bronze and banded with iron all the way to the top. The Knights' banners, deep blue strips of cloth touting painted golden eagle heads, cascaded down either side of the door. No one stood guard outside the building, and as far as Kadorax knew, there hadn't even been a need. The Priorate Knights certainly had their fair share of sworn enemies, the Blackened Blades chief among them, but not even those rogues and assassins were brazen enough to attempt an assault on the chapter headquarters in Oscine City.

"Didn't the Priorate Knights put a bounty on your head once?" Syzak remembered.

Kadorax stopped just short of knocking on the driftwood door. "You know, they actually did. I wonder if anyone would remember it?" he mused. Without giving the issue another thought, he knocked on the door and took a step back.

A few short moments later, the driftwood swung inward. "Yes?" a young knight wearing the telltale blue and gold tabard of the priory asked.

"I'm—"

"Kadorax," the young knight interrupted. "The Lord of Darkarrow, leader of the Blackened Blades. You've come to turn yourself in? Or are these two here for the bounty themselves?"

"Well, they remember the bounty," Kadorax laughed. He looked the knight up and down. The younger man couldn't have been older than sixteen, which meant he shouldn't have even known who Kadorax was, much less have heard of his importance. "We've come to offer our services, actually. May we speak with the prior?"

The knight stood in the doorway and blocked their passage. "A dangerous criminal like you wants to join the Priorate Knights?" he scoffed.

Kadorax ensured that his character sheet wasn't being hidden. "We're level six," he explained. "We aren't here to raid you or start anything. I'm no longer affiliated with the

Blackened Blades. Check my sheet. I'm not even the Lord of Darkarrow anymore."

The knight read his stats, gave the other two a condescending sneer, then reluctantly stepped aside to allow them entry. "Wait here," he commanded. "I'll summon an escort. The prior wouldn't want you traipsing around the priory unwatched."

Kadorax shrugged. He didn't really care if a bunch of a self-absorbed knights wanted to babysit him. As long as he was able to see the prior, he was confident he could get what he wanted. Like the outside of the huge building, the interior was beautifully appointed and altogether not a bad place to spend a few minutes waiting. Everything was white marble, dressed in blue and gold, and the center of the foyer was dominated by a huge sculpture of an eagle with its talons and wings outstretched, fiercely positioned against any who entered.

Several moments after the young knight left, a troop of lightly armored soldiers came pounding their way up a staircase to the right of the foyer, spears and swords at the ready.

"That's a bit much, don't you think?" Kadorax asked.

The knight in charge of the platoon only glowered.

"The prior will see you," the young knight who had fetched the squadron said. The rest of the knights surrounded the three adventurers like they were a group of Agglor's most feared assassins, and the young knight led them down two hallways to an open-air balcony overlooking the ocean below. The smell of saltwater mingled with two heavily perfumed candles mounted to either side of the balcony.

In the center of the balcony, the prior waited with a smile on his face. He was an old man, probably close to the natural end of his life, but he held a strength and confidence about him that made him appear far more capable than his wrinkled skin would imply. "Thank you," the prior said warmly to the young knight. Formal bows were exchanged, and then the retinue of guards clanked away to stand watch somewhere out of earshot.

Kadorax noticed the impression of a sword hilt poking at fabric of the prior's robe. He also took note of the distinct lack of armor the man wore, even down to the sandals on his feet. "I appreciate the audience," he said as genuinely as he knew how.

"And to what do I owe the pleasure?" the prior asked. His voice was old and strained, but it did not quaver. "It is a rare day indeed that the leader of the Blackened Blades pays a prior of the Knights a visit."

"I'm not their leader any longer," Kadorax told him.

"So I have heard," the prior went on. "Slain by the jackals and their god, yes?"

"There wasn't a jackal alive in that temple when I died," Kadorax answered.

The prior's smile widened. "Just their god, then."

"Right," Kadorax agreed. "And that's why we're here. We heard you've aligned with the Blackened Blades and the Miners' Union. We want to help."

The prior took on an inquisitive look. "At level six?" He let his gaze drift back out toward the ocean, an inquisitive hand on his chin. "The youngest knight I'm sending is level thirty. From what I've heard, the Blackened Blades are only sending their best as well. Perhaps you would try the Miners' Union?"

Kadorax couldn't help but laugh. For as much as the assassins and knights refused to get along, virtually *no one* tolerated the Miners' Union. Their reputation was that of petty thieves and highwaymen, always taking advantage of those who hired them and didn't know any better.

The prior laughed as well, letting the absurd suggestion die in the air. "I know you're bound to be more capable than your level would indicate," he said. "And if you die on the front lines, I do not think it would cost me any sleep."

"So there's a job?" Kadorax asked.

The old man's smile took on an almost imperceptibly sinister quality. "I have something in mind, yes," he answered. "I assume you have adequate means of transportation?"

Brinna stepped up and pointed down the shoreline. Against the horizon, the *Grim Sleeper's* central mast was barely visible. "We have a ship and crew," she declared.

"Good, good," the prior said. "I have a message for you to deliver to the priory in Skarm's Reif."

"I'm not your little messenger boy," Kadorax scoffed. He turned to leave, shaking his head in disappointment. A simple delivery quest, especially by boat, wouldn't yield anywhere close to a noticeable amount of experience.

The prior laughed and wheezed at Kadorax's back, making him turn back around with a scowl on his face.

"Don't you want to know what the message would contain?" the prior asked.

Kadorax fixed him with an even stare.

"Skarm's Reif is where our forces are gathering for the real assault on the jackal god. The prior there is serving as our field general, and my letter would be a means of introduction for you and your little band of hapless adventurers," he said, laughing all the while. "But if you don't want it—if that sort of thing is *beneath* the mighty Kadorax—no one is forcing you to accept."

Kadorax's face flushed with embarrassment. He should

have expected at least one such caper from the man who had been his nemesis for so long. "Fine. We'll take your letter to Skarm's Reif. At least you aren't trying to send us all the way to Vecnos."

"Are there dangerous, man-eating jackal gods in Vecnos, hmm?" the prior went on through more of his own laughter. "Last I heard, some upstart kid was trying to make a name for himself there. Trust me, if he ever becomes a threat, you'd be the first one I would look to send."

"If I ever set my sights on that forsaken land, I'm taking you with me. They'll never find your body all the way out there," Kadorax retorted.

"Perhaps we'll take a trip there sometime, only the two of us." He sighed, a slight smile on his face. "But Skarm's Reif isn't far enough to get my hopes up that you might not return. I would send a contingent of my knights to guard you along the way—the gods know you'd need them at level six—but I wouldn't want one of them to get greedy and claim the bounty on your head, so you'll have to make the trip of your own accord, I'm afraid," the prior said.

"Perfect," Kadorax mumbled. "We'll wait at the door for the letter." He left the balcony, assuming the other two would follow close behind.

Back in the interior of the building, the squad of guards snapped to attention, then quickly fell into step alongside the three adventurers. The ring of their boots echoed off the high walls and vaulted ceilings.

Only a minute or so later, the prior appeared at the foyer. The armored knights stood as straight as they could possibly manage, not a hair was out of place as they solemnly waited for the final bits of formality to conclude. Somewhat satisfying to Kadorax, the prior didn't even seem to notice the soldiers as he passed by with a wooden scroll case in his hands.

"Here," the old man said. "I marked the case with Skarm's Reif as the destination, though I'm not convinced you can read, so do try to remember the name. And when you get there, the priory will be the tall building dressed in blue and gold. I'll pray that you find it before the Priorate Knights return victorious with the beast's head. I wouldn't want you stumbling around Skarm's Reif like a lost puppy when my army comes marching through."

"And my bounty?" Kadorax asked, trying his best to ignore the stream of insults thrown his way.

The prior dismissed the notion with a wave of his hand. "The bounty was only for the leader of the Blackened Blades, not a level six would-be hero."

"And when the Gar'kesh is dead, you'll just go back to the old ways?" Kadorax wondered.

With a devious smile, the prior answered, "Of course. Priorate Knights have hated the Blackened Blades since long before either of us were ever born. Though we've put aside our differences for now, the truce means nothing in the grand scheme of things."

"So be it," Kadorax stated. He didn't offer the prior any formal goodbye—he just turned on his heel and pushed his way out the driftwood door.

"Well, that was as fun as I had expected," Syzak announced when the door was fully closed behind them.

"I take it you two have tried to kill each other in the past," Brinna said.

Kadorax shook his head and tried to rid himself of the dour mood the prior had brought down on his head. "Knights and all their high-minded notions of honor and hierarchy," he spat, pointedly avoiding the question. "Assassins are free men and women, beholden to very little. Membership in the Blackened Blades was paid in blood, not gold, and everyone was equal. I was their leader, yes, but no one else had a rank, no chain of command. The assassins were free to come and go as they pleased, accepting only those contracts they really wanted. No one can *order* them to do anything. They either chose to go, or they chose not to go. Knights take orders like obedient dogs—slaves, really."

"And the Miners' Union?" Brinna went on. "How do they fit into everything?"

The mention of such an inept group of mercenaries went a long way toward lifting Kadorax's spirits. "They're a bunch of idiots," he laughed.

"I thought they just worked the Boneridge Mines. They fight?" Brinna asked.

"Just a bunch of orcs, hermits, goblins, and other brutes loosely organized under the banner of some elf lord who lives so high up the mountains he sees snow every day of the year. They work the mines, that's for sure, but they've been known to hire out conscript militia to certain causes," Kadorax explained.

"The cheapest, rowdiest, and worst-trained mercenaries in all Agglor," Syzak added with a snicker.

Kadorax agreed, and Brinna just laughed.

The journey back down to the main portion of Oscine City was just as slow and arduous as the ascent had been. They had to move backward, constantly checking their footing and taking dozens of breaks to ensure their balance on the side of the jagged rocks.

"We have a day to kill," Kadorax announced when they were all on solid ground once more. The waves lapping at his boots played a gentle rhythm underneath his words.

"You need better gear," Syzak told Brinna. "Skarm's Reif is about as remote a place as you'll find in Agglor. The animals living in the woods are all at least level ten. You're not a fighter, not yet."

The rogue agreed. She took her daggers from her boots and handed them over for inspection. "These are all I've ever had," she said sheepishly.

Kadorax twirled one of them over in his hand, then tested the sharpness of the blade against his palm. It didn't draw any blood. He tilted the point against the meat between his thumb and first finger and pushed down, gently at first, and then harder. It *still* didn't draw any blood.

"This is basically a knife you'd use to cut meat in a tavern," Kadorax concluded. "And it wouldn't even be adequate for that."

"I know," Brinna said, her eyes cast down at the rocky shore. "I never really needed much, you know?"

"Let's get to Darkarrow as soon as we can," Kadorax told her. "The Blackened Blades always kept some weapons stashed there, and we'll be able grab a few things. For now, let's go see how the captain is faring. Maybe we can get Ayers to at least add an edge to these daggers."

Enjoying the stiff, cool breeze coming in off the ocean and basking in the undeniably serene beauty of Oscine City, the three took their time as they headed back to the *Grim Sleeper*. The ship felt a bit out of place moored next to the other, mostly larger ships in the harbor. Such a gruesome figurehead stuck out like a whore at vespers.

Ayers was hard at work in his cramped smithy, and a thin plume of dark smoke escaped from the chimney he had built into the deck above his head. Without windows, he had to use a pair of taper candles and the light of his forge to see. "The captain has me working on a couple projects for him," he said when Kadorax and the others entered. "I won't be able to make you anything new until those are finished."

Brinna tossed her pair of daggers on the man's anvil next to the iron he was working. "Think you could sharpen these?" she asked.

The blacksmith didn't need more than a glance to know the quality of the daggers. They were beginner weapons, and they hadn't even been maintained. "Aye," he answered. "Leave 'em here. I'll get an edge on the pair, though you really need new ones altogether."

"What would it cost?" she asked, though she had no gold of her own.

Ayers thought for a moment, scratching his head. "Hold up your hand," he said.

Brinna complied, and Ayers measured the size of her palm and fingers against one of her own daggers. "You've got small hands," he told her. "There are enough scraps here for me to make something that tiny, I'm sure."

Kadorax drew his blade and held the hilt in Ayers' direction. "Any chance you could add a deeper fuller?" he asked.

"Not on such a thin weapon," Ayers answered. "It would break the first time I hit it." He shook his head and sighed. "You lot are sorely in need of better weapons."

"There's no doubt about that," Kadorax agreed.

"Give me a couple days, and I'll see what I can do. And I could use some better iron, if you come across any. The ingots I brought from Coldport are so impure they might as well be lead." Ayers took the two daggers on his anvil and set them on a new wooden shelf behind him, then twisted the bar he was working into the coals.

RESPAWN

Back on the top deck, a handful of sailors were making their way slowly up the gangplank, the captain hobbling between them. Lord Percival was flushed, and both of his legs were bandaged with fresh, white linen, though he did appear in far better spirits than before.

"How'd it go?" Syzak asked from the railing.

The first mate grunted as he hefted the captain by the shoulder over the last section of the ascent. "Cost him all he made from killing the werewolf and then some, but he'll walk unaided again. Maybe even soon," the man replied.

"Fancy a trip to Darkarrow?" Kadorax asked when Percival finally recovered his breath.

The captain regarded him with weary eyes. "My . . . yes, I . . . Where? I suppose," he muttered incoherently.

"Have a plan after Darkarrow?" the first mate asked. "I'll do the thinking for the crew over the next couple days. Just until the captain regains his wits."

"Good idea," Kadorax answered.

"We've no more contracts, and Oscine City will basically be asleep all winter. I'd like to get us out of port sooner rather than later," the first mate replied.

Kadorax put his arm around the captain to steady the man's feet as he hobbled to a chair near the wheel. "Darkarrow for a day, then on to Skarm's Reif. Have you ever been there?"

The first mate nodded. "Skarm's Reif is a good ways out, but that'll give the captain here a few needed days to recover."

"Perfect." Kadorax shook the first mate's hand, excited to

be returning to his home for the first time since the wretched jackal god had sent him back to a respawn. Well, it wasn't *his* home, he reminded himself. One of the other Blackened Blades would have taken over. On Earth, the prospect of someone else sleeping in his bed would have been a horrible affront. On Agglor, it didn't actually bother him. That was the way of life. He had been killed in combat, had lost everything, and his former title alone awarded him absolutely no luxury. Darkarrow was not his.

CHAPTER 8

The *Grim Sleeper* cut through the ocean, its bow pointed east. They had to round the edge of the Boneridge Mountains, then they'd dock at either Virast or Black Harbor. From either city, Darkarrow was a two days' hike inland, or three if the heat was bad, which it likely was. The southern end of the Boneridge Mountains was speckled with low volcanoes, and the wind coming over the peaks from the west trapped all their heat in the basin below. Summers in Darkarrow were brutally hot. The winters weren't much cooler, at least not during the day.

Despite the overall inhospitable nature of the region, Kadorax had loved living there. Black Harbor and Darkarrow had both been named for their presence next to the volcanoes, since the ash clouds produced by every eruption—even the minor ones that barely brought any lava—hung low in the sky and cast dark, eerie shadows over everything for several days. Some of the older legends said Black Harbor had been cursed by a banshee, and the thick blankets of ash that gave the place its namesake were actually her death shroud. Whenever the city became dark, the old folk would shutter their windows and hang flowers from their eaves in an attempt to ward away the spirit.

Kadorax had never been particularly interested in science during his time on Earth, but he knew enough about volcanoes to have never feared a banshee. That folksy superstition had made Darkarrow the perfect location for the Blackened Blades. If a would-be attacker wasn't deterred by the mere fact that they were assaulting an estate full of assassins, they were probably insane enough to buy into the mysteries of the darkness. Plus, the veil helped keep some of the Blackened Blades' more questionable activities safe from prying eyes.

When the *Grim Sleeper* pulled into port at Virast, the skies were clear. In terms of beauty and splendor, the smaller port town couldn't compare with Oscine City. Virast was much older—built, destroyed, and rebuilt dozens of times over the last several centuries so that the architecture was a hodgepodge of different styles and techniques. "Think anyone will recognize you, my lord?" Syzak asked with a playful tone.

Even before, when Kadorax *had* been a lord, he had never required Syzak to use the honorific. "In Virast, I doubt it," the man replied. "But they'll know me in Darkarrow, that's for sure."

"Let's just hope the new leader has more fond memories of us than grudges."

The two had been equal parts beloved and notorious during their tenure at the head of the organization. Succession, after all, was rarely initiated via retirement. Kadorax had taken his title with a bit of thin wire in the middle of the night. There had been a few members, even after all the years, who remembered his ascension with a grimace.

Kadorax, Syzak, and Brinna stepped off the *Grim Sleeper* around midday. The weather was cool and cloudy, but they could feel the heat whenever the sun broke through to find their backs. It was going to be a hot journey inland, of that they had no doubt. Carrying supplies exacerbated the high temperatures. Before long, Kadorax and Brinna were both sweating.

"If you're ever back in Virast without us," Syzak explained to the rogue, "never go in there." He pointed to a rickety tavern with mold and moss growing on the slanted roof. The sign hanging above the door was so old that all the paint had faded away.

"I don't think you'd have to worry about me willingly entering a place like that," Brinna answered. She turned her nose up at the smell of the place as they walked by. Luckily, there were no windows.

It took them a couple hours to walk the entire length of Virast. There were no guards posted or gatehouses manned at the edge like Oscine City had to regulate those entering and leaving. Instead, the buildings simply became more and more sparse until all that was left was farmland accented by the occasional house breaking up the monotony of crops. A road, poorly built and never repaired, cut north through the heart of the farmland toward Darkarrow. For whatever reason, the road had been built twenty feet or so to the right of a decently sized ridge, causing more and more of the paving stones to wash away every time it rained. A fresh layer of mud coating the path told Kadorax that such a rain had passed recently.

Their boots sloshing through the muck and grime, the

three trudged onward without complaint. There were several other cities besides Darkarrow, some of them quite large and opulent, farther to the north, and travelers sharing the road passed by rather frequently. Most of them hauled finished goods, typically barley wine, in heavy oxcarts that left deep ruts in the mud and stone. As the Lord of Darkarrow, Kadorax had once sent a group of his workers to try and repair the road, but it had been pointless. All the barrels of ale that came down the road had quickly undone all the repairs his men had made.

There were a few roadside inns along the path, none of them reputable or conforming to any sense of comfort whatsoever. Kadorax led them to one such establishment to spend the night.

"We're not staying at the usual spot?" Syzak asked.

"Not tonight," Kadorax answered. "Too many of my own assassins spend their nights at The Blue Ax. I'd like to make it into Darkarrow unannounced."

"I don't know if switching inns along the road will be enough," Syzak said honestly. In truth, he had the sneaking suspicion that they had already been seen by one of Darkarrow's sentries.

Kadorax nodded in agreement. "If any of them learned anything from me, we've been followed since Virast."

"Might as well make the best of it, then," Brinna added.

The inn Kadorax had chosen was the roughest of them all, featuring nightly brawls, all manner of debauchery, and the occasional murder. The only redeeming quality of the place was that they let out their rooms for free so long as the patrons bought a few mugs of beer before turning in. Kadorax didn't have many coins in smaller denominations than gold, just a few pieces of copper he had gotten from one of the sailors aboard the *Grim Sleeper*, but chances were the owner wouldn't bother to notice his lack of patronage.

Luckily, it was still too early in the night for the tavern to be crowded with travelers, so Kadorax bought one round at the bar and claimed a room at the back of the building.

In the morning, the three adventurers were the first patrons awake. "We'll be at Darkarrow before nightfall," Kadorax stated as they emerged from the building, boots squishing in the mud.

"Why do I keep getting the feeling that we're willfully walking into our own demise?" Brinna asked. "I don't even have my weapons..."

"We'll be fine," Kadorax said confidently. Though he was being sincere, he knew his words were far from comforting.

He didn't notice the first sentry shadowing his movements until he was just barely within sight of the Darkarrow compound. The man, covered in dirt and leaves off to the side of the narrow trail branching from the main road, had sneezed. Kadorax smirked to himself, careful not to expose his own awareness, and wondered if the low-level scout would be beaten upon his return to the Blackened Blades. When he had been in charge, the scouts had always worked in pairs and had always been eager to expose the shortcomings of their partners in hopes of gaining an advantage in the cutthroat world of murder-for-hire.

Still smiling to himself, Kadorax decided not to rat out the hapless scout, though it did make him cringe to think that Darkarrow had fallen to the point of using untrained initiates to watch their roads. They reached the perimeter of the estate with the scout still tailing them. The outer wall, only eight feet tall and made of stacked stones, gave way to a large, open courtyard where anyone approaching would easily be seen before they ever neared the door.

Emerging into plain view, Kadorax let out a deep sigh. He was happy to be home, but also felt a pang of sorrow that he wouldn't be staying. His memories were emboldened by the fact that most of Darkarrow had not changed in his absence. The estate was large and low to the ground, illuminated sparsely by torches on the interior of the wall and near the entrances, just as he had left it.

"Not any further," the scout said behind the group. Brinna was the only one who reacted with any amount of surprise.

Kadorax turned, his eyebrows raised. "Allergies?" he asked sarcastically.

The man's face went white with fear. "You—"

"Don't worry," Kadorax reassured him. "I won't say anything. I'm just trying to get in to see whoever it is leading the Blackened Blades these days. Care to walk us to the door?"

The man gulped, but he quickly stepped ahead to lead the way nonetheless.

Unlike the days of Kadorax's tenure, the front door was not rigged with a poisoned crossbow bolt. In rather mundane fashion, the scout simply knocked four times, and then the door was opened. Another man, perhaps even more a novice than the first, answered.

"Get the boss," the nervous scout said. The other man nodded before disappearing deeper into the complex.

A few minutes silently passed before anyone else came to the door. "Please, come in," a level four rogue beckoned.

The three adventurers stepped into the dark, dreary room just beyond the entrance. It was far from a proper foyer, and it was so much the opposite of the grand entry at the priory in Oscine City that any knight accidentally stumbling upon it would have figured it for nothing more than an abandoned home. Everything was shrouded in gloom. Only a pair of paintings hung on the walls, both of them depicting bloody executions, and there were no tapestries or carpets, no statues or busts. Even the floor beneath their feet creaked with every step, and whole planks of it were missing outright in the corners.

"Ah, Jaczkz," Kadorax said. The assassin standing in the room was tall and clothed in pitch-black leather armor, the edges of which were trimmed in silky feathers and fine thread. "I'm glad to see you. It has been too long."

"Kadorax?" the assassin questioned. He scanned Kadorax's character sheet just above his head to make sure. "Ha! You're back! I hope you don't intend to retake your position, my friend."

"I would never," Kadorax said warmly. His thought derailed for a split second as he realized he had lied, but he carried on regardless. "I'm glad to see someone capable like yourself in charge of my glorious brethren."

Jaczkz shook his head, looking dismayed. "I was the only one of a respectable level they left behind to watch over Darkarrow while so many are deployed against the Gar'kesh. I'm basically in charge of nothing. Elise has command of the Blackened Blades now. I trust you remember her."

"Elise?" Kadorax repeated, hoping desperately that he had heard Jaczkz incorrectly. "Who let that happen?"

Jaczkz had visibly relaxed, discharging all the tension from the room. "When you went missing, she was the first to scramble for leadership. Two others challenged her, at least as far as I heard, and she killed them both. So there you have it. Elise has command of the Blackened Blades."

Kadorax groaned. Of all the skilled assassins he had

previously overseen, Elise was perhaps the one who harbored the most hatred for him on a personal level.

"I assume Elise won't be eager to see your return?" Brinna asked.

To her side, Syzak scoffed. "Elise tried to kill him twice."

"I can deal with her later," Kadorax added. "How many have departed for Skarm's Reif?"

Jaczkz spread his arms out wide to indicate the lack of activity in Darkarrow. "Almost everyone has gone. There are thousands of jackal packs all over Agglor. Some of them have started summonings of their own, though the beast you fought was by far their strongest. If Agglor is going to survive, we'll need everyone we can get, even the knights."

"Saving Agglor would be nice and all, but the experience points we'd earn slaying a handful of Gar'kesh would be insane," Syzak said.

Brinna didn't look so confident or eager. "If everyone went out to Skarm's Reif to fight, they probably didn't leave many weapons behind, did they?"

"Not much," the assassin replied. "Darkarrow is a ghost town."

"Well, we're heading to Skarm's Reif next," Kadorax said. "The temple where we died is the ultimate goal, but we heard in Coldport that the Gar'kesh had moved on to other villages, rampaging through the countryside. Where was it last seen?"

Jaczkz rummaged through a short bureau, one of the only pieces of furniture in the dark room, and pulled out a torn bit of scroll. "This was the last report, though it's a week old now. We were going to burn it tonight with a few other missives, but it's yours if you need it."

Kadorax read over the report quickly and handed it back.

"The Gar'kesh is still pretty far north. We'll focus on the jackal temples and hideouts around Skarm's Reif."

"I'd offer to send more assassins with you, but we need at least one person to stay here and await your return," Jaczkz said.

"Ha, I don't think I'll be taking over the Blackened Blades again, my friend," Kadorax told him. "I just need to pay a visit to my old room and recover a few things, then we'll be on our way."

The rest of Darkarrow was just as drab and dreary as the entryway. Jaczkz led the three through Darkarrow to the room Elise had claimed as leader at the back of the compound. Kadorax had been the one who had selected the room a long time ago. Returning there was bittersweet. Part of him hated not being in charge—and an even larger part hated that Elise had been the one to take his title—but there was still a bit of relief that came from only being a visitor.

The room was still much like Kadorax had left it, even down to the traps rigged in the ceiling above the door. Inside, the bed, dresser, knife rack, and other fixtures were still in their places. "Well, she took the obvious weapons," he said.

A layer of dust on the back edge of the dresser told him that Elise hadn't discovered the small cache he had hidden. He reached behind it, pushed aside a false bit of wood, and plucked a key from a small hook. Inside the dresser's bottommost drawer was a tiny little panel. Kadorax moved it aside to reveal a keyhole, then pushed the key all the way to the back of the lock. "Right, left, right," he remembered aloud. A clicking noise came from behind the dresser, and then a little wall cubby in the back of the drawer released from its chains by an inch, allowing enough room for Kadorax to get his fingertips inside and pull it open.

"Everything is still here," he said. "But I hadn't left much inside. Just some essentials." He pulled out a leather pouch with fifty gold pieces, a pair of small, poisoned darts, and a single curved knife built in the classic style of the Blackened Blades. Running his finger over the knife's hilt, he gave it a moment of reminiscence before handing it to the rogue.

"Thanks," she said, holding it gingerly like some relic from a holy temple.

"Just be careful with it. You won't want to keep it in your boots. The blade itself is obsidian, and it has a pretty nasty enchantment. Stick it in someone for longer than a second or two and you'll heal from it," Kadorax explained.

Brinna's eyes grew wide. She focused on the weapon to read the official details of the magical enhancement:

Talon Dagger - Rune slots used: 1 of 1. Theft of Life Rune: Rank 9 - Penetration into living flesh for more than 1.4 seconds casts Theft of Life on the target, draining their life and transferring it to the wielder for up to 6 seconds. Effect: profound. Cooldown: 1 day.

"I . . . I can't accept this," Brinna said. "It must be worth a fortune."

Kadorax nodded. "Oh, it is. Just be careful with it. If you accidentally cut yourself enough to activate the rune, I don't really know what will happen. And the blade's too small for combat anyways. Talon daggers are made for close, quiet assassinations. Keep it on your belt until someone gets close and you need it."

The three adventurers didn't hang around Darkarrow much longer. They shared a brief farewell with Jaczkz, took some food from the cellar, then hit the road. Virast was too far to make the trip in a single day, but Kadorax kept them moving late into the night. He wanted to be back on the *Grim Sleeper* and heading for Skarm's Reif as soon as possible. As far as he was concerned, every minute spent away from the front lines in the war against the jackals was time wasted.

A bit of rain fell as they neared closer to the city in the early morning haze. The clouds were low, dark and brooding, with pregnant undersides that threatened a storm.

Lord Percival was awake and at the railing when they returned to the ship. He still wasn't standing, but his spirits had greatly improved, and that was progress. "We're off to Skarm's Reif, is it?" he asked. A few days of resting in a hammock to recover had taken a toll on his voice, making it come out raspy and dull, a stark contrast to his usually bright demeanor.

"That's the closest port to the jackals' territory. The Gar'kesh is still much farther north, close to their highest temple. The other jackals, though—they've been performing summoning rituals of their own all around Skarm's Reif. The Blackened Blades and the Priorate Knights have joined forces there as a basecamp of sorts. They're making expeditions into the jackal temples," Kadorax explained.

"Without my warlock, I'm not sure where my crew will be needed," the captain said sullenly. "We can't really accept bounties unless we hire on a crew of mercenaries, and I don't have much capital left."

"I'm sure there will be shipping contracts to support the war effort," Kadorax told him.

The captain shook his head, wincing at the pain that shot up from his hips as he moved. "You're probably right, but the *Grim Sleeper* has never really been a shipping vessel. Not recently, at least. I need to start choosing combat talents when I level," he said.

The *Grim Sleeper* cast off from the docks of Virast right as the storm brewing overhead began in earnest. The rains pounded down on the top deck, and peals of thunder made the mast shake. Fortunately, the storm was relatively localized over the city. The ship sailed slowly away from the tumult, rocking side to side in the swells, until it found calmer waters an hour or so later.

"You've been to Skarm's Reif more recently than I have," Lord Percival said to Kadorax below deck. They only had a few candles burning since two had fallen from the table and been extinguished in the rainwater sloshing around at their feet. "The maps have two approaches. One, the western channel, is closer. The eastern approach is probably cleaner. How difficult is the west?" He pointed to a section of the map labeled with a heavy amount of coral and a sand barge jutting out beyond the bay.

Kadorax had to think back to his previous life. "I don't think I've ever bothered to pay attention to the direction the ships came in. I'd say more of them docked on the east, but that's all I know."

"I'll let the pilot know when we get closer," Percival said.

Avoiding the storm added an extra day to the journey. Lord Percival had spent the entire time restless and weary, confined to a bunk for all but an hour or so each day. Ayers was at least able to add a respectable edge to Brinna's daggers, though he grumbled incessantly when he gave them back, saying something about disrespecting his skill as a smith by having him work on dinnerware.

No matter their quality, Brinna was glad to have her blades where they belonged, tucked neatly into the inside flanks of her leather boots. The talon dagger was small enough to fit into her belt without the hilt poking out and giving it away.

Ships constantly came and went at Skarm's Reif. The city itself was situated on an offshoot of the actual ocean, facing a rocky, uninhabited island directly to the south. Unlike the cities and settlements of Agglor closer to the Boneridge Mountains, Skarm's Reif had never been formally planned. The city had organically grown over the years from a collection of several fishing villages to a scattered, disorganized heap of buildings and streets all piled on top of each other. Being so close to the ungoverned realms of the jackals and other non-humans, Skarm's Reif had never been important.

It was easy to see that everything had changed. The blue and gold banners of the Priorate Knights flew from almost every window. The knights had transformed the ramshackle layout of the city into a well-organized machine ready for war. There were spiked ramparts built everywhere, even in places that didn't make any sense like unused alleyways and main thoroughfares. Kadorax wasn't sure exactly how close the nearest jackal settlement was to Skarm's Reif, but he was fairly certain there wouldn't be any fighting in the streets.

"Doesn't hurt to be prepared, I guess," he said as he disembarked from the *Grim Sleeper*.

"Well, I think we'll find the priory chapter quite easily," Syzak said.

A little ways up the hill from the docks, a huge stone structure dominated the entire city's skyline. Blue and gold pennants flew from its three towering steeples. Several groups of armored men were being led on drills in front of the priory's door, a loud sergeant on horseback barking orders to them.

"And where are your Blackened Blades?" Brinna asked. "Everything that isn't clearly of priorate construction looks dingy enough to be your headquarters."

Kadorax shot her a sidelong glance, then shook his head. "You know, there's something to be said for inconspicuousness. You're a rogue. You shouldn't even like all that pomp and visibility."

"Ha, you're right," Brinna laughed. "All the splendor and majesty gets a little grating after a while, I suppose."

Letter of introduction in hand, Kadorax led them through the streets toward the priory. They passed several groups of knights along the way as well as all manner of civilians trying to sell their war provisions. Most of the weapons and armor being vendored were barely good enough to even use as scrap, but Kadorax did see one shop displaying high-quality arms in their front window.

"I'll need a sword later," the bastion mused to himself, making an effort to remember where the shop was located.

When they reached the priory, they found the doors already opened and a line of what appeared to be peasants carrying supplies inside. It took a moment for Kadorax to find a knight who wasn't already occupied.

"You, knight," he called unceremoniously. "I'll need a word with your prior." He extended the scroll out to the man, but the knight did not take it.

"Prior's out on a raid," came the curt response.

"Well, who's next in charge? I've a letter from the priory in Oscine City."

The knight looked him over, then inspected his character sheet as he wrinkled his face in disgust. "You're not a knight," he said with a heavy dose of condescension. He snatched the scroll from Kadorax's hand and opened it. "None of you are knights or any other class the priory would hire."

Kadorax wished he still had his title as Lord of Darkarrow attached to his name. Maybe then he'd get somewhere with the stubborn knights. "Just tell us where to go to find someone with a little more authority," he said.

The knight's expression soured even further. "I'm the commanding officer here while the prior is away. All this letter says is to not kill you, hope that no one kills you, throw your body in the sea and never speak of it if someone *accidentally* kills you, and otherwise order you to the front lines. Who are you?"

For once, Kadorax was rather glad his reputation didn't precede him.

"You—" Syzak started. Kadorax stopped him with a hand across his chest.

"Don't worry about it. Just tell us where we'll find some action." Kadorax tried to put on his most disarming smile. He had a strong hunch that it didn't work.

The knight handed the scroll back while showing as little interest as possible. "Fine, then. To the front you go. There's a trail out of the Reif to the east, lots of knights there all the time, you can't miss it. Take the trail out five or six miles, and you'll see the command tent clear as day. If the prior's back, you'll find her there."

Kadorax considered thanking the man for the directions,

then the silence between them stretched to an awkward length, so he simply turned and left.

"Grab a sword from in town and then find that camp?" Syzak asked.

Kadorax and Brinna both gave their assent. "I just hope Elise isn't there. Knowing her tremendous ability to remember those she hated, we might not find the Blackened Blades to be as welcoming as we would like," he said.

"And the Miners' Union?" Brinna added. "No one's even bothered to mention them. I thought they were supposed to be caught up in the war as well."

Syzak looked around the street, but he didn't see any non-humans other than a pair of gnomes standing in front of a bar with clay jars in their hands. Their scrawny builds and fine attire easily placed them outside the ranks of the Miners' Union. "We might find some of them at the forward camp, no doubt profiteering from all the raw materials coming into the city, but don't get your hopes up on fighting side by side with miners. They're industrious—they aren't adventurers."

"I've never met a proper dwarf or orc before," Brinna said with a nod, her mind far away. "And Santo was the only elf I had ever known. Assir feels so . . . far away . . ."

Kadorax found the weapon shop once more and stepped inside. A man dressed in blue and gold was busy haggling with the attendant at the counter, so the bastion took his time going through the weapons that weren't locked at the front.

Glancing at the prices, Syzak kept his voice low. "Way overpriced," he said.

Silently, Kadorax agreed. He found a sturdy short sword with a deep fuller in a slotted wooden bin and lifted it, surprised by the weight. He had to remind himself that his *Strength* score was terrible compared to the stats he was used to as an assassin. "Seventy gold," he nearly gasped. It didn't take him long to return the blade to its wooden home and be gone from the store.

"Well, the *Grim Sleeper* shouldn't have any trouble finding work transporting cargo, and Ayers' workshop will be fully stocked and operational in a week," Kadorax observed. He could just barely see the top of the ship's center mast from the street.

"Aye," Syzak agreed. "Let's find some jackals."

CHAPTER 9

The path to the forward camp, as it turned out, was even marked with a priory archway and a set of flapping banners. It was heavily used, perhaps even more so than some of the streets in Virast. The walk took a few hours, and they passed hundreds of other adventurers, merchants, and even a few members of the Miners' Union along the way. Some of the adventurers were in pretty bad shape as they went by. More than one of the groups they saw pulled along a sheet-covered corpse in a wagon.

More blue and gold banners flapped happily in the wind at the camp. The road sort of ended in a sea of tents, hastily constructed wooden buildings, and latrine lines dug into the ground. From what they could see of the other side of the camp, a few more trails began there and wound their way into the wilderness. There was a thick forest to the road's right side and jagged, rock-strewn plains to the left. In the center was a priory building, a compound of tents, wooden shacks, and a brick fireplace to one side that held several spits of roasting meat.

It didn't take long to find the Blackened Blades among the constant bustle of the camp. Their outpost was plain and dreary, flying no heraldry or colors at all, with a single man standing watch in front of the door. Behind the low building were two rows of palisades complete with sharpened spears and shallow pits. The ring of several blacksmiths' hammers sounded from a series of thatched roofs over a collection of anvils next to the Blackened Blades. Each of the smiths was busily shaping arrowheads and passing off buckets of them to fletchers who fit them to shafts in the next building.

Before Kadorax could knock on the door, it opened, and the guard stepped politely to the side. Elise stepped out into the sunlight, stretching her back. Then her eyes found Kadorax and she stopped midstep.

"You," the woman said flatly. Her right hand hovered near the hilt of her sword, a magnificent weapon dripping puffs of black shadow into the air from its unsheathed tip.

Kadorax brought up the woman's character sheet. Sure enough, *Lady of Darkarrow* was clearly present right after her name. Beyond that, Kadorax saw her level as well: *Elise Stormdottr, Lady of Darkarrow, Level 41 Assassin.*

"You're alive," she said. The guard from the door recognized the tension, and he stepped forward with his own blade in hand.

"Yes," Kadorax finally said, dismissing Elise's stats from his vision. "We've come to help . . ."

Elise raised an eyebrow. She was a tall woman, built, and her eyes glimmered with violence. When she smiled—something that almost never happened—Kadorax thought even her grin appeared sinister. Everything about the new

Lady of Darkarrow spoke of malice. "I suppose that is fitting. It was you, after all, who put Agglor in such a mess."

"I caused it?" Kadorax laughed. "If you've forgotten, I hate jackals. I didn't summon their god and start a war."

Elise ignored his words with an ugly snarl. "You were there. You failed to kill the Gar'kesh. Probably got cocky and made a mistake."

Kadorax decided to let her think whatever she liked about his demise. Telling her the truth wouldn't make her believe it. "Just tell me when the next mission leaves," he said.

She motioned for the guard to relax, then stepped forward and placed her hands on Kadorax shoulders, making him jump a bit at the unexpected touch. "If this is some ploy to win back your title, you're far too late. The Blackened Blades are *mine*." She was several inches taller than Kadorax, and her breath was hot on his forehead. "If you take a single step toward me that I don't like, I'll paint the walls of my tent with your innards."

Kadorax knew she meant every word. Her grip on his shoulders was starting to bring a bit of pain, even through his armor. "You can have the Blackened Blades," he stated as he turned away from her vise-like grasp.

Finally, the woman eased away, a smirk replacing her scowl. "Good. There's an expedition leaving this afternoon," she told the group. "Two assassins and two knights. You're welcome to join them, though I don't know what they'd need with a bunch of low-level has-beens. Meet them here shortly, and they'll give you the details."

Elise stalked off without waiting for a reply.

"Well, there you have it," Syzak hissed.

Brinna watched Elise's back as she left. "If the only choices for a new adventurer were the Priorate Knights and that insufferable woman, I think I'd take a closer look at the Miners' Union."

Just then a fresh cart of ore and other supplies rolled into the forges next to the Blackened Blades' command post. A short, hairy goblin wearing a pointed felt hat led a pair of ponies, frivolously shouting commands at the clearly untrained beasts until they came to halt. A bedraggled human, or perhaps a mix of human and elf, followed behind with a stick in his hand. The Miners' Union didn't have any particular colors or uniform, but the side of the cart was stamped with their group's logo: a short, stubby arm holding a mining pick.

"Now's your chance," Syzak said, pushing Brinna toward the haphazard delivery crew. "An exciting life of unloading carts and digging through pitch-black mines awaits!"

Brinna watched as the goblin ordered the human around. It was a strange sight considering the stark height discrepancy between the two. "I'll take my chances with the jackals," she said.

The Miners' Union workers spent the better part of ten minutes squabbling as they slowly unloaded the supplies at the front of the forge. By time the four adventurers arrived at the command post, the goblin and his companion were arguing over who would get to ride in the cart on the way back to Skarm's Reif, though it was obvious that the cart had plenty of room for the both of them.

"We're joining up," Kadorax told the higher level of the two Blackened Blade assassins. They were both human, lithe of build, and similar enough in appearance to be sisters. The knights, on the other hand, were older than everyone else and covered in scars. Each of them wore a steel breastplate and matching tassets. Their armor bore no less than a hundred dents and scratches each.

"Glad to have you along," the assassin replied, sizing them up. "I'll never turn down an extra hand."

"We're heading east to a new temple," one of the burly knights cut in, lacking all tact.

"You ever fought jackals?" the other knight asked.

Kadorax nodded, but he didn't turn to include them in the conversation. "How many are there?" he asked the pair of assassins.

The level twelve smiled with a hint of recognition as she read Kadorax's name from his character sheet, then answered, "We don't have much information. We only heard about the new temple yesterday from some of the outrunners. Once they establish a temple, it takes about three days to complete their summoning, or at least that's how it's been going so far. We've only been out here for about three weeks. If we leave now, we can hit the temple by nightfall."

Everyone agreed, and the group left the forward camp on one of the small trails that began north before turning east to enter the forest. The trees on either side of the path were tall enough cast a bit of gloom as they blocked out the light. As far as Kadorax knew, there weren't any real cities east of Skarm's Reif, and it was clear that the forest had never been harvested en masse.

A few miles into the forest, one of the assassins halted the group and consulted a crudely drawn map, then marked an X on one of the trees to her right. "This way," she said confidently. "We're looking for a cave entrance. The scouts said it was built up around the outside with minor defenses, so it should be easy to spot. We just need to remember how to find the trail when we come back."

The two assassins marked a handful of other trees before setting off. They moved slower without a path to follow, stopping frequently to mark their path and check the map. The two knights stayed at the back of the group, walking side by side and remaining quiet, their faces constant masks of seriousness.

A low wall of stacked stones was the first indicator that they had found the newly established jackal temple. The wall wasn't long, maybe thirty feet in length, and only waist high. "Check for sentries," one of the assassins whispered to the rest of the group. They were crouched behind trees about fifty yards from the wall, waiting as quietly as they could.

"See anything?" Kadorax asked.

"I have *Improved Perception: Rank 3*," the assassin whispered back. "Nothing yet. Let's get closer."

No one needed a reminder to stay low and quiet as they stalked toward the temple. They arrived at the wall without being spotted, still crouched and listening. "There's nothing," one of the assassins whispered. She waited a moment longer before standing up.

There was a cave entrance not far from the low wall. It was low and dark with several stakes crudely in place around the outside. The assassins crept up to the entrance on the balls of their feet, avoiding even the smallest of sticks lining the forest floor.

"You need to raise your *Sneak* to whatever rank theirs is," Kadorax whispered to Brinna.

One of the assassins paused to listen while the second took a quick glance inside. Neither of them reacted. They waited another moment, then performed the same maneuver again. The one who had been listening waved for the others to join them at the entrance.

"I only heard one," the woman said.

The other assassin nodded. "There's a single room with

an exit at the rear. It just looks like an entrance, nothing more. It was dark, so there might be a second jackal in there I didn't see."

One of the knights drew a torch from his gear and lit it, keeping the flame away from the cave entrance. "We will lead the way," he declared, his voice a bit too loud. "Keep the advantage and don't slow down in the first chamber. We'll handle however many are in there as the rest of you push through quickly. Take them by surprise, and we'll all make it back to camp unscathed."

Without waiting for anyone else to offer their acknowledgment or consent, the knight bounded into the cave with his sword in one hand and his torch in the other. The rest of them had to go one at a time as they followed the meager light. Kadorax was thankful that most jackals didn't have proficient eyesight in total darkness, and he glimpsed a bit of light as soon as he burst into the first room.

"For the priory!" the lead knight shouted.

"Way to alert the whole temple!" Kadorax yelled at him, though he figured it probably wouldn't matter. The temple was small, or at least what he knew of it was small, and the fighting in the first room was already loud.

The torch-bearing knight hacked and slashed wildly at a terrified jackal in front of him, and a second dog-headed creature emerged from the shadows with a knife, flanking the knight. To the right of the cramped combat, an opening in the cave wall led to the next chamber.

The two assassins didn't hesitate. They darted through the passageway without giving the knights a second thought, and fighting quickly erupted from that chamber as well.

"Move!" Kadorax yelled, pushing Brinna behind him. Somewhere in the brief flash of chaos that was the beginning of the fight, he had let Brinna get ahead of him. The woman didn't seem too upset about being forced back to her previous position in the line.

The second room was far larger than the first. It had been carved out, or perhaps natural water had turned it into the hollow, spherical chamber that it was, but the stone altar in the center was certainly a late addition. Four jackals stood guard in front of the altar. Two of them were lightly armored, one wore a glinting necklace and nothing in the way of clothing, and the fourth, probably their leader, was already engaged with both assassins, fending them off with mighty swipes of his claws. The second assassin broke off to challenge one of the jackal fighters, leaving Kadorax, Brinna, and Syzak to handle two, a sizeable task considering their low level.

Before Kadorax could even close the distance, Syzak's *Spike Trap* appeared right under the feet of the jackal holding a knife, and the beast let out a yelp of pain as it scampered out of the magical pit. Kadorax and Brinna stuck together, weapons in hand, and circled toward the right of the altar where there was the most unoccupied room.

The jackal limped and dripped a bit of blood from its left paw, but it came at them all the same. Behind it, the last enemy was fiddling with a wand it had plucked from the altar. "Take the caster," Kadorax commanded Brinna.

Surprisingly, the rogue didn't ask questions. Brinna broke off the side, vaulted over the spike pit with one graceful leap, and then was rocketed backward by a blast of icy magic directly to her chest.

Kadorax didn't have time to see how badly she was injured. He slashed from his right with his sword, his bastion's whip still hanging from his side, then reversed his cut to catch the jackal's knife by the handguard. He tried to rip his weapon away to disarm the doghead, but he wasn't quick enough, and the failed move left him temporarily exposed. A jackal claw raked against his side a split second later.

Kadorax's *Cage of Chaos* activated in response to the hit, summoning a rather anticlimactic gust of wind that only served to very briefly confuse the jackal. Kadorax spun to his right with his sword tucked in close to his side in case any attack was there to meet him when he completed his turn, but the jackal had scampered back a step. He barely had time to react to the throwing knife hurtling in at his gut. Thankful for his boots raising his *Agility* score, he was able to dodge the knife, but only by an inch. A second knife followed the first and clipped him just above the groin, eliciting another magical response from *Cage of Chaos*. A little burst of fire erupted at the site of the hit, accomplishing absolutely nothing.

The jackal pounced forward with supernatural speed. Kadorax didn't know what talent the creature had activated, and he didn't have time to care. With the knife still hanging loosely from his armor, the tip having penetrated his gut, he brought up his sword and attempted a *Riposte*. The blades met, but the talent didn't activate. The jackal's *Agility* score was simply too high. Luckily, what the jackal possessed in *Agility* it lacked in *Strength*, and Kadorax shoved all his weight into his hilt, throwing the creature out wide.

Neither combatant had seen Syzak creeping up behind the bastion, claws spread out at his sides. The snake-man lunged at the same time the jackal stumbled, and the gambit worked. A full dose of *Paralytic Envenomation* surged through the creature's veins, and its body stiffened, freezing a fearful expression on its snout. Kadorax ripped the knife from his leather, threw it to the ground, then solemnly ran his blade through the stunned jackal's back.

As soon as he was sure the jackal was dead, Kadorax doubled over in pain and exhaustion. Next to him, Syzak was out of combat spells. They both still had a lot of fight left in them, but not without at least a moment's respite.

In front of the altar, Brinna hadn't fared well. The jackal had fired off two more magical attacks into her chest. The woman wheezed on her back as she rolled side to side, both of her daggers scattered on the ground at her feet.

To the left and near the opening where they had come from, the two assassins had the armored leader down, and they were taking calculated, coordinated stabs at the only jackal remaining against them.

"Come on," Kadorax growled through gritted teeth. He could still hear the knights fighting in the first room. "Hurry!" he shouted in their direction.

The spike pit dissipated from the floor, and Kadorax ran forward to help Brinna. He slashed down hard with an overhead swing, fully anticipating a magical attack to meet his brazen assault, but none came. At the last possible moment, when there was already no chance for Kadorax to stop his momentum, he caught a glimpse of frosty white shimmering within the mat of the jackal's dark hair. *Ice Armor*.

Kadorax's blade touched the jackal's shoulder, and then he was frozen in midair, completely encased in a solid sheet of ice. At incredibly high levels, *Ice Armor* would last long enough to suffocate a person, a fact Kadorax knew well. Judging by the relatively painless level of cold the spell brought with it, he knew his icy prison wouldn't survive more than a handful of seconds. Still, even a handful of seconds would likely prove to be too much.

The jackal mage finally showed signs of exhaustion as it cast another spell toward Brinna. A slow-moving arrow of energy emanated from the creature's finger. Kadorax could just barely see the spell from the corner of his frozen eyes, and despite the blurred details obscured by the ice, he knew what it was. The jackal had cast *Pinning Arrow*, a complex incantation designed to impale an already immobile target. His mind whirled as he considered the implications of the jackal's defensive enchantment. The *Pinning Arrow* had been meant for whoever the *Ice Armor* had frozen. Had it been single combat, Kadorax would have easily lost.

The arrow was headed right for Brinna's lower back. The woman was unarmored and too wracked with pain to know to get out of the way.

Syzak saw what was about to happen. The arrow would tear through Brinna's body, living up to its namesake and pinning her to the cavern floor where she would die a miserable death. He hissed, his bloody fangs bared, and dove to meet the slow, ethereal projectile. The *Pinning Arrow* caught him in the ribs and blasted him down with enough force to drive the air from his lungs.

At the same time, Kadorax was released from his frozen restraint and landed on the ground with a thud, spinning quickly on his heels. Behind the spell caster, he was already in the perfect position, and all it took was a single horizontal stroke to sever the jackal's left leg from its body. The creature collapsed to the ground, and Kadorax finished it quickly, sinking his sword through the caster's hairy throat.

Syzak grunted in pain on the stone floor. His tongue flickered out rapidly over his lips, and his eyes had rolled back in their serpentine sockets. Slowly, Brinna struggled to regain her feet. Her back and chest were both soaked in magical ice, and her upper arms had been singed as well.

"Can you heal yourself, Syzak?" Kadorax asked, dropping to his knees next to his badly wounded companion. His own gut, along with all the muscles of his legs, neck, and back, throbbed with pain. Somewhere behind the altar, he thought he heard another jackal coming to join the fight.

Painfully, Syzak reached a hand down to his belt and tapped his potion. Kadorax ripped it from its pouch in a hurry, barely pausing to uncork it before pressing the glass to Syzak's lips. The potion went down smoothly despite the taste. A moment later, Syzak regained a bit of his focus, just enough to cast *Cure Minor Ailments* on himself. Much to his obvious relief, the combination of the healing potion and the magic was enough to seal up the wound on his side to the point where he could get to his feet and perhaps fight a bit.

The two knights had emerged behind them, one a bit battered and the other looking no worse for the wear. They had their weapons pointed across the chamber, directing Kadorax's vision. Another jackal wore a backpack, and it was scrambling over a roughshod barricade and into a dark tunnel. The assassins had just killed their final opponent with a deft two-blade strike to its abdomen. They were naturally the most fleet of foot, so they both sprinted across the chamber in pursuit.

Kadorax and the others waited for several long, painful moments before relaxing and returning their weapons to their sheaths. The small temple was empty, and they only had to wait for the assassins to return from chasing down the runner. Slowly, Syzak and Brinna both got to their feet. The knights helped them limp out of the cavern and back into the daylight, where they could rest against the low stone wall.

RESPAWN

"I'll go back in and see if there's any loot," Kadorax said, though he wasn't really sure he trusted leaving his wounded friends in the care of two knights he didn't know who belonged to an organization he'd never trusted. Still, they were allies, and betraying two wounded allies would besmirch the knights' honor. If there was anything Kadorax knew for certain about the Priorate Knights, it was that they valued their outmoded concept of honor even more than their own lives.

With a sigh, Kadorax returned to the cavern. The knight's torch sputtered on the ground, so he grabbed it and lifted it high. The room he was standing in wasn't very large. A few crates were stacked against one wall, and the other corner was full of straw, an old blanket, and other bits of smelly bedding.

Kadorax rooted through the crates with one hand. They were mostly just filled with straw, but he did manage to find a single short ingot that had the daunting heft and familiar sheen of steel. After he tucked it awkwardly into his pocket, he emerged from the cavern to find his friends still alive.

The distant sounds of combat drifted to their ears from somewhere beyond their vision, deeper in the woods.

The unwounded knight grunted and rose from the wall, starting to draw his sword.

"No," Kadorax told him, sitting the man back down with a hand to his breastplate. "They're two against one. They'll be fine. We need you here more than they need you out there. If any more jackals arrive, we're easy pickings." As much as he hated to admit it, Kadorax needed the knights, though they did not need him. In times like those he envied the knights in their heavy steel armor. They were far slower than him, sure, but they didn't take a beating in every single fight, either.

Ten or so minutes later, the two assassins crested a small hill and came into view. One of them was injured. Kadorax couldn't tell how bad it was, but judging by the expression on the woman's face as they neared, it was serious. He went out to meet them, slinging the wounded woman's arm over his shoulders to help her walk.

"The jackal got away," the uninjured assassin stated. "There was a trap hidden under the brush. We should have seen it. *I* should have seen it. Or at least I should have looked . . ."

Kadorax wanted to offer some words of comfort, but none came to his mind. The woman between them was bleeding mightily from her foot. Her boot was torn and ragged, like a set of powerful jaws had torn through the flesh.

"Do you have any healing left?" the healthy woman asked.

Silently, Kadorax only shook his head.

"She's going to bleed out. I have bandages, but she needs a tourniquet and magic—an experienced medic at the least."

They joined the others and propped the bleeding woman against the wall. She was barely conscious.

"There's . . . nothing we can really do," Kadorax said softly.

Neither of the knights were carrying anything more than standard field dressings. Bandaging the garish wound would be little more than a waste of good supplies.

"Wait," Brinna said quietly, still clutching a burn on her arm. "Here." She drew the talon dagger from her belt and held it aloft.

"*Theft of Life*," Kadorax explained grimly.

Brinna nodded. "Have her stab me with it. It'll work, right?"

Kadorax took the dagger away from her before she could do anything foolish. "I'm stronger. She can take it from me," he said.

The healthy knight stepped forward, grim determination on his chiseled face. "Let me bear the burden. Even for an enemy of the priory, offering some of my life is the right thing to do."

"To know chaos is to understand pain," Kadorax repeated. He thought of Ligriv, his strange warden awaiting him in the chaos, wherever or whatever that place really was. He pressed the talon dagger into the assassin's hand, then guided the blade up to the outside of his thigh where he figured he could sustain the most damage before being seriously maimed.

"Are you s—"

Kadorax drove the blade in, instantly letting go of the assassin's hand at the same time.

Bond: 7 flashed before Kadorax's eyes. A moment later, another message appeared. *Encroaching Insanity: Rank 2*, it said.

He blinked, and the world was different. His body didn't hurt any longer; his muscles didn't ache.

"Chaos," Kadorax whispered.

"Very astute," Ligriv said, stepping out from nothing to materialize before him. The trees and other features of the forest began to take shape within Kadorax's vision, but they were all cloaked in some sort of metallic, shimmering silver that shifted and danced depending on how he looked at it.

"To know chaos is to understand pain," he said flatly. "I suppose I'm here to recover, right?"

Ligriv seemed pleased. "Perceptive indeed." The shadowy, inscrutable figure paced back and forth for a few moments. "The assassin, Jaris is her name—she took a lot from you. She will live."

"And I'm here for my reward for such a noble deed?" Kadorax jested. He didn't think of chaos as a place where rewards were frequently bestowed upon anyone, noble or otherwise.

The shifting humanoid laughed. "No, I have never favored nobility over any other trait. If that is a path you seek, well, you're already acquainted with the Priorate Knights, correct?"

"So is this just a day spa? Do you have a few healers lined up to stitch these wounds?" Kadorax asked.

"Not exactly," Ligriv answered. "Though you will recover at least modestly. While the mind has fled the body, the body is not hindered by the mind, and therefore it can heal much quicker. But no, the purpose of your visit is the same purpose as all bastions who visit here. You've learned more of pain, and so you now learn more of chaos."

Kadorax tried to parse some logical meaning from the being's words, but ended up only shrugging. "So you're rewarding me for experiencing a ton of pain, even though I basically brought it on myself?"

Ligriv nodded, and a dark, nefarious smile spread across his entire face.

"Damn," Kadorax said with a sigh. "I can see how bastions go insane. That's pretty messed up."

"Knowledge and understanding are two of the gifts begotten of pain, bastion," Ligriv went on. "Now you may reap the rewards."

The strange guide held out both his palms, and a small

ring sat on each. The black band on the left held a square emerald, while the silver band on the right glimmered with a sapphire stone in the shape of a teardrop.

"What are they?" Kadorax asked. He could feel the world slipping away as he spoke. Reality was blending back into focus faster than he could think to try and make it stop.

He focused on the rings, but all that would display were their names:

Radiant Band
Chasm Star

Ligriv's hand was starting to fade from view. Kadorax could see a bit of the sky shining through his translucent palm, completely out of place.

"I'll probably regret my choice either way," he grumbled. As chaos fully slipped from his conscious awareness, he swiped his fingers through Ligriv's right palm and snatched away the ring.

His eyes fluttered open, and then his chest blossomed in pain, his soul rod the epicenter. He was rocking back and forth and at first, the motion made him think he was somehow back aboard the *Grim Sleeper* in one of the hammocks below deck. But he smelled the familiar scents of the forest lingering beneath the scent of his blood. When he was finally able to focus, he saw that he was being carried on a stretcher by the two knights.

"What happened?" he asked.

"You're awake!" Brinna said before either of the knights answered.

Kadorax rubbed his head. There was a headache brewing right behind his eyes. "How long was I out?" Slowly, painfully slowly, the memory of offering the assassin the chance to steal his life force came back.

"Only thirty minutes, maybe less," the woman responded. "But . . . you lost a lot of blood. You shouldn't be awake yet. Not for a day at least."

"Yeah, let's just say I used a class-specific ability," Kadorax said. If it weren't for his headache, he knew he would be able to stand and walk on his own. For whatever reason, being in the chaos had healed him almost completely. He lifted his hands to rub his eyes once more, and there he saw the ring he had taken firmly around the middle finger on his left hand. As an assassin, he had never worn rings for fear of them clicking against the hilt of his weapon and giving him away.

Back in Agglor, he could finally read the entire description:

Radiant Band - Grants the wearer low-light vision, +1 Spirit, and heightens the effects of Encroaching Insanity. Cannot be removed. Passive while worn.

"That doesn't sound good," Kadorax said under his breath. He let the knights carry him all the way back to the camp as his headache slowly retreated into the recesses of his mind. The two men didn't say much between them, and they didn't complain about carrying Kadorax's weight, either. At the back of the little train of adventurers, the assassin who had stolen some of his life was still limping, helped along by her fellow Blackened Blade.

Elise met them at the headquarters. A woman Kadorax assumed to be the prior from Skarm's Reif was with her. He could stand, but his feet were wobbly.

"The temple was eradicated?" Elise asked, foregoing any semblance of decorum or introduction.

The prior was a bit nicer. "You're injured," she said, pulling one of the knights to the side and inspecting his armor.

She laid her hands on the wound, silently mouthed a few words, and a wave of healing magic washed over the man at once.

"One of them got away, my lady," the higher-level assassin said. Her eyes stayed focused on the ground.

Elise let out a sigh. "The last time one of the jackals was allowed to flee from a temple, they retaliated. We can expect another such attack." She turned to the prior with a scowl on her face. "Prepare the defenses."

The prior smiled as she bowed. Her billowing tunic of blue and gold fanned out in the wind, revealing the embroidered eagle stitched into the front. "The Priorate Knights will be ready, Elise. We shall defend the northern flank if you and yours will guard the east. It will be like the last time. We'll push them back into the woods, and none shall fall."

The leader of the Blackened Blades didn't share the prior's penchant for platitudes. "If we mobilize the camp in time, perhaps you will be right," she stated.

The two women didn't shake hands before the prior left. There was no love between them, barely even respect, and Elise's expression said she kept all that negative emotion pent up inside her like a tightly wound spring ready to furiously uncoil all at once.

As the quest officially came to a conclusion, experience points flashed in each person's vision. Kadorax, Syzak, and Brinna all advanced to their next levels. The other four earned a decent chunk of their way toward leveling, but they were already too high for a handful of jackals to earn them a new talent.

For Syzak, the decision was easy. He selected *Rat Trap: Rank 1*, an ability that would summon a nest of venomous rats to attack his enemies should they stray too near.

Brinna chose a passive, *Faster Recovery: Rank 1*, which let her body heal from wounds quicker when out of combat, as well as replenish her stamina and muscles while still in combat.

Since Kadorax hadn't used his skills enough to unlock the next ranks of any of them, he was presented with three new options:

Sealed Doom (Fate 20): Rank 1 - The bastion may react to an incoming attack, forming a magical bond with the enemy. Upon being hit, part of the force of the attack is shared with the target as though they were hit as well. At higher ranks, the bastion may transfer all of a single attack. Duration: 20 seconds. Cooldown: 1 day. Effect: Moderate.

Chaos Step: Rank 1 - After a 1 second charge time, the bastion steps into the chaos and reemerges somewhere else. May cause the user to experience disturbing images upon reentry into reality. Range: 10 feet. Cooldown: 1 day.

Sleight of Hand: Rank 1 - Hiding objects comes naturally to one possessed by chaos. The bastion can use misdirection and minor sleights to conceal small objects from view. Higher ranks allow more complex sleights and for larger, louder objects to also be hidden. Passive.

Sealed Doom, Kadorax knew, was likely the smartest choice. Being able to transfer incoming damage to an enemy would be wildly useful and help keep him alive, but he also knew the dramatic advantages afforded by any talent that was similar to teleportation. His assassin build had used *Dark Jaunt* pretty frequently, allowing him to shift through thin walls and other objects as long as he knew the other side was safe. He couldn't remember exactly how many times that ability had saved his life or allowed him to complete a contract without being seen.

Kadorax focused on *Chaos Step: Rank 1* and added the ability to his rapidly growing list.

He was tempted to activate it immediately, but quickly pushed the notion out of his thoughts as his mind wandered to the incoming attack Elise had warned of. If he was being honest with himself, he didn't expect the jackals to be dumb enough to try an assault on the fortified camp. Her kind of 'always prepared' mentality was a hallmark of the Blackened Blades, though, and he couldn't deny that the possibility was strong enough to warrant being ready.

The jackals didn't arrive until sometime late in the night. Most of the camp was asleep when the first outrider came back from the woods, shouting from horseback to rouse the fighters and warn the civilians. Kadorax, Brinna, and Syzak had been asleep in the Blackened Blades' main building, more a collection of poorly made huts linked by covered walkways than any real headquarters, when the alarm was raised.

Half-dressed and quickly strapping on sword belts and bits of armor, the Blackened Blades assembled in front of their building to await Elise's instruction. The three adventurers stood out at the back of the group, their unmatched and non-conforming leather clashing with the dark, stained armor of all the assassins and rogues. There were roughly twenty Blackened Blades assembled, and Kadorax figured more of them were away from camp, deployed against the various temples and jackal strongholds throughout the region. A trumpet call rose up from the Priorate Knights' compound, and it was quickly followed by the ring of steel against steel as the knights all moved in practiced unison.

Elise strode forward in pitch-black leather that blended in seamlessly with the dark night. There were only a few torches planted here and there, and Elise was nearly invisible when she found the dark patches between them. "Blackened Blades," she began, pacing at the front of the assemblage as she spoke. Behind her, the outrider's call to alarm still rang throughout the camp. "We're after their leaders! Let the knights handle the brunt of the assault and the lower-ranking, untrained jackals. Our place is not on the front lines. Remember your training, wait for the bulk of the jackal forces to engage the knights, and then find your targets one at a time. Each doghead leader we kill is worth at least ten of the soldiers."

Kadorax couldn't deny the smile on his tired face. The strategy was the exact one he had taught to Elise, the only difference being the presence of the knights instead of some city's formal guard or militia. A few stray howls lifted up through the trees all around.

"They're almost here," Elise continued. From her left, a small contingent of knights marched into view and spread out, forming a line behind crude wooden barriers. "Remember: don't engage them head-on. Even if you see them breaking through and reaching the camp, just stick to the plan and hunt their leaders."

There was a murmur of assent from the gathered assassins and rogues, and then the first wave of jackal attackers reached the palisades only ten paces or so from the Blackened Blades' buildings.

"Let's go!" Kadorax yelled to his two companions. He had every intention of following Elise's instructions to the letter. The knights could handle the assault en masse, and he didn't have a shield—not that he'd know how to effectively block with one anyways.

Next to the two seasoned adventurers, Brinna looked

almost out of place. She wasn't a combat veteran like Kadorax and Syzak, and her hands shook no matter how much she tried to hide her fear. She kept pace, though Kadorax wasn't entirely sure how well he could count on her given the scale of the battle erupting on the front lines. He had been the same way when he had first arrived in Agglor: constantly scared for his life. Stopping for only a second to offer the woman a shred of confidence, he placed a firm hand on her shoulder and nodded, his jaw set like stone. "Keep your head down. Wait for them to come to you. Don't waste your talents."

Around them, the Blackened Blades sprang into action all at once, darting for the darkest glimmers of shadow. The three adventurers took a wider path around the rest of the fighting. Keeping single-file, they wove through trees and over exposed roots at a slow pace, placing the chaotic sounds of the battle far to their left.

"What are jackal leaders like?" Brinna asked, her voice shaking less than Kadorax had expected. "Were there any in the temple?"

Syzak shook his head, though none of them could see him in the darkness. "Their leaders are usually magic users, but not always. You'll know the real leaders easily because they'll always have a few members of their pack close by. The bodyguards will be warriors, and they'll protect the leader to the death. We just have to get close without being seen."

"Neither of you have any *Sneak* talents," Brinna reminded them, fear in her voice.

"Then you'll have to do most of the heavy lifting," Kadorax told her grimly. "You'll do just fine."

As they stalked along the forest floor, Kadorax ran

through the skills they'd have left at their disposal. He had consumed nothing more than a few activations of *Cage of Chaos*, and he figured he had at least one more use of it left. Syzak was the most depleted. All the snake-man had left was *Summon Rain* and *Rat Trap*. Luckily, Brinna relied mostly on passive abilities that didn't need time to recharge.

With his new ring allowing him vision enough to at least see where they were going, Kadorax led them for some time, occasionally stopping as groups of jackal warriors scampered by on all fours. They changed their direction after every group they saw, trying to keep the jackals always to their left so they'd make a wide arc around whatever leadership they would manage to find. After what felt like far too long in the woods, they found a ring of jackal soldiers protecting two others in robes. A pair of unarmored jackals served as runners, bringing information to the robed dogheads and confirming Kadorax's suspicion that the group was indeed that which they had sought.

"What the hell is that?" Kadorax whispered, pulling Syzak down hard to the forest floor with him.

Brinna practically yelped with fear as she dropped to her stomach as well.

"What?" Syzak whispered, his snake eyes scanning the scene over and over. "Just jackals. What did you see?"

Kadorax rubbed his eyes, but everything he saw did not change. "I . . . You see it, right?" He couldn't figure out how to describe the World War Two-era object to his medieval-minded companions. The vehicle's engine was still on, gently idling in a small clearing, and there was a huge black gun mounted toward the rear of the frame. "At least they're on our side, sort of . . ." Kadorax muttered as he noticed the white star painted on the hood.

"What is it?" Syzak whispered. He peered as intently as he could, then shook his head.

"Run," Kadorax said, pushing himself backward. "They'll fire on us. They'll kill us all."

Brinna shook him hard on the shoulder. "What do you mean?" she quietly demanded.

"The Jeep!" Kadorax urged. He pointed right at it. "How can you not see it! There's a Jeep from Omaha Beach sitting in the middle of the forest, and one of the jackals it standing on the back with a fifty cal looking in our direction! Get out of here! Go!"

The rogue woman backed off, clearly terrified.

"Syzak! Run!" Kadorax implored. He didn't bother trying to cover his steps or prevent his footfalls from making all the noise in the world as his mind tried to come to grips with reality. He'd been in Agglor for thirty years. He hadn't thought of Earth history since the day he'd woken up with a stat sheet blinking before his vision. *If people could show up here, why not other objects? Why not a car? A tank?* His mind reeled with possibilities. He'd never seen anything from Earth in Agglor before, just the occasional Earth-born person he had met on his travels, most of which had been homeless and entirely ill-equipped for life in a fantasy realm.

"Where?" Syzak yelled at him, both scaly hands on Kadorax's chest. "What is it?"

The jackals had heard all their commotion, and the ring of soldiers began stalking in their direction with their weapons and claws at the ready.

"There's a fucking *gun!*" Kadorax screamed. His brain was delirious snapping through a thousand different scenarios all at once. "They'll cut the forest to ribbons! We're all going to die! Just *RUN!*"

Syzak chanced a single look over his shoulder before joining the mad retreat of his companions. They didn't get more than fifty feet before Brinna's foot caught on a root and sent her sprawling to the ground in a heap of arms and legs, tripping Kadorax in the process. The jackals weren't far behind.

"They're on us," Syzak breathed, hoisting the two to their feet. "We don't have a choice. Time to fight." Buying time, he summoned a cloud of rain in the space between himself and the jackals, but it wouldn't last long.

"The gun! The Jeep! They have a damn car!" Kadorax continued to bawl.

Syzak stepped forward, letting his friend collapse back to the ground. He gave Brinna the most confident nod he could muster. "I only have one trap left. There's six of them. Time to earn your keep, rogue."

The woman nodded back, but her face told a completely different story. She was terrified. Her knees shook, matching the trembling of her hands and arms. She had both of her daggers out, her knuckles white around the hilts. "He's—"

A jackal burst through the magical rain Syzak had created and cut her off. The creature's sword was aimed right for her chest.

In a flash, both of Brinna's daggers launched up and crossed, and the small handguard on the dagger in her right hand deflected the jackal's attack at the last possible moment. Syzak lunged at the enemy with his fangs bared and caught the jackal by the neck, wounding and scaring it, but doing little else. He was out of venom, and the beast didn't need long to free itself.

A second jackal stalked into view just as the last of the magical rain subsided. It wielded a spear between its fur-covered paws.

RESPAWN

Syzak shoved the first jackal away in order to focus on the second. He trusted Brinna to fight, but his trust was all he could give her. She'd have to survive on her own.

A nest of rats—dark, beady-eyed vermin with patchy hair and broken whiskers—erupted from the ground in a flurry of dirt and filth. They clawed up the spear-wielding jackal, biting and scratching him, causing the jackal to stumble backward and use his spear to keep his balance. Syzak lowered his head and ran forward, pushing the jackal backward. He got lucky, and a smile spread on his face as the jackal fell into one of its compatriots who had been a step or two slower in the pursuit. Both jackals landed hard on the ground.

Syzak emerged a moment later with jackal blood running freely down both of his scaly claws. Sadly, his rats dissipated back to the realm of magic whence they had come, leaving him with no spells whatsoever to cast. Behind him, Brinna was not faring well.

Brinna turned and kicked as the jackal slashed after her again and again. She had blood on her face—someone's blood—and a lot of it. She kept moving farther and farther backward. At the rate she was giving up ground, she'd be on top of Kadorax in a matter of seconds, likely knocked to the ground and then swiftly killed.

The snake-man waited for his moment. There were more jackals coming, but they were still a few paces from reaching the fighting. He waited, and when the jackal lunged for what should have been a killing blow at the exact moment Brinna tripped over their prone companion, he slammed his claws into the creature's shoulder blades. The jackal howled and jerked, but Syzak held fast. He pulled the jackal in close to his body and tore at the hairy neck with his fangs, ripping out chunks of bloody hide and letting them fall all over the jackal's own chest.

The little clearing was quiet a moment later. "Come on," Syzak urged, lifting Kadorax by the shoulder. "Either fight or run, no other option." The rushed words mixed with his natural serpentine hiss to produce a sinister sound.

Finally, Kadorax began to figure out how to clear his mind. His face still clearly displayed his bewilderment, but the lack of thunderous rifle shots cracking through the air was starting to bring his mind back into reality. Brinna fell down to her knees at his side, clutching the top of her scalp, and the sight of her wound brought him fully back.

Kadorax grabbed his whip from his belt and planted his feet, accepting the next jackal's charge with an activation of *Torment*. The jackal's torso spurted a thick line of blood into the air. Before Kadorax could strike again, the creature turned with its tail between its legs and fled. Another two were there to take its place, each of them holding a spiked mace and baring their large, white fangs that glimmered in the moonlight.

"*Chaos Shock!*" Kadorax yelled, clenching his left hand into a fist and pulling out a seashell-sized bit of coagulated undeath from the chaos. He rammed it forward, catching the lead jackal on his forearms where the creature had attempted to block.

The jackal's flesh began to melt away where the undeath had touched him. His skin and hair oozed, sloughing off of the bone and onto the ground. Kadorax dropped his whip and grabbed his sword, slicing the edge along the jackal's exposed skeleton as he drew it.

The second jackal was not as reckless. Having seen the utter destruction that had been visited upon its friends, the creature took a more cautious approach, circling and pawing the ground instead of committing itself to a charge. Kadorax waited as well, measuring his enemy's steps and constantly scanning the forest any new attackers. Finally, Kadorax was the first to break the standoff. He skittered forward and feinted to his right, then cut back to his left, willingly exposing himself to the jackal's sword on his right flank. He took the hit, dulling it with his armor and expending his last charge of *Cage of Chaos*. The reactive ability shot a narrow line of silky spider web at the attacker, entangling the jackal's blade. Not wasting a single breath of time, Kadorax used *Chaos Step* and suddenly appeared on the jackal's opposite side, behind his head and completely out of view. A single downward stroke of his sword left the jackal dead at Kadorax's feet.

"The leader," Syzak said, his eyes locked on the tree line. Behind him, Brinna clutched at her jaw. Her eyes had rolled back in her head to show only the sclera, and the smell coming from her shirt said she had thrown up on herself.

Kadorax gave the rogue one last glance before running back through the trees. "I . . . I don't know what I saw," he growled to Syzak as they ran. "Maybe it was real, maybe it wasn't. If it was, we're still going to die."

"Not without a fight," the snake-man said between breaths.

They reached the small copse where the jackal leader had made his command and skidded to a stop. The leader was dead, and two Blackened Blades stood in the center of the trees, blood dripping from their daggers.

"The Jeep," Kadorax muttered. The vehicle was nowhere in sight. He stepped from the concealment of the undergrowth with his hands held out before him. "Did you see something here? Something strange?"

The two assassins looked relieved to see him. "Thanks for pulling all the guards," one of them said.

The other took a moment to look around the clearing, then shook his head. "What do you mean?"

Encroaching Insanity: Rank 2 - The seed of chaos living within your soul rod. As the bastion increases in level, the power of the chaos grows, further weakening Bond. At Rank 10, Encroaching Insanity becomes Living Nightmare.

Kadorax dismissed his stat sheet and looked down at the ring wrapped firmly around his finger. "It wasn't real," he said more to himself than any of the others. "The Jeep wasn't real. It was all in my head. I'm losing it."

Syzak put a bloody hand on his back in a weak effort to comfort him. "Just tired, that's all," he said.

Both of them remembered Brinna lying in the dirt at the same time. They made sure the two assassins didn't have any other jackals in the area they'd need help dispatching, then returned to fetch their friend. They could hear the sounds of battle a little ways off toward the camp, but nothing else reached their ears beyond the normal sounds of the moonlit forest.

Brinna was unconscious when they arrived. "We need a bandage or another potion," Syzak stated. He propped the woman's head up on his knees and grabbed her forehead to stymie the bleeding.

"Here." Kadorax ripped off a bit of one of the jackals' sword belts and handed it over. "Better than nothing," he said.

As Syzak applied the meager bandage, Kadorax wondered what *Encroaching Insanity* would do next to alter his mind. He began to question everything he had seen in Assir. The grave-armored centipede had been something more akin to nightmares than even the mythical creatures of Agglor, though the others had reacted exactly as he would have expected from such a gruesome amalgamation, telling him it had been real. But what other things could have been the machinations of his tainted mind? The endless possibilities—the things he might *not* have noticed—were nearly as frightening as the one hallucination he had so clearly seen.

The two assassins regrouped with Syzak and Kadorax a moment later. "Did any of them escape?"

Syzak surveyed the battlefield once more as he thought. "I don't know."

The assassin scowled, but the expression was born more from frustration than disappointment. "The leader had a scroll," he said. "It looks important."

Syzak took the scroll and unfurled it in his grasp. He held in plain view for Kadorax to read as well, but the bastion was lost in his own thoughts. "Ah, I can't read any of this," Syzak said. The language of the jackals was the same as everyone's on Agglor when spoken, but many of the races had developed their own independent scripts for the sole purpose of sending messages that were harder to intercept and decode. The jackal script, written by beasts with paws instead of hands, looked so erratic that it bordered on nonsense.

"There's a drawing on the back," the assassin said, indicating the other side of the parchment with a point of his dagger.

Syzak flipped the sheet over. The back of it had a drawing of some sort of siege contraption next to one of the standard jackal altars, but something was different. Several creatures that vaguely looked like the Gar'kesh were coming out of the altar. Even more curious than the drawing's overt imagery were the straight lines, each labeled with a number, extending from the machine. "It looks like . . . mining equipment? A siege engine of sorts? Whatever it is, it seems complex," the shaman said. He grabbed Kadorax by the shoulder and held the scroll in front of his face to capture his attention.

"Something new to summon more than one of their gods," he said after a quick glance.

The assassin took back the scroll and tucked it into his belt. "Jackals don't build siege engines. Jackals don't build anything that even remotely resembles machinery."

Both Syzak and Kadorax nodded in agreement. "Let's get her back to the camp," the bastion said, bending over to lift Brinna from the ground. "There's only one group I know of that would sell machinery to jackals."

Syzak lifted Brinna's legs, and then they set off, hoping the majority of the fighting would be concluded by the time they reached the camp.

One of the assassins sheathed his weapons and spat on the ground in disgust. "Bastards probably sold us out," he said. "Elise needs to be told."

Kadorax wasn't sure if the unconscious woman in his arms was going to make it. The knights guarding the perimeter were still holding quite well by the time they arrived in view of the camp, but the fighting had not concluded. A group of twenty or more jackal warriors augmented by several spell casters was busy assaulting the front, and the other entrances to the camp were either too far away or heavily barricaded with sharpened palisades. There simply wasn't any way to gain quick, easy access to the camp without being seen by the jackals and possibly picked out as targets.

The two assassins had slipped through the barricades a ways down the camp line in search of help, but that had been minutes ago, and Brinna was continuing to bleed.

"I need a field medicine talent," Kadorax said with frustration.

"The first thing we're buying when this is all over is a bandage kit, a proper one. And I guess I should be more conservative with *Cure Minor Ailments* so I don't waste it," Syzak replied.

Kadorax readjusted the makeshift bandage across Brinna's scalp. If he was being honest with himself, he knew the bandage did nothing. "No, you didn't waste the spell," he said. "We were unprepared. We should have known better."

Syzak caught a glimpse of something dark moving in the shadows. "They're back," he said, pointing at the figures.

One of the assassins returned with a Priorate Knight healer, a chaplain as they were called, jogging to keep up behind him. The chaplain clinked and rattled in his heavy battle armor, and the man looked close to complete exhaustion.

"Can you heal her?" Kadorax peeled back the bloody bandage and tossed it aside.

The chaplain rubbed a hand across his sweat-covered brow as he inspected the horizontal gash above Brinna's eyes. "Probably," he said after a moment.

"Probably is good enough," Kadorax told him. He stepped away, as did the others, to let the chaplain work.

"*Stitch Together*," the healer cast, holding his hands over the wound with his thumbs laced together. A gleam of white magic emanated from his palms and seeped into Brinna's head. Fortunately, none of the jackals attacking the shield wall seemed to notice the bright flash, and the small group of adventurers remained undiscovered.

Brinna's forehead closed, and the chaplain fainted to the ground, completely drained.

"Great, now we have to carry both of them," Kadorax mused.

Syzak grabbed the chaplain's legs and looked over his shoulder before beginning to pull the man back toward the palisades. "He's wearing armor. Dragging him won't hurt."

The rogue balanced on their shoulders between them, Kadorax and the assassin made slow progress toward the nearest opening in the camp's defenses. By the time they finally found themselves on the safe side of the barricade, the fighting at the front had concluded, and a good chunk of experience flashed across everyone's vision. Kadorax had been either directly involved in or near enough to major battles to have seen the peculiar phenomenon of the winning side reaping a bounty of experience before. Since every combatant and support caster received their experience at the same time, the battlefield took on an eerie, unsettling quiet for a few moments as every other activity ground to a halt.

Kadorax advanced to level eight, unsurprising considering the sheer size and implications of the battle compared to his relatively low level, but he quickly pushed the notifications from his vision and sought out the Blackened Blades' barracks. He was too tired to worry about talents. Beyond that simple fact, Brinna needed further medical attention sooner rather than later, and the three adventurers weren't exactly sure where they were supposed to take the passed-out chaplain snoring at their feet.

Finally, perhaps only an hour or so before dawn broke,

Kadorax and Syzak managed to stumble into a pair of cots at the rear of the barracks, where sleep quickly overcame them both.

CHAPTER 10

Kadorax was the first to rise. The sun was several hours into its descent beyond midday, and the rest of the camp was alive with activity. He decided to let Syzak continue to sleep and made his way to the center, spotting a few cookfires burning underneath several racks of meat. A handful of the soldiers, men and women from both the Priorate Knights and the Blackened Blades, sat on low stools around the fires as they finished what was left of their lunches. Kadorax joined them, eager to fill his stomach and clear his head.

"Any news on the rogue we left in the priory?" he asked the nearest knight.

The woman, glittering in her polished mail hauberk, didn't have an answer. More than one rogue had been brought to the priorate healers, and most of them had not recovered enough to have left yet.

Kadorax made his way to the priory when he had finished

his meal. There were knights all around it, though none of them tried to prevent his entry, so he pushed through the wooden door and headed in the direction of a few groans, not that the building was terribly large to begin with. There were only three rooms, and the wounded were being tended to in the second one.

A chaplain, dressed in blue and gold robes, knelt over one of the cots against the far wall as he applied a cloth to a wounded man's chest. Near the door, Brinna was asleep on a cot of her own. A fair amount of dried blood coated the white linen bandages around her head, but she looked otherwise stable and recovering. Her chest moved up and down with a steady rhythm.

Placing a hand on her shoulder, Kadorax gently shook her awake.

"How do you feel?" he asked.

Brinna ventured a hand up to her forehead, felt the bandages, then closed her eyes again. "I'll make it," she said. "Just a headache now."

"That'll take some time, I think," Kadorax said. A wounded knight in the next cot called out for the chaplain with an upraised arm, his wrist jutting out at an unnatural angle.

Kadorax was never one for hospitals. He didn't like large congregations of the sick, either on Earth or Agglor, as they always made him feel a little too close to death himself. Offering Brinna a meager pat on the shoulder, he stood and turned to leave. He had to wait a moment as the chaplain carried a large, cumbersome bag to the wounded knight and blocked his path, and then Kadorax left the building quickly. Standing once more in fresh air, he crossed the camp again to reach the forges and the Blackened Blades.

Elise and her cohort were standing in a half-circle around

a pile of looted weaponry and scavenged armor from the fight. Most of the pieces were too dented and poorly made to be of any use, and two of the assassins were actively sorting them into piles to be smelted down and recast later. Next to the pile, occasionally picking through it to inspect something that caught his eye, was the assassin who had found the strange schematic on the dead jackal leader.

"Anything new with the scroll?" Kadorax asked. Behind the assassin, Syzak emerged from the building, rubbing his tired eyes.

The assassin shook his head and stepped to the side. "I think you were right," he said in a low whisper. "Elise agrees, though we're to limit those who know."

"Certainly. What's the plan?" Kadorax asked.

Both of them had turned and were looking at the forges across from the loot where the Miners' Union had set up their workshops. "One of them is selling secrets to the enemy," the assassin said.

"Do miners ever actually have any enemies?" Kadorax asked. "The group doesn't necessarily swear allegiance to anyone. Not even to Kingsgate."

The assassin smiled in agreement. "Could be any of them."

Syzak spotted a few things in the scavenged equipment and pulled them out, brushing some of the blood from one of the pieces on the grass.

"So, are the Blackened Blades going on a little hunt?" the bastion asked with a sly grin.

His eyes watching Elise not far away, the assassin whispered, "You know the plan more thoroughly than I do, my lord."

Kadorax had to turn to hide his surprise. "You know

better than to use that title with me," he stated flatly. "Don't get yourself killed. Elise runs the show now."

"There are still a few who disagree."

"No," Kadorax said, putting on his most serious tone. "I'm not your man. I'm not even an assassin or a rogue in this life. Hell, I haven't even officially joined back up."

The assassin shrugged. "Just know that we're ready for you, sir, should you choose to come back. In the meantime, have any interest in catching a miner and ripping a few secrets from his flesh?"

"Now you have my attention," Kadorax replied. "The Miners' Union isn't known for tactical genius, but they aren't flagrant idiots, either. Whoever it is will need to check in with their jackal masters. It'll probably go down tonight. You in?"

The assassin extended his hand. "The name's Pennywise. Happy to make your acquaintance."

"Pennywise . . . Pennywise . . ." Kadorax mused, trying to remember where he had heard the name before. "Shit, are you Earth-born?"

The man's smile lit up and blanketed his whole face. "Never thought I'd meet another. Been here almost twenty years now. Yourself?"

"Thirty," he replied. "And you really renamed yourself Pennywise?" He finally located the memory in his mind, and images of a gruesome dancing clown floated to the surface.

Pennywise laughed. "Not exactly. My last name was Penn, and that's what everyone called me in college. It just didn't really fit well with the vibe here, you know?"

"Ha, I couldn't agree more. My name was Kasper—a stupid hipster name, I know—but that's who I was. Kasper Ansel. And Syzak, the snake-man rummaging through all the broken armor, he's Earth-born too; my pet snake, actually," Kadorax explained.

"We've a lot to discuss, I imagine," Pennywise said. He followed one of the miners as the stout goblin gathered some pieces of iron in his arms and dumped them into a wooden barrel. "Meet me here at dusk. We'll find our miner with his hand in more than one pocket."

Smiling to himself at having found another Earth-born citizen of Agglor, Kadorax left Penn to investigate the loot for himself.

"Judging by the whispers, I'd say you learned something of the scroll," Syzak said, glancing up from his small stash. He had a dagger, a short sword, two sets of battered metal bracers, and a bent-up piece of iron that could have once been a breastplate if it weren't for being shorn off at the top.

Kadorax nodded, but he said nothing in response. They were too close to the forges for him to risk even hinting at collusion against the Miners' Union. "Find anything useful for Brinna?"

From their years working silently together in the bowels, undercrofts, and rafters of nearly every kind of building on the continent, Syzak understood the full weight of Kadorax's refusal to address his question. "Nothing here is that good," he said. "Just a bunch of doghead junk. I'll take it back to Skarm's Reif, and if the *Grim Sleeper* hasn't left port yet, I'll let Ayers make what he can. Any requests?"

"I wonder if Brinna could use a shield. Never seen a rogue with a heater before," Kadorax jested.

"Armor for the rogue," the snake-man happily agreed. "She certainly needs it."

"You should probably take her with you back to Skarm's Reif. She needs to stretch her legs and get some fresh air as soon as possible. Lying on a bed in a priory is a great way to wake up as a knight or a chaplain. Their proselytizing knows no bounds. I don't want her there any longer than she has to be." Kadorax angled himself to get a better view of the forge while still not looking at them directly.

"We'll leave once she's ready. Just don't do anything stupid while I'm gone," Syzak told him. When the shaman had all the metal scraps gathered under his arms, he left for the priory, keeping an eye on the workers busy in the small forge as he went.

Sitting near some of the other Blackened Blades and with his back pointedly turned toward the forges to reduce any potential suspicion, Kadorax settled in to look at his eighth-level talent choices:

Chaos Shock: Rank 2 - The bastion pulls two slivers of chaotic energy into the world and thrusts them forward, creating a random magical effect augmented by a second impact quickly following the first. Effect: minor. Cooldown: 28 minutes.

Torment: Rank 2 - The bastion's weapon magically extends to a second target beyond the first, and Torment inflicts slightly more damage than rank 1. Torment has an increased effect when used with a whip. Effect: moderate. Cooldown: 28 minutes.

Ghostly Strike (Blade Training: Rank 2): Rank 1 - Becoming momentarily incorporeal, the bastion's weapon slides through the gap between space and time, bypassing armor for a fraction of a second. Effect: moderate. Cooldown: 1 day.

Kadorax spent a long time reading and rereading the details of *Ghostly Strike*. Everything about the maneuver, the flashiness and overall intimidating impact it would have, begged him to select it. As an assassin, Kadorax had no doubt it would have been his choice above the others. Still, he couldn't deny the doubts lingering in his mind. If the 'fraction of a second' line meant his sword could get stuck in armor when it rematerialized, the skill would be useless. On top of that, he already had *Chaos Step* which produced a somewhat similar—perhaps not as viscerally pleasing—effect.

In the end, he focused his vision on *Chaos Shock: Rank 2*, confident that the chances of getting two lackluster magical effects when he rolled the dice would be slim. Adding the second effect meant he could use the ability without quite as much trepidation, and that peace of mind was worth more than a flashy sword trick.

Kadorax spent most of the afternoon training with a handful of Blackened Blades, a few of which remembered and recognized him from his previous life, but his mind wasn't really focused on the combat practice. Every time he got into a good mental groove, wooden training sword in hand, his mind would wander back to Penn. The man knew him, that much was clear, but they had never spoken before.

Whenever Kadorax thought of Earth, an old longing inevitably crept into the back of his head and took root there, sometimes requiring several weeks to dislodge and bury itself once more. He didn't long for his old life or even his family from back home, but rather his spirit yearned for something—*someone*—more carnal. In his fifth year on Agglor, he had met an Earth-born woman. He had fallen in love with her, or at least that's what he had thought it had been, though they had traveled together for only a month before she'd died. Kadorax knew she would still be alive somewhere, having respawned in some dreary inn, maybe even looking for him. Estelle—that had been her name. She was from Spain originally, and she had been terrible at life in a fantasy realm. Kadorax still found a few persistent tears welling up in the corners of his eyes when he thought of her death . . . at his own hand.

He had just joined the Blackened Blades as a recruit, and one of his first assignments had been to protect a minor dignitary from some city whose name he couldn't remember. He had slept in the shadows outside the dignitary's room with his dagger in his hand, but Estelle had always known his hiding places. She had come to him in the night with a drink and some food, creeping quietly on the balls of her feet so she didn't make a sound, and then she'd playfully jostled his hair.

Kadorax had been so terrified of getting his own throat slit that he sank his knife into Estelle's gut out of pure reaction. He still remembered the look in the beautiful woman's face as she stared at him. She hadn't screamed or made a noise. She had only watched as her own life flickered away.

The Blackened Blades broke for a bit of food toward dusk, concluding the training and asking Kadorax to join them. The bastion waved them off and hung his head, trying his best to hide his emotion. If there was any skill he'd had back on Earth that had stayed with him through the spatial dislocation, it was the profound ability to mask his emotions from the world. A life of video games, filing government paperwork, and studying history from the comfort of his single-bedroom apartment had seen to that.

An hour later and Kadorax was still standing awkwardly behind the barracks with a wooden sword in his hand and his real weapons resting in a little pile at the edge of the practice circle. He tried to shake the memories of Estelle from his mind, but there they stayed. He heard her laugh echo in his ears, and he saw her smile flickering in the dim light of a Kingsgate tavern.

"Hey," came a raspy whisper.

All Kadorax could see was the wavy amber of Estelle's hair flowing over the back of his hand, illuminated by nothing more than moonlight filtering through the muddy glass of a rented room in the back of that same Kingsgate tavern.

"I'm sorry . . ." he muttered.

"Hey, Kadorax!" the voice whispered a little louder.

Finally, Kadorax looked up and brushed a bit of dampness from his eyes. Penn motioned for him from the side of the barracks.

"What the hell are you doing?" the assassin asked under his breath. They both crouched low in the shadows. Their view of the forges was limited compared to the original spot they had agreed upon, but moving would have been too obvious to be worth the risk.

"Sorry," Kadorax repeated. He wasn't really sure if he was talking to the assassin at his side or the woman clinging so fiercely to his memories.

Penn dismissed the apology with an inaudible exhale. "Nothing's happened yet. You're fine."

"No," Kadorax replied. "I shouldn't have been late. I just . . . I just got caught up in something for a bit. Speaking of which, you said you've met another Earth-born, right?"

"Just you," Penn whispered back.

Kadorax felt his heart sink a little lower into the abyss. "Sure." All the questions he had wanted to ask, the practical interview he had looked forward to conducting, had slipped from his mind completely.

Instead of trading question after question of life back on Earth, the two sat in silence as they watched the forge workers making their small shop ready for the night. They counted five Miners' Union members in total—the goblin and human Kadorax had seen earlier were gone, likely returned to Skarm's Reif, leaving two dwarves, a gnome who appeared to be in charge, and a pair of burly orcs that got to do the heaviest of the manual labor. Unlike all the games Kadorax had played and all the books he had read back on Earth, orcs weren't treated any different than the other intelligent races of Agglor, something that struck him as a bit odd. Humans did tend to give the orcs a wide berth in taverns and on the streets, but that was simply due to the orcish superstition that forbade them from bathing.

A little after midnight, when most of the torches in the camp were neglected and burning low, there came a bit of movement from the forge. The gnome and one of the dwarves exited the building with slow, measured steps. To any of the Blackened Blades, their movements were easily recognized as poorly executed tradecraft.

"They don't even have *Sneak* talents," Penn whispered under his breath. "They're idiots. Trying to skulk away in the middle of the night when they're surrounded by rogues, thieves, and assassins is illogical, even for the Miners' Union."

Kadorax scanned the area for any signs of a trap before skittering up to the next shadow. "I think you're giving the Union a bit too much credit," he said over his shoulder.

"Let's hope," Penn replied. Both of them were on high alert as they followed the pair of miners around the camp.

The gnome and dwarf remained silent, skulking from building to building, finally leaving the camp altogether.

They departed on the western side of the encampment near the priory, careful to avoid the guarded paths in the north. There was still the matter of climbing the palisade guarding the western flank, a tall order for two of Agglor's shortest races, and the venture lasted a painful ten minutes. The gnome even managed to cut his arm on one of the sharpened stakes, though to his credit he did not make a sound.

When the two conspirators were finally over the barricade, Kadorax and Penn waited a few moments before vaulting it easily in a single silent leap. The gnome bordered on *too* nervous as he frantically looked all around before running into the woods.

"I don't know," Kadorax whispered. "It doesn't feel right. No one is so obvious."

Penn stopped and crouched low, the leaves beneath his feet crunching ever so quietly. "You think we're being led into a trap?" he asked.

"I don't know. It has to be, right?"

"We'll follow them a little longer."

"Alright," Kadorax agreed. "Stay a little farther back. Just in case."

The gnome and the dwarf kept up their pace long into the night. They seemed to know exactly where they were headed, but they did stop once to consult a map. Kadorax made a mental note of where the gnome had stored the map in case he needed to pilfer it from the creature's corpse later.

After an hour or more in the forest, the gnome finally came to halt. No one else was around, so Kadorax and Penn had to wait some distance off. They crouched behind a few small trees, grateful for the darkness and the lack of awareness of their prey. Had they been stalking someone trained who knew what to look for when being tailed, their cover would have been entirely insufficient.

"They said they'd meet us here," the gnome said. The two were far enough away that the dwarf's response was lost to the trees.

A few moments passed before the gnome spoke again. "How long should we wait?"

Kadorax was wondering the same thing himself. He covered his mouth to keep his voice from drifting. "You really think these are our guys?" he asked.

"They have to be, right?" Penn answered. "Why else would they be out here? Someone's selling equipment to the jackals. Has to be them."

A faint howl rose up from somewhere far off into the woods.

"Did you see the dwarf flinch?" Kadorax asked. "He's afraid. Maybe they aren't here to meet dogheads."

"Or he's a coward, simple as that," Penn quietly replied.

Another twenty minutes passed without anything happening. The two miners sat with their backs against a tree and talked quietly to themselves, though about what Kadorax and Penn could not hear.

Then a new sound caught everyone's attention. Footsteps grew louder, rapidly approaching from the north. "Must be a lot of them," Kadorax whispered. He tried to pick apart the sounds of the individual footsteps to measure how many there were, but whoever it was moved too quickly, and the sounds all ran together.

A pack of jackals came to a skidding stop in front of the miners. Kadorax quickly counted eleven of the hairy beasts. Every one of them was armed to the teeth.

"The delivery hasn't made it," one of the beasts growled.

RESPAWN

Panic written on his face, the gnome fidgeted and looked all over the forest before answering. "We . . . we'll have it tomorrow, I promise."

"You promised today," the jackal said. The creature stood a full head taller than the gnome, probably on equal height with Kadorax. The creature held a cruel barbed mace in his paw, though his claws were easily long enough to make quick work of unarmed opponents.

"J—just one more day," the gnome stammered. "I'll have it tomorrow night!"

The jackal menaced over him, glowering and baring his canines, letting a bit of drool escape the corner of his snout and fall on the gnome's head. "We lost some of our pack because of your delay," he barked.

Two of the other jackals pounced on the dwarf, eliciting a yelp of pain and terror from the stout miner. They pinned him to the ground, and the alpha jackal grabbed the gnome fiercely by the shoulders, spinning him so he could watch his companion's fate.

"Don't move," the jackal commanded, passing off the gnome to two of the others. With the miners both held firmly in place and surrounded by enemies on every side, the leader set his mace to work on the unlucky dwarf's legs.

Screams filled the night air. The jackal's mace flung torn, ragged flesh all over the nearby trees as it shredded the dwarf, hit after bloody hit.

"Let's go while they're occupied," Kadorax suggested. He had seen enough tortures—committed his fair share of them as well—to know how it would all end.

Penn nodded and motioned toward the direction they had come. The two left just as they'd arrived: quietly, quickly, and unnoticed.

Syzak and Brinna still had not returned to the camp by the next day. Kadorax trusted his lifelong companion, and he didn't think anything of the extended absence. He and Penn had decided to tell Elise as little as possible. They spent the morning loitering around the forges and waiting for the terrified gnome to finally make a move. Neither of them were surprised that the dwarf was nowhere to be seen.

When the knights and assassins congregated around the main fires in the center of camp to eat their lunch, the gnome finally made his escape. He had a smithing hammer tucked into his belt, both eyes full of fear as he walked toward the road that would take him to Skarm's Reif. The little gnome hurried, constantly glancing at everyone he passed. It didn't take long for a sheen of sweat to break out on his pale forehead.

Kadorax and Penn followed from such a close distance that it almost didn't feel fair. Any intelligent mark would have seen them at once, but the gnome was so focused on his own footfalls that he never turned all the way around to check his rear.

They waited until no one else was within sight before stopping the gnome on the road. Kadorax came up behind him, muffling his steps on the softer patches of dirt along the side of the path, and grabbed the frightened miner by his collar.

The gnome screamed like a wounded animal staring down a hungry predator. It was an awful noise, pathetic even by civilian standards, and made Kadorax's distaste for the

Miners' Union grow even deeper. "At least have the decency to keep your bowels and bladder in check," he sneered, stepping around in front of the gnome. He held the small creature aloft with one arm.

"I don't know anything!" the terrified miner said all at once.

Kadorax laughed in his face. "The interrogation hasn't even begun!" he said with a disarming smile.

The gnome flailed and kicked, but his feet only scraped at some of the gravel on the road. "Please . . . Just let me go! I won't do it!"

"Do what?" Kadorax asked. He raised an eyebrow, genuinely curious to see how much of his plan the gnome would willingly spill. Penn stood guard behind him, out of view, and watched both ends of the road for any passersby.

The gnome's eyes were as wide as they could go without falling out of his head. "Whatever it is, I won't do it!" he yelled.

Kadorax was honestly impressed by the miner's attempt at misdirection. Even such a lame statement was more than he had expected. "You work at the forge, right?" Kadorax asked him. The gnome nodded in his grasp. "Perhaps you could help me out. I was looking for a dwarf who worked at the forge as well. I think he might be in trouble, and I only want to help."

Somehow, the panic on the gnome's face managed to increase. "He . . . it wasn't me! I didn't do anything!"

Kadorax's forearm was beginning to seriously tire, so he dropped the gnome back to the ground. "What were you selling to the jackals?" he demanded.

The gnome backpedaled a few steps, and then he bumped into Penn, and the full gravity of the situation finally washed over him. "It was a drill," he stated, his eyes downcast and his voice quavering. "I knew a jackal in Skarm's Reif before all the temples started cropping up around Agglor. We were friends, you know?"

"What kind of drill?" Kadorax pressed onward. He didn't care much for the sappy details of a ruined friendship.

Heaving a great sigh, the gnome continued, "I designed a drill that runs on steam. It isn't very large, so it could be portable on the battlefield during a siege or something. It was supposed to be a project for the Union, but I could never get it strong enough. It won't go through rock or ore."

"But it will move through dirt, and it leaves a path large enough for a jackal to fit through, right?" Kadorax finished for him.

The gnome nodded.

"Traitor's trying to get us all killed," Penn added. "I say we gut him here, find the drill, and burn it."

Kadorax had to laugh at the stereotypical Blackened Blade response. Assassins and rogues hated machinery and the engineers who made it. The true thief in the night trusted only a blade and a sturdy set of quiet leather to get the job done. Anything more than that meant the killer was making up for lack of skill with tricky gadgets. Still, Kadorax wasn't one to let such an obvious advantage go to waste. "Where did you hide the drill?" he asked.

The gnome faltered and hesitated a moment before answering. "I left it at the forge, hidden under a few empty boxes," he said softly.

Kadorax and Penn turned the gnome around and gave him a less-than-gentle shove in the direction of the camp. "Let's go see it," the bastion stated.

They walked with the gnome all the way back to camp,

and it didn't take any extra convincing to get the miner's full cooperation.

The notion of giving Elise an update on their findings danced temporarily through Kadorax's mind as they arrived back at the forward base and headed right for the forge. In the end, Kadorax couched his decision on the mere fact that he was not an official member of the Blackened Blades and therefore owed the woman no real vow of allegiance.

The gnome grew more and more nervous as he led the two adventurers into the forge and to a stack of wooden crates haphazardly piled against a wall. After a moment of digging, the gnome pulled out a heavy metal contraption with a circular blade attached to the front and a series of empty hoses hanging from the back. "Here," the miner said. There was another worker in the forge close enough to see what was going on, but the tall orc didn't seem to take much interest in the affair.

"I'd like to see it in action," Kadorax said. There was a small cart on wheels connected to the main body of the drill where the coal and water would be kept during operation, and the whole assembly was certainly intriguing.

"Where's the jackal pack that you've been dealing with?" Penn wanted to know. "Let's take the drill there and give it a little test run."

The gnome shook his head, his face showing nothing but terror. "I always met them in the woods. I don't know where they live."

Kadorax knew the explanation was plausible. "Then set up another meeting," he said. "We'll go with you, unseen, and give the drill a test."

The gnome shook in his boots. Finally, after a gentle

prod in the back from Penn, he acquiesced. "I'm meeting with them again tonight," he said under his breath.

"Perfect," Kadorax replied. "Deliver the drill to them exactly as you're supposed to. We'll go to the meeting place in advance of the jackals arriving and wait. Maybe we can tail them back to their den. Eradicating an entire pack of dogheads would go far in advancing the cause."

He looked to Penn for confirmation, and the assassin returned a grim nod.

"It's settled, then," Kadorax said. "We'll find their den and turn the drill against them. Risky, but it'll work."

Penn smiled with a bit of malice glinting in his eyes. "I'll sharpen my daggers. If we're going to sack an entire doghead den, we'll need more men. Let me handle Elise. I don't think she likes me, either, but she's never tried to kill me. She'll give us a squad."

"I like the idea," Kadorax said. "We'll take them out all at once."

Nightfall cast a thick shroud over the swarm of hidden assassins and rogues scattered through the forest. The gnome stood in the middle of a little unmarked clearing with his drill laid out before him. He'd brought a bit of coal and a tank of water, and all the machine needed to get moving was a touch of flame and a few moments for the steam to begin to build.

A small pack of jackals ran into the clearing not long after. They were armed and armored, but there weren't quite as many as there had been the day before. Kadorax counted eight. He had over a dozen Blackened Blades assembled behind him. Despite his protest against her presence in the field, Elise was among those hidden. He knew her true motivation lay in her mistrust of Kadorax. When Penn had told her the plan, she had immediately jumped on it, far too eager to join in the assault than she should have been. She was there to watch him, and everyone else knew it.

None of Elise's misconceptions bothered Kadorax. If she was waiting for him to recruit an army to overthrow her, she'd have to wait far longer than a single night in the woods.

The alpha jackal, the same leader as the previous night, took his time and inspected the drill as though the terrified gnome wasn't even there. Finally, he stood straight and looked the gnome in the eye.

"I—"

The leader stopped. His snout turned up to the air, sniffing quickly and swiveling from side to side. "What do I smell?" he growled back to the other jackals behind him.

The warriors drew their weapons and spread out.

Stay down! Kadorax silently urged. Perhaps a high-level mage or sorcerer would have been able to telepathically transmit the message to all the Blackened Blades, but Kadorax was neither high-level nor a mage.

"Kill them!" Elise shouted, emerging from the darkness with an enchanted dagger held in her hands. The rest of the group followed suit, taking the clearing by storm.

Kadorax watched and waited. He knew the Blackened Blades would make quick work of the jackals due to their overwhelming numbers and, ultimately, his own blade wouldn't be needed. But jackals had a notorious reputation for sending a runner scampering away to warn their other groups and organize counterattacks, something Kadorax knew all too well.

The initial clash of blades, teeth, and claws was too chaotic to follow. The jackals naturally collapsed from their outspread positions to form a tight ball between the trees. Fighting against such a formation was something the assassins were completely unused to. A small handful of knights would have stampeded over the jackals in no time, their training and equipment designed perfectly for frontal collisions and violent clashes on the front lines, but the Blackened Blades had to dance and roll, parry and dodge, to keep from suffering serious losses despite their impending certain victory.

A minute into the battle, half the jackals had fallen. At least two of the Blackened Blades were on the ground and clutching wounds. Kadorax was still fully camouflaged when one of the jackals broke rank to flee.

The bastion leapt into action. The jackal was fast, probably faster than him if they were in an open field, but the tangled roots and fallen branches of the forest floor slowed them both equally, allowing the gap to be closed in mere moments. Kadorax fell on the runner's back and called on *Chaos Shock* at once. He thrust his hand forward into the jackal's lower back, where a small sliver magical ice erupted from his palm. The jackal staggered and tripped, dropping to all fours. *Chaos Shock* activated a second time and generated a ghostly prism of energy, but his hand was too far from the jackal's hide for the second emanation to bring any effect.

Pawing at the ground with large, sharp claws, the jackal growled and bared its teeth. Kadorax came on hard with his sword, keeping his whip coiled at his side due to the tight quarters, and the jackal sidestepped with magical speed.

"*Torment!*" Kadorax yelled, and a sheath of darkness wrapped itself around his sword as it arced through the air.

Again, the jackal's reflexes were simply too fast. The beast jolted to its left and then came forward in a blur with its claws leading the way. Kadorax had no choice but to accept the hit on his chest. His armor blunted most of the force, but he was still pushed backward hard enough to send him crashing to the ground as his foot tangled on a protruding root. Had it not been for the reactive magic of *Cage of Chaos*, the bastion would have been rent to pieces by the jackal's claws.

A burst of foul, necrotic energy swept up from the armor like a cloud of accelerating spores, pushing the jackal back for just long enough to offer a moment of respite. Quickly running out of talents to use, Kadorax activated *Chaos Step*. The single second of charge time before the talent teleported him away felt like an eternity.

With a flash, Kadorax appeared behind the jackal, but he was still on his back. As the jackal spun to find his target once more, Kadorax was able to get to his feet, still a few seconds from being able to strike. He knew he was outclassed. The jackal was a higher level, clearly had more combat experience than Kadorax in his current life, and he was smart.

Kadorax had to think of something quickly. He looked toward the rest of the fight in hopes of finding rescue in the form of an assassin creeping up behind his attacker. All the Blackened Blades were engaged with the mass of jackals, and none of them were even looking his way.

The jackal pounced and ripped at Kadorax's stomach, shredding the bottom of his leather armor. *Cage of Chaos* triggered once more and sent a bolt of magical stone directly at the jackal's face. The stone smashed into its jaw, rocketing it backward, giving Kadorax just enough time to push away and get his footing.

Squared off on equal ground against the jackal once more, Kadorax didn't have time to pay attention to the throbbing pain in his gut. He knew he was bleeding, he knew he was hurt—but he could not submit. Without *Torment*, his last option was to time a *Riposte* that could land solidly enough to end the fight with a single blow.

The jackal was battered and a bit dazed from the magical assault it had suffered. Undefeated, the beast leapt forward, growling and showing its teeth.

Kadorax didn't recognize the talent the jackal had activated, but he had fought similar opponents enough times in the past to know what the next move would be. He took a chance, placing his life in the hands of a risky gambit, and turned to his left, leaving his back exposed to the jackal's claws. As expected, the creature darted forward with impossible speed—directly through the place where Kadorax had stood just a second before.

Kadorax's sword sliced down along the jackal's right flank, deep enough to carve a chunk of bloody meat from the bone beneath. The jackal howled and pounced again, moving slower without the aid of a talent.

Claws rang against Kadorax's blade, and his *Agility* was finally higher, thanks to the wound he'd inflicted, allowing him to execute a flawless *Riposte*. He turned the sword in his hands, flung his arms sideways through the attack, then cut back with all the strength in his body.

Both of the jackal's front paws fell to the dirt. Kadorax stepped forward, turning slightly on his heel to bring his body in line with the bloody, whining creature. With a single thrust, he claimed the jackal's experience points as his own.

"Finally," he wheezed, falling to his knees as the adrenaline of the battle left his veins. Pain flared up from his torso, radiating from every inch of his body and thrumming with wave after wave whenever he took a breath. He lifted the tattered bottom portion of his armor and saw that it wouldn't be fatal by any means—his innards were all where they were certainly supposed to be—though the knowledge did very little to stymie the pain.

He looked back toward the clearing where the rest of the Blackened Blades were still fighting. The assassins held the upper hand, of that there was no question, but the cornered jackals fought well. Their numbers had dwindled to less than a handful. Kadorax watched as one of the rogues, a class more suited to open combat than his assassin comrades, capitalized on an opening left by a recently felled jackal. The man lunged toward the left side of the jackal formation and tore through the nearest enemy, showering himself in gore as he continued to slash. The jackal line faltered and then fell. When everything was calm and the last beast had been silenced, the rogue who had so brazenly attacked stood amidst a circle of bodies. Blood ran from his daggers as well as his arms.

Only a few of the Blackened Blades appeared harmed, and Elise was quick to order her underlings to attend to their wounds with potions and bandages. "Over here," Kadorax shouted, still clutching at his stomach.

One of the assassins with a few potions on her belt helped carry him back to the others. She handed him a bottle, which he greedily devoured. After a few moments, the pain faded into a dull throb that Kadorax knew his mind would ignore before long. There were only two Blackened Blades who could not be brought back by healing magic.

Both of them were face down on the forest floor, blood coating their armor and disheveled hair.

Elise finally made her way to the dead bodies and rolled them over. The first one she touched was Pennywise. It looked like a jackal claw had torn through his neck, ripping out his throat. "At least you didn't linger in pain for days, my friend," Kadorax quietly lamented to himself. He had barely known the man, but still his loss was painful.

Deep down, in the dark reaches of his mind where all the thoughts and memories Kadorax wished would simply die lurked, he knew why he felt a pang of sorrow when he looked at the man's bloody face. The Earth-born assassin reminded him of home, and home reminded him of Estelle. He felt the old despair creeping up again, stalking him from the darkest corners of his brain, and he focused on the pain in his stomach to try and force it all away. All the effort accomplished was to make his pain a little worse.

"None of them escaped?" Elise asked the recovering group of Blackened Blades.

Kadorax met her gaze. "I took down the runner," he said.

The woman nodded and looked away. "We can follow their trail back to their den. If they get no warning, they won't be ready. They won't even suspect their group is missing until morning. We move."

Murmurs of assent spread through the group, and everyone began checking their gear and getting ready to move. Kadorax knew they wouldn't bury the dead. He didn't bother to look. More likely than not, the corpses had already been looted of anything useful they'd had on them when they died. Pragmatism was the ultimate lesson of the Blackened Blades, and it was probably the main reason the organization had been so profitable under Kadorax's ruthless leadership. Still, leaving them to rot in the elements felt disrespectful, even though everyone knew the two men would respawn somewhere else on Agglor before long.

No matter what Kadorax wanted, the Blackened Blades wasted little time. They were moving through the forest, following the trail the jackals had left, before the little miner gnome had even had a chance to inspect his machine to ensure it had survived the battle undamaged. As they walked, Kadorax inspected his character sheet. He hadn't earned enough experience points to level, though he needed to get a solid handle on which of his abilities would be ready without a full day's rest. Attacking a den of jackals head on was going to take everything he had to offer if he didn't want to end up like Penn.

Torment and *Chaos Shock* would both be ready by the time they found the jackal den, but that was it. His *Riposte* and *Chaos Step* needed a full day to recharge, and he wasn't really sure if he had expended all of the magic in his *Cage of Chaos* talent. Since it was still in the first rank, he wasn't confident there would be any strength left to whatever random elements it happened to conjure forth in the middle of a battle.

The trail wasn't hard to follow. There had been a lot of jackals, and they had trampled the leaves as they went, clearly not worried about the gnome or anyone else following them back to their home. In most places around Agglor, jackals kept to themselves, so little was known about their society or cultural norms. A few jackals, strays who had likely been exiled from their own packs, lived in all the major cities, though assimilation had been one of the major factors leading to their acceptance by the human community as a whole. Still, most of the jackals living in Kingsgate or Oscine City were outcasts and beggars. Few of the hairy beasts ever progressed through human society to make anything noteworthy of themselves, but everything was different in the wilds.

Kadorax had spent a significant amount of time lurking unseen in a jackal city—or what passed for a city by their standards—some years ago. He and Syzak had been paid a hefty sum to deliver a certain jackal head to a certain unnamed, wealthy jackal client, and the target had been the type to never leave his own home. The city had really been more a collection of low sheds, underground burrows, and crude pens of livestock than anything else. When not fighting or interacting with other intelligent races, most of the jackals preferred to live their lives as quadrupeds, more akin to their canine ancestors than their human pedigree.

The den they found in the middle of the darkest part of the forest was small, and for that Kadorax was glad. He wasn't sure if Elise was wise enough to turn away from a battle where the odds wouldn't be in her favor. Fighting against a hundred or more jackals, even with the element of surprise on their side, would certainly be a battle best left abandoned. Kadorax had always been sure to demonstrate such calculations when approaching contracts when he had been the leader, but that was a different time, and Elise was a different Blackened Blade. Her ruthlessness was equally matched by her recklessness, like the two wild emotions were locked in a constant struggle for priority within her mind.

Elise halted the group a good distance from what appeared to be the den's entrance. There weren't many torches, only a few scattered here and there without a thought given to their placement, so the entire compound was shrouded in thick darkness. Like the ring on Kadorax's finger, most assassins had some way of seeing well in the dark, be it magic or talent. Jackals saw quite well at night also, so the torches were likely in place to help either the very young or the very old of their breed, or perhaps they marked something else altogether.

The woman pulled a bit of onyx from a pouch on her armor and crushed it, then spread it between her hands and on her face—the reagent required for an assassin's most powerful spell. "*Sweeping Darkness*," Elise whispered, her eyes closed and a smile spreading on her face. Dark shadows began crawling through the trees to their position. The shadows were thick, blacker than they had any right to be, permeating the darkness of the night with something altogether unholy and vile.

The talent was one that Kadorax knew well, though most of the lower-level members of the Blackened Blades had only heard of it in murmurs and rumors, spoken of like some unhallowed god whose name would invoke some measure of inexorable wrath. Kadorax had used the same ability himself. The preternatural darkness would cover their bodies, clinging to their clothes and weapons like a sticky miasma. It would last for hours, depending on the rank, and the inky fog would hide every movement and sound the Blackened Blades made. They would become invisible to anyone not standing within five or so feet of them. Even then, when their prey came close, their outlines would be obscured and their features would appear hazy, like specters or hallucinations. In Kadorax's experience, there was no single talent that could ever match the usefulness of *Sweeping Darkness*. Accordingly, the cooldown time was measured in months as opposed to days.

Perhaps one day he would get to see a high-level prior or chaplain cast some epic, battle-altering spell of their own, but until that day came to pass, Kadorax was utterly amazed by the inky darkness swirling around his waist.

But the darkness did not cling to him as it gripped the others.

When the rest of the Blackened Blades were covered head to toe in magical darkness, all of them were left regarding Kadorax and the gnome with quizzical expressions.

Elise stepped forward and waved a bit of the fog from her arm toward Kadorax, and the darkness lingered for only a moment before dissipating into the night. "You aren't one of us," she said flatly. "The spell will only cover assassins and rogues, true members of the Blackened Blades. Your class . . . a bastion of chaos incarnate, whatever that means, is not affected." She glanced at the gnome with the same pitiful expression. "Such a shame."

Elise turned back to her underlings and began to lay out her plan as Kadorax and the gnome backed off to the side.

"Can you start that thing?" Kadorax asked.

The gnome was quite literally shaking in his boots. His hands gripped the sides of the machine so hard that his knuckles had been white for probably an hour. The gnome's collar was soaked with sweat. "Y—yes," he stammered. "I think so."

"Look," Kadorax started. He knew the exact plan Elise was explaining to the others, for he had been the one who had explained it to her. Complementing that plan would be tricky without a shroud of darkness of his own, but he knew it could be done with a little creative thinking. "They're all going to slip into the den at different points, moving slowly and silently through the compound, slitting throats as they go. Inevitably, one of the lower levels is going to rouse an alarm one way or another, and then the whole thing will collapse into open combat. The shroud won't mean much when that happens."

To his credit, the gnome was smart. "That's when we start the drill?" he asked with a nod.

"Exactly. Once the cover of silence is wasted, we can make as much noise as we want. Just be ready to fire it up the moment we need it." Kadorax still wasn't exactly sure if the drill would be useful or not, but he didn't want to squander a perfectly fine opportunity to find out.

The gnome checked a few levers and gears before responding, "It'll work when we need it. But where? There's isn't much fuel, so it won't cut that large of a path before running out."

Kadorax waited for the Blackened Blades to spread out around the den. One of the jackal huts in particular looked more defended than the others, with large wooden spears guarding the low entrance along with sturdier walls than all the rest, and it was located directly in the center. Kadorax pointed to it. "That's where the alpha is going to be," he said. "Think the drill will make it there?"

An inquisitive hand on his chin, the gnome tapped his foot as he thought. "It should. It'll get close, I know that."

"Perfect," Kadorax replied. "We'll come up right beneath the alpha. He'll be worth the most experience points, you know?"

"*We?*" the gnome basically gasped. "Here, let me show you how the device works, and I'll explain what to do if anything goes wrong or if the blade slows down for some reason. Really, it isn't that hard to operate, I think . . ."

Elise gave a signal, and the Blackened Blades moved from their positions all around the jackal compound, slowly infiltrating it from a handful of places at once, daggers in hand. Their grim work would begin in a few seconds.

"Come on," the bastion said, grabbing the side of the drill and lifting it into the air.

The gnome instinctively took hold of the other side and began walking forward in pace with Kadorax. "You can't expect me to go with you," he muttered under his breath when they set it down just outside the nearest building.

Kadorax gave him a confident pat on the back. "You'll be fine. Just operate the drill and bring me up under the alpha, then run back through the hole to safety. Easy as that."

"But that means I'll be the first one to the surface . . ." the gnome said.

"And the alpha won't be ready for you, so you'll have plenty of time to make an escape!" Kadorax reminded him. "Jump to the side, let me climb out and get my footing, then run back."

The gnome's eyes were full of just as much fear as when he had been accosted on the road to Skarm's Reif. "It won't be running. Crawling," he urged.

Kadorax shrugged. "Do you think the alpha will chase after you when I'm in his house and his pack is being slaughtered outside his walls?"

With a heavy sigh of resignation, the gnome finally nodded. "I just bought a new enchanting talent last week. If I die before I get to use it, I'm going to find you in my next life and . . . pay someone to slit your throat," he said.

Kadorax had to stifle a laugh. The gnome, traitor though he was, was beginning to grow on him. "You'll be fine, trust me," he said.

They only had to wait a few moments longer before a jackal, clearly wounded by the sound of its raspy howl, raised the alarm. "Light it!" Kadorax commanded, and the gnome burst into action.

Sparks flew from a handheld contraption the gnome produced from his coat, and the coals were burning before long. Next, he smashed a glass vial onto the coals, instantly stoking the flames to a wild intensity. He dropped a few pinches of some foul-smelling compound into the water in the holding vat above the coals, and the drill's blade began to turn. The machine was slow at first, but it gained speed with every passing second. When it was moving too fast to follow, the gnome operated a pair of levers which angled the bit downward until it made contact with the ground.

Dirt flew up in every direction, pelting Kadorax and the gnome with a relentless torrent of small rocks and clods of grass, leaves, and sticks. "We need goggles," the gnome shouted above the raucous din of the steam engine.

"Yeah, no shit," Kadorax yelled back. Ahead of them, the compound was alive with the sounds of battle. Kadorax was beginning to think the drill would be too slow and the alpha would already be out in the open by the time they reached his hut. Still, coming out behind the alpha and catching him unaware for a quick, clean execution was a prospect worth pursuing.

The gnome tilted the drill completely vertical, and the blade began to sink into the ground. It was several feet below the surface when the gnome operated a different lever to turn it horizontal. He pushed the small cart of coal in behind it, dropped down into the hole, then waved for Kadorax to follow. The device bored a tunnel about three feet in diameter, enough for Kadorax to crawl without fear of getting stuck, but it was a far cry from a comfortable journey.

Blinded in the sheer darkness of the dirt and soil, Kadorax had no idea if they were moving in the right direction.

"How will we know when we're there?" he shouted to the gnome who was busy at the controls in front of him.

The miner only nodded in response. Whether the nod meant they would be fine or meant they would be taking a wild, potentially deadly guess, Kadorax had no idea. No matter the outcome, he was in the tunnel and not about to turn back. The drill continued to spit a constant stream of dirt and debris back on his face as it chugged along, and there was nowhere for the smoke to go in the confined space.

"This thing . . . needs some redesigning," he hacked between coughs. Kadorax wasn't sure how much more he'd be able to take without getting a clean breath from somewhere. They kept going, and Kadorax kept slogging on behind it.

When they were maybe halfway to the alpha, or so they hoped, the ground beneath them began to rumble more than it should have. The gnome eased off one of the levers to slow down the machine, but the rattling and shifting did not relent.

Kadorax braced himself for a fall. "Some of the jackals live underground!" he shouted, but it was no use. There was nothing either of them could do.

Panicked, the gnome slammed his levers all the way forward, throwing his weight behind the machine and urging it on. They rumbled farther into the compound, and then the floor beneath them gave way, and the tunnel collapsed.

Kadorax, the gnome, and the drill fell through the air, surrounded by a smoky cloud of dirt and rock, and landed painfully on a hard stone floor some fifteen feet below the surface. The drill shattered on impact, sending hot coals and boiling water all over the unfortunate jackal caught beneath it. Kadorax and the gnome were in a jumble of arms and legs not far from the jackal. They both groaned as they tried to fill their lungs amidst the choking cloud of dust blocking the air.

Unlike the forest above, the subterranean chamber was illuminated fully by a ring of torches. The room looked surprisingly similar to the small temple Kadorax had raided earlier. Then he noticed three more jackals, each of them wearing robes and clutching various canine holy relics. They were on all fours off to one side, and they looked surprised.

"A summoning chamber," Kadorax said. He swung his feet in front him, wincing at a sharp pain in his right ankle, and pushed himself up from the ground.

The gnome didn't get to his feet. He was alive, but the fall had knocked more than the wind out of him. He'd lost a few teeth, and a piece of broken rock had been lodged underneath him, punching a nasty wound into his flesh on the back side of his ribs.

Kadorax didn't have time to worry about the gnome's health. The jackals were advancing, and at least one of them was already beginning to cast a spell. He dove to his right, away from the wreckage of the drill, and landed in a roll, barely dodging an icy blast that rocketed into the stone. Another of the jackals was a shaman, a fact Kadorax quickly learned as a magical pit opened up directly beneath his feet, offering a short drop onto a pile of burning embers.

The flames singed Kadorax's armor and seared the hair from the back of his arms. He scrambled over the edge of the pit as quickly as he could, then took a blast of ice to his chest. *Cage of Chaos* responded to the direct attack with a burst of harmless light, and then the talent was depleted. Kadorax silently cursed himself for choosing the fifth-level passive ability. The sheer randomness of the effect was so unreliable that any benefit it conveyed was offset by the number of times it had failed to help at all.

Sprinting for the wall where the casters stood, Kadorax uncoiled his whip from his belt. The longer range coupled with the relatively slow movements of mages and shaman compared to normal jackal warriors meant he had a good chance of landing *Torment* on the nearest enemy.

With only one good opportunity before the next spell was certain to come flying toward him, he cracked his whip and activated *Torment*, lashing the nearest jackal across the snout and sending the creature fleeing with its hands up in the air as though it was on fire. The other two jackals hesitated for a moment, watching their comrade's retreat, giving Kadorax enough time to strike again.

The mundane hit from the whip caused nearly as much devastation as *Torment* had inflicted. The second jackal reeled backward as its spine and side broke open in a stream of blood. Yelping, it fell over its own legs in its haste to scramble away, though the third jackal wasn't nearly as fazed.

A blast of fire buffeted Kadorax backward, forcing him to shield his eyes. The blast was quickly followed by heavy concussive force that slammed into his upper torso with enough weight to knock him to the ground. Or it would have knocked him to the ground had there been any stone on which to fall. Instead, Kadorax fell into another trap.

Punji sticks pierced his back and legs. He hadn't fallen from a great enough distance for the stakes to impale him more than an inch in any one spot, but the painful wounds were numerous. Thankfully, the armor on his back took most of the damage and kept him from being killed. Kadorax struggled to get his arms free enough to push up from the ground. He was at an awkward angle, and his armor was so entangled that it kept him down longer than otherwise, but he was able to scramble free of the pit and roll to the side, heaving. Blood flowed freely from at least a dozen places on his back and legs. The back of his head felt like someone had taken a hammer to it.

Kadorax had to brush a bit of his own blood from his eyes in order to see. In front of him, the jackal had a small knife, something that looked more ceremonial than designed for combat, indicating that its wielder had either run out of spells or simply preferred to finish the kill up close and personal.

Somewhere in the tumult, Kadorax had dropped his whip. He drew his sword and climbed to his knees, using the blade as a cane as he pushed himself up to his feet. He knew he wasn't going to last long. The muscles in the back of his legs had been shredded.

The jackal smiled as it stalked forward.

From the corner of his eye, Kadorax saw the gnome finally regain his composure. He wasn't steady by any means, but he was standing—an improvement. Across the room from the shattered remnants of the drill, the second jackal was finding its courage.

The jackal released *Pinning Arrow*, firing the slow projectile right for the gnome. The terrified miner saw it coming, but he didn't know what to do, frozen in place by fear with his hands shaking at his sides.

"Run!" Kadorax yelled.

Finally, the gnome took off for the other side of the room, narrowly avoiding the devastating spell. Kadorax had to turn his attention back to the jackal coming for him. He hated to leave the gnome vulnerable, but there was nothing he could do. The jackal pounced at him, and Kadorax caught the creature's muscled shoulders with his hands, throwing him to the side. The quick grapple barely did anything to the jackal other than divert its course momentarily, allowing Kadorax a few seconds to continue moving away.

From all fours, the jackal came on again. Like the first time, Kadorax only defended himself, pushing the jackal's body wide, but not hurting it at all. He stepped backward as he fought off the attacks, positioning himself closer and closer to the wrecked drill. After the fourth jumping assault from the jackal, he started to feel his strength fading. His legs wouldn't hold him up much longer.

The jackal lunged in again, slashing with its knife and biting the air with its huge teeth, and Kadorax deflected, shoving down hard with his hands and sword. His plan worked, and the bloodthirsty jackal didn't realize it was landing directly on the drill blade at their feet. The blade itself was horizontal and therefore didn't cut the jackal at all, but the creature lost its footing as the metal slid across the stone floor, issuing a loud shriek.

Kadorax, tired and bloody, swung down with his sword to end the jackal in front of him. As the beast thrashed and tried to scamper away with a partially severed spine, it wrenched the blade from the bastion's hands and sent it skittering across the stone. Defeated as well, Kadorax slumped down against the floor.

The gnome had his back turned and was running frantically around the edge of the circular chamber, dodging magical blasts as best he could.

"You have to fight!" Kadorax tried to yell. His voice only came out as a faint, hoarse, incomprehensible gargle. Running would mean the gnome's death, and the gnome's death would certainly ensure his own. "Fight! Turn and fight!"

Luckily, the jackal mage was wounded as well, leaking blood from the garish laceration caused by Kadorax's whip. Searching for some answer to ward off the inevitable, Kadorax gathered up a small pile of coals and some of the magical powder the gnome had doused them with earlier. There wasn't much, but a bit of a plan started to form in his mind nonetheless.

His whip was still lying on the ground not too far away, and the space between himself and weapon had returned to solid stone once more after the *Spike Trap's* dissipation. Kadorax dragged himself across the ground. He left a thick, red smear in his wake. When he grabbed onto the whip's handle, he started pulling himself closer to the remaining jackal, trying hard to not make any noise and draw any attention to himself.

A blast of some invisible magical energy knocked the gnome to the ground. The miner squeaked as he hit the stone, scrambling for his life to get back to his feet, and Kadorax made his move. He cracked his whip forward and connected with a torch right behind the jackal mage. He yanked his arm back, exhausting what little was left of his strength, and the torch fell free from its sconce to land at the jackal's feet. Before the beast could react, Kadorax threw his little pile of coal and enchanted powder at the flames.

A huge burst of flame—temporary, and more dramatic than effectual—erupted from the jackal's feet. Had the creature been standing quadrupedal, Kadorax knew the blast would have probably done a good deal of damage. Against the bipedal target, it only managed to distract and scare the creature, but then the jackal fell over in its panic. It landed directly on the torch, and a bit of unburnt powder must have still been clinging to its robes. A howl of pain and rage filled the chamber as the jackal burned.

When the scream subsided a moment later, Kadorax couldn't open his eyes. He had lost too much blood. "Healing?" he managed to ask, but he knew his head was not facing the correct direction for the gnome to hear.

Kadorax awoke in the chaos. He could smell the burning sulfur and smoking pitch before he even opened his eyes. As before, Ligriv was smiling down at him, his ethereal form flickering and wavering at the edges.

"So nice of you to join me again," the strange guide said.

"Ugh," Kadorax groaned, rubbing his temples. "Did I even survive?"

With a laugh, Ligriv nodded and continued, "Of course you did, otherwise you would not be here right now."

Kadorax realized he was shirtless, and the soul rod lodged in his chest throbbed with pain. Part of the rod's metal rim was dented and nicked. "I don't suppose you're going to fix that, right?" he asked.

"Not at all," Ligriv replied. "You must learn to protect yourself better if you wish to survive. Though your body will regain some of its composure while you remain in the void, your soul rod, the most important aspect of your class, will not."

"What does it even do?" Kadorax asked. "If the damned thing is so important, what do I get for lugging it around?"

Ligriv looked surprised. "You haven't figured it out?" he answered with a raised eyebrow.

"I don't have time for your games."

"Tsk, tsk," Ligriv chided. "Haven't you thought it odd how you've been consistently fighting enemies far stronger than your level should allow? You're smart, yes, and you have more than enough experience on your side, but at the end of the day, your stats are simply subpar. Every jackal you've killed has been stronger than you. The undead you slew in Assir was more than four times your level. Anyone else would have been carved to pieces a dozen different times by now. You have survived."

"What's that have to do with the soul rod?" Kadorax asked, though he could more or less anticipate the answer.

"Bastions are stronger than the other classes on Agglor," Ligriv explained. "Speaking of which, you'll be level nine when you return to the material plane. But think about what you've accomplished already. All of that cannot be luck, and all of that cannot be attributed to your experience. As I said before, bastions are stronger than other classes. The soul rod implanted in your chest becomes active during combat, channeling your abilities and enhancing your senses."

"Everything at a cost, right?" Kadorax assumed.

Ligriv nodded. "Right you are. Many of Agglor's strongest personalities have chosen the path of the bastion upon respawning, though few have succeeded in making a name for themselves. Several priors and more than one leader of the Blackened Blades have all attempted to take on the mantle of the bastion. Few have made it to the point of adopting a second class. Fewer still have risen to the level of their previous lives. None have fulfilled their destiny as a bastion."

The scene was beginning to fade from Kadorax's vision. "Not even multiclassed?" he repeated. "That's only level ten . . . and a destiny? I've no time for your riddles."

Ligriv flickered out of view before responding, leaving the world in utter darkness, accented by flares of pain from Kadorax's legs and back until he finally lost consciousness altogether.

CHAPTER 11

Kadorax awoke in the camp, and he immediately knew something was wrong. His body hurt, but that wasn't it. There was too much noise. He could tell there was no battle raging just outside his dark room, no jackal invasion moments from bringing his end—just a tumult foretelling action on a large scale. Rubbing a bit of headache from his eyes, he got out of his small cot as quickly as his wounded body would allow.

As he expected, the camp was awash with activity. Both groups, Blackened Blades and Priorate Knights alike, were scrambling to and fro as they collapsed tents, gathered supplies into piles for transportation, and disassembled some of the fortifications. "What's happened?" Kadorax asked of the nearest soldier, a tall man dressed in the telltale dark leather of the Blackened Blades.

The man stopped only for a moment to respond. "Some sort of jackal attack on Kingsgate," the man said. "Elise and the prior are leaving a few stationed here to protect Skarm's Reif, and the rest are headed to the port to get on ships."

Kadorax knew an attack on Kingsgate would throw all of Agglor into war. Maybe that's exactly what they needed. He spotted Syzak helping with some of the operations near the forge. "Syzak! What's going on?" he called.

The snake-man looked relieved to see him. "We just got back an hour ago. There's word from Kingsgate that the royal heir was kidnapped by jackals somewhere on the ocean. She was en route to Oscine City to meet with a tutor or something like that when her ship was seized. Rumors say the jackals left the whole crew alive, but forced them to go to different cities so they could spread the word, though I'm not sure I believe it. Sailors have been known to lie."

"Was Kingsgate sieged?" Kadorax asked. He thought of the drill the gnome had tried to sell to the dogheads and what kind of damage it could wreak if dozens of them were unleashed all at once.

Syzak shook his head. "I didn't hear anything of it. Everything I know comes from Lord Percival. He had run one short delivery for Skarm's Reif, just transporting some messages to a priory outpost somewhere along the coast, and the crew ran into the information from a guard. No one is sure what to believe."

"It could all be an elaborate campaign of misinformation," Kadorax added. "If the jackals are planning on summoning more of their gods out there in the wilderness, they'd want the knights and Blackened Blades to leave, chasing some phantom all the way to Kingsgate."

"You're right," Syzak said.

"If everyone goes now, Skarm's Reif will probably be sacked and razed within a week," Kadorax continued.

RESPAWN

Syzak stretched his back and took a break from moving crates to rest for a few moments. "Elise and the prior are keeping a contingent here to protect the city, though most of the people are fleeing as well. Word of the brazen attack on a royal family member has traveled quickly. People everywhere are going to be scared. They'll flock to the largest cities for protection," he explained.

"We'll go with the *Grim Sleeper*," Kadorax stated, rubbing his forehead in concentration. "If there's an attack somewhere else, we need to be mobile to get to it." He thought of Ligriv's strange words about the now dinged soul rod implanted in his breastplate. "We're too low level to really be any use here anyways, especially if the heavy support is packing their bags and hitting the road as well."

Syzak nodded his agreement. "Brinna stayed with the ship. Ayers made her a new pair of daggers, and one of the crew's been showing her how to use them. He has a few things for you as well, and when I heard the news from Kingsgate, I didn't feel like dragging everything out here just for you to have to haul it back."

"Good thinking," Kadorax said. "Let's get whatever we need and be gone. If there's going to be a mass exodus out of Skarm's Reif, I want to be on one of the first ships to leave the harbor."

Owing the Blackened Blades and the Priorate Knights no allegiance meant Kadorax and Syzak could leave the camp whenever they wanted. They didn't have to wait for orders like most everyone else, and neither of them felt any particular duty to help the camp prepare for the absence of the majority of their fighting force. Kadorax spoke once more with Elise to learn what had happened after he had blacked out in the bottom of the jackal den and to thank her for dragging him back to camp, and then he and Syzak were off.

The road from the forward camp to Skarm's Reif was crowded with soldiers. Most of the men and women they saw along the way were knights, clinking along in their heavy, reflective armor, though they saw more than a handful of civilians going the other direction. Most of them were either would-be adventurers looking to swell the ranks or else profiteers trying to sell supplies, though there were a few men they passed who actually looked like they'd seen a fight before.

Back in the town, everything was even busier than the camp had been. Ships were constantly coming and going from the port, more departing than arriving, and shop owners were busy boarding their windows as they made their own preparations to leave. The poorer folk had all gathered in a giant mass near the docks to beg the ship captains to take them away. They offered everything they had, most of which the captains quickly turned down, though Kadorax did see more than one young peasant woman accompanying a sailor aboard a ship.

The *Grim Sleeper* was one of the tallest vessels in port, and its twisted, gruesome figurehead kept all but the bravest beggars from going anywhere near it. Kadorax and Syzak pushed through the crowd and spotted the captain at the railing, his typically ostentatious clothing making him easy to spot. Brinna was on the deck as well, sparring with one of the soldiers, and the rest of the crew was waiting to cast off the moment the two were back on board.

"Welcome home," Lord Percival said, clasping Kadorax in a warm embrace. "I've healed up quite nicely since we last saw each other. Turns out the priests in Oscine City know a thing or two about their spells."

"Thank you, sir," Kadorax replied.

"Before you get too settled, please accept my invitation to visit the galley. I've been told the chef has food prepared in anticipation of your arrival, and then Ayers has also requested a word below deck, if you aren't too tired." The captain doffed his hat and then had to clutch at the railing as the ship lurched away, caught momentarily by an unexpected wave.

Kadorax stood for a moment to watch Brinna train, impressed by how far she'd come and the level of dedication she showed. He laughed silently to himself when he realized that the woman didn't have a choice. Everything she'd ever known had died back on the other side of the Boneridge Mountains. She was an adventurer, and whether the choice had been hers to make or one born from pure necessity, it did not matter. From then on, the quality of her life depended on her skill with a blade. Kadorax had seen such determination in himself when he had first arrived in Agglor and come to accept his fate, and he enjoyed watching that determination in action.

A small group of other crewmen were eating in the galley when Kadorax and Syzak arrived. They also found a handful of knights sitting to one side by themselves. Breaking their well-known stereotype as walking metal hulks covered in armor, all of the knights wore only simple clothing with their blue and gold tabards, though every single one of them had a weapon on their belt. "They've purchased passage?" Kadorax asked without giving the issue much more thought.

Syzak explained how the group of knights was going to be dropped off in Oscine City as he grabbed two plates full of grilled meats and the hard, seasoned bread that seemed to be the only food consistently available on the ship.

They had their fill, ignoring the knights in the corner all the while, and then made for Ayers' smithy toward the rear of the boat. The burly man was shirtless and covered in sweat, and his workshop smelled like he hadn't left it in days. The heat coming off the forge didn't help.

"Just in time," the man said, grinning from ear to ear. "I've made enough improvements and repairs to the ship to get *Minor Runecrafting: Rank 2*, and Syzak brought me plenty of materials. I've made a few things since I saw you last."

"That's *exactly* what I want to hear," Kadorax replied. Just like in the video games he used to play back on Earth, getting new gear was one of his favorite pastimes.

Ayers began by lifting a large leather breastplate with a front piece of scalloped metal onto his anvil. "This thing will take a few blows, that's for sure," he said. "It'll offer a lot more protection than the leather you currently have, and I reinforced the very center over your . . . uh, your rod, or whatever it is."

"You know about my soul rod?" Kadorax asked. He didn't remember ever showing the blacksmith his chest.

Ayers nodded. "I did a little research, asked around a bit. Not too many people have heard of your class, but one of the knights we took on board knew it. He said one of the old priors had been a bastion."

"Well, I could certainly use more armor," Kadorax told him. Focusing on the gear, he brought up the stats in his vision:

Reinforced Leather Vest - Empty Rune Slots: 2. Reduced

incoming concussive and piercing damage. Effect: moderate. Passive while worn.

Kadorax began undoing the tattered armor he was wearing, eager for the upgrade. When he had given the old vest back to Ayers to salvage into materials, the smith brought out a matching set of iron-banded leather greaves that would lock into place over the tops of his boots.

"These will come in handy, I think," Ayers said as he slid the greaves across the anvil.

Guardian's Enchanted Steel Spats - Grants the wearer immunity to all harmful ground-based effects up to level 20. Effect: profound. Passive while worn.

"If only I'd had these before I shredded my back on a pit of spikes," Kadorax lamented. "But they'll be perfect. Though with all this metal, I should probably avoid falling overboard any time soon."

"Ha," Ayers laughed. "Tell that to the knights. The only reason they've taken off their armor is for fear of not being able to swim. I swear, that lot likes to live inside their steel."

"You—"

Kadorax stopped as Ayers drew a sword, a proper sword, from a fine sheath he had been hiding underneath a shelf to the right of his anvil. "Saved the best for last," he said with a sly grin.

Kadorax took the weapon gingerly and tested its weight in his hand. He still wasn't entirely used to wielding a short sword, and he much preferred a dagger when given the chance, but the hilt felt *right* in his palm.

"I had to make more nails and horseshoes than I care to admit just to bargain with a merchant in Skarm's Reif for the recipe I used to make that sword, so don't go swinging it into rocks and destroying the edge," he said.

"I'll save it for skulls and spines, then," Kadorax replied. He turned the weapon over to inspect the high level of craftsmanship. The dagger he had lost in the jackal temple in his previous life had been worth more than the entire *Grim Sleeper* and all that it contained, people included, but the weapon Ayers had made was still better than anything the bastion could have expected.

"A deep fuller, too, as you like," Ayers added.

Kadorax gave it a few slow test swings through the air. "I can't thank you enough," he said.

"Bah, you already have," Ayers laughed. "I've seen more of the world from this ship than I ever would have stuck in Coldport. I just wish I didn't have all those ranks in *Advanced Carpentry*... And look, there on the hilt, already have a rune in there."

Kadorax inspected the rune with a bit of wonder. He had used hundreds of runes in his life as an assassin, and their magic still captivated him. A high-level smith or enchanter could make runes out of almost any material, though the one in the hilt of his new sword was stone, the typical variety, engraved and painted with ancient arcane symbols he did not understand. Summoning the weapon's details, he was eager to find out exactly what the rune was capable of:

Assir's Edge - Increased damage inflicted against enemies who have recently wounded the wielder. Minor Rune of Vexing: Enhances the wielder's ability to both resist and inflict fear abilities. Effect: moderate. Passive.

"You've been busy," Kadorax said, his voice full of admiration. "And I like the name. Well done."

Ayers offered a slight bow. He dug into one of the pockets on his apron for a moment and then pulled out three small stones, each of them a carved and enchanted rune.

"Don't use them all yourself, you greedy bastard," he joked, sliding the runes over and beaming with well-earned pride.

Kadorax inspected the runes only momentarily before offering them all to Syzak. "I have enough for one day," he said. "Split them with Brinna."

"She needs all the armor enhancements she can get, and *Minor Rune of Protection* should help quite a bit," the snake-man replied.

"I have plenty of leather to make her a set like the one you have," Ayers said to the shaman. He rifled through a bit of his scraps and found a few pieces that would work.

"She'll have two rune slots, then," Syzak added. "I'll give her the *Minor Rune of Escape* and keep the *Minor Rune of Chance* for myself."

"Keep at it," Kadorax told the smith as he left. He was ready to be gone from the heat and mustiness of the cramped room. Beyond that, he still hadn't looked at his own stats since returning from the chaos, and Ligriv had told him he had advanced a level. He liked waiting to progress levels sometimes, but only when the chance of battle was extremely low. Something about knowing the advancement was waiting for him, waiting for his decision to make it permanent, brought a glimmer of satisfaction to his smile.

Leaving Syzak to his own devices, Kadorax casually made it above deck where the sun was shining brightly and the air smelled of salt. Lord Percival was at the helm, and Brinna was still busy training with one of the crew, taking far more hits than she managed to deliver. Kadorax strolled to the railing and watched as Skarm's Reif became smaller and smaller on the horizon. So many other ships were departing alongside the *Grim Sleeper* that the city was sometimes hard to see, bobbing in and out of view as the ships crossed paths.

Basking in the sunlight, Kadorax brought up his character sheet to investigate his ninth-level options. The first thing he noticed was that *Encroaching Insanity* had progressed another rank. He was still a ways from acquiring *Living Nightmare*, but the rapid degeneration of his mind was not something he could ignore. Unfortunately, there also wasn't anything he could do to abate the debuff. He tried not to let the realization get him down as he read through his newly available skills:

Chaos Shock: Rank 3 - The bastion pulls two slivers of chaotic energy into the world and thrusts them forward, creating a random magical effect augmented by a second impact quickly following the first. If neither of the slivers hit an enemy, there is a small chance that Chaos Shock will not be expended. Effect: minor. Cooldown: 24 minutes.

Guardian of the Deep: Rank 1 - The bastion reaches into the depths of chaos, beckoning forth a hideous amalgamation of tentacles, magic, and destruction. The guardian will attack the first living thing it senses, and it will not stop until it is killed. Higher ranks allow the guardian to receive basic commands. Effect: profound. Cooldown: 10 days.

Bathed in Silence: Rank 1 - Surrounded by the eternal quiet of chaos, the bastion no longer needs to announce when abilities are used, and words spoken softly cannot be heard by enemies without enhanced perception. Passive.

Kadorax was at a loss. On one hand, he fully understood the absolute necessity of a passive talent that removed his requirement to speak during fights. A similar passive had been one of his highest-ranked skills as an assassin, and it had shaped everything about his entire combat style. On the other hand, *Guardian of the Deep* sounded too incredible to ignore. Under normal circumstances, he would have been able to find someone else of his class to ask for advice and to help plan his entire build, but he had not met another bastion of chaos incarnate. As far as he knew, he was the only one.

Standing at the *Grim Sleeper's* railing, he read through the two abilities several times. "If I knew when—or if—I'd get another silence talent..." he muttered to the wind.

For a second, Kadorax thought of asking Syzak for advice. But he knew what the stealthy, slithering snake-man would say. The silence talent would *always* be useful. *Guardian of the Deep* would only be useful once every ten days. Kadorax pounded a fist onto the top of the railing, immediately picking up a splinter and regretting his stupid outburst. "Stupid railing..." he growled, though he wasn't really upset.

Doing the only thing he knew made any sense, Kadorax dismissed his character sheet and postponed the decision altogether, content to simply watch the waves and enjoy the feel of the warm sun beating down on his back. It would be the dead of winter before long, and while the ocean around Skarm's Reif and Kingsgate would remain quite warm, the rest of Agglor would see snow before the month was out, if they hadn't already.

The *Grim Sleeper* pulled into the frantic Oscine City harbor amidst a slew of other ships. Security on the docks was massive. City guards patrolled everywhere, and several large groups of knights were organizing even larger groups of militia into regiments to be deployed.

"Here we go," Kadorax said solemnly. Syzak nodded at his side. "All of Agglor is going to war. We just need to figure out where we're going to fit in among all the fighting."

"Need to identify where the jackals are coming from first," the shaman reminded him. "Let's talk to the knights. They look like they know what they're doing."

"Agreed."

Brinna adjusted her leather armor. "Think I'm ready for a war?" she asked.

The woman had gained a level from her training with the crewman, and her newfound confidence showed clearly in her voice. She was eager, though eagerness often got people killed—especially in war.

"Once we know exactly what's going on, we'll figure out where we need to be and what we need to do. Just try to keep your head down until then," Kadorax said.

The three adventurers followed the *Grim Sleeper's* contingent of knights down to the docks, where they met up with others from the Oscine City priory. The armored knights marched through the crowd, leading them up into the pristine city so alive with panic and excitement. The prior was standing with a circle of his retainers and officers outside a tavern that was still in the process of being converted into a priorate outpost. Blue and gold banners flapped in the wind from one of the second-floor windows.

"We meet again," the prior said with a grin as he recognized Kadorax approaching. "I thought you'd had your fill of knights the last time you were in Oscine City."

Kadorax laughed off the subtle abrasiveness, trying to defuse the situation in order to gain as much information as he could. There wasn't a large Blackened Blade presence in any of Agglor's cities, and he knew any he found in Oscine

City would likely be from Skarm's Reif like himself, so the knights were his only source of reliable intel.

"What's the latest on the jackals?" the bastion asked.

"That depends," the prior replied, his eyes narrowing. "What do you know?"

Kadorax had to wait while a group of knights brought information and supplies to the tavern and received orders from the prior. "We heard the king's daughter was kidnapped, but that information is old and might be unreliable."

The prior's expression was one of surprise. "Then you know nothing, it seems."

"I'm sure you're a busy man," Kadorax prodded.

"Yes, yes, of course," the prior said after a curt laugh. "What you heard was the initial report, nothing more. The king's daughter was kidnapped, that much is true, though that was only the beginning. A Gar'kesh was with the group of jackals who captured the princess. My knights slew the beast as it tried to come ashore not far from here, and alas, the body was washed out to sea."

Kadorax wasn't sure he believed it. If every Gar'kesh the jackals summoned was as powerful as the one that had laid him low, there was no way a group of unprepared knights from Oscine City had slain one. He imagined the bit about the corpse washing out to sea was just a convenient way for the knights to do a little boasting without being called out on their lie. "Have any others been spotted? Are there any more Gar'kesh roaming about?"

"Oh, there's a vile beast alright, and here in Oscine City, no less," the prior said. His sly smile spoke volumes toward the secrets he harbored. "You remember Atticus Willowshade, yes?"

Kadorax had only heard the name a few times. Atticus,

if that was even the man's—the *creature's*—real name, was a warlock of some renown. Or perhaps infamy was a better way to describe him. No one knew exactly what to believe, but one of the most retold rumors in Agglor detailed a war some hundred years ago. Along the northern rim of the mainland, there had once been another kingdom. Now, no one went to the north. The land was desolate and barren, a waste inhabited only by Agglor's gruffest and meanest of intelligent races. The rumors said that only Atticus knew the names of the cities and kings who had once ruled the north. He knew their names because he had been the one who had brought them down, single-handedly, and within a single night as well.

"You're telling me that Atticus Willowshade is here in Oscine City?" Kadorax asked.

The prior nodded.

"And the citizens haven't fled for the Boneridge Mountains?"

"Not yet," the prior replied. "A contingent of knights found Atticus in those very mountains, as it turns out, so I'm not sure that's the first place the people would want to run."

Kadorax let out a long sigh. He had hoped the Grim Sleeper would have been the last warlock he would have to fight alongside. "Where's he staying? I want to know which part of town to avoid."

The prior laughed and pointed toward the north. "He wouldn't accept our offer of refuge in the priory, so he's holed up under a collection of sticks and leaves at the edge of the city for now. It seems he prefers the wilderness to the trappings of modern civilization."

"And how much did you have to pay him?"

Again, the prior laughed in response. "Someone like that

isn't motivated by the number of gold pieces jingled in their direction. No, all he asked was that he'd be allowed to keep any Gar'kesh corpses he came across throughout the war. Only the gods above know what he intends to do with them..."

"Wonderful," Kadorax said dryly. "Well, what's your plan? Where are we needed?"

The prior's mouth was open on the verge of issuing a response when a low rumble permeated through the entire city. For a split second, the whole mass of people in and around the docks went quiet. Then a roar echoed off in the distance, quickly followed by a second, and then a deafening cacophony erupted all at once as every civilian in Oscine City was overcome by panic.

Kadorax, Brinna, and Syzak had to press themselves in close to the prior and his knights to not be crushed by the tumult in the streets. "Is that your warlock?" Brinna shouted over the crowd.

The prior's white face and wide eyes gave them all the answer they needed.

"We're under attack!" Syzak yelled.

Kadorax nodded and grabbed the front of the prior's shirt. "Get your knights!" he screamed. He was close enough to the old man's face for some of his errant spit to land on the man's cheek. "Organize! To the north!"

The prior nodded, and Kadorax let him go. The knights protecting their leader struggled to get a small shield wall established around the tavern, like a beachhead rising above the water in the midst of a violent summer storm.

The three adventurers felt like the only people in the city moving toward the noise instead of away from it. They pushed and shoved, staying close to the buildings on their left so they at least had part of an open path and wouldn't be lost in the sea of fleeing civilians flooding the streets like a swarm of flies racing toward a fresh corpse.

Oscine City was large, one of the largest settlements in all of Agglor, and it took what felt like an eternity to reach to the northern sector of the town. A wide swath of the houses to their right had been utterly destroyed. A few small knots of armored knights were scattered about the streets, cowering more than mounting a defense, and a veritable horde of jackals was swarming toward them on all fours.

Behind the swarm, Kadorax saw a dark, towering outline marring the horizon. It was a Gar'kesh, and it finally confirmed beyond any doubt in Kadorax's mind that there was indeed more than one of the jackal gods. Even though Elise and the priors he had met had spoken as though the multiplicity of the Gar'kesh had already been clearly established, some part of him had refused to believe it. Such power was not meant to exist, and it was certainly not meant to exist in pairs or trios or any other quantity exceeding one.

"Stay back," the bastion ordered his companions, but he was already the closest to the Gar'kesh's flailing arms and bulging eyes, ahead of the others by more than ten feet. He ran back to rejoin them and tried to swallow back his fear.

"The priory chapter here is huge," he began. "We wait for the knights. Maybe Atticus. For now, we need to look first to our own survival."

"We should join the knights," Syzak stated. His serpentine eyes hadn't left the silhouette.

Kadorax scanned the streets in hope of finding some answer waiting to be exploited. No such answer presented itself. "If we're caught by ourselves when the jackals hit, we're dead." He pointed to the nearest group of knights. It was impossible to really tell due to all their armor, but he swore he saw their shields shaking in their hands. "We'll join the knights. But we still need more. If we could wall off each street . . ."

Another guttural roar broke through the morning sky. Kadorax didn't wait to finish laying out his plan. He took off for the nearest clump of knights, and the other two followed him without question.

"How do we kill it?" Brinna shouted from behind.

Kadorax didn't look back over his shoulder as he answered her. "I don't think we can," he said, and he meant every word.

ABOUT THE AUTHOR

Born and raised in Cincinnati, Ohio, Stuart Thaman graduated from Hillsdale College with degrees in politics and German, and has since sworn off life in the cold north. Now comfortably settled in the warmer climes of Kentucky, he lives with his lovely wife, a rambunctious Boston terrier named Yoda, and four cats who probably hate him. When not writing, he enjoys smoking cigars, acquiring bruises in mosh pits, and preparing for the end of the world.

ACKNOWLEDGMENTS

Special thanks go out first and foremost to all the fans. Without eager readers picking up copies, telling their friends, and leaving reviews, I wouldn't be able to keep writing books and penning new adventures.

I'd also like to thank Anna, Josiah, and Tony for putting up with all my bullshit and still pushing me to write. You guys are the best.

One final tip of the cap must be given to a few authors as well: Orson Scott Card, David Dalglish, and R. A. Salvatore inspired me to be a writer. Without those three, I'd have a lot more free time.

WANT MORE EPIC FANTASY?

Sign up for the newsletter at www.stuartthamanbooks.com to be the first to get your hands on all the new releases, exclusive content, and tons of book giveaways.

If you enjoyed this book, please take a moment to leave a review. Even just a few kind words can do wonders for a book's visibility, helping other readers discover their own love for epic fantasy.

Be sure to check out Stuart Thaman's other series available in paperback, eBook, and now audiobook!

Interested in contact? Send an email to stuartthaman@gmail.com

Printed in Poland
by Amazon Fulfillment
Poland Sp. z o.o., Wrocław